CLOSE
QUARTERS

Published by Kandi Steiner
Edited by Elaine York, Allusion Publishing
www.allusionpublishing.com
Cover Design by Staci Hart
Formatting by Elaine York, Allusion Publishing
www.allusionpublishing.com

CLOSE QUARTERS

KANDI STEINER

PROLOGUE

I knew now what it was.

That feeling I'd had that first day on the boat, when the sun was high and warm on my neck in Barcelona — the way my stomach had somersaulted like we were in a deep sea storm even though we were still tied up at the dock.

It was a warning.

I didn't see it then, didn't recognize it as anything more than nerves and maybe a little sorrow swimming in my gut.

But now, with the blood pooling around my head, soaking into the teak and my hair all the same, I understood.

It was a warning.

The universe knew long before I did the way this all would end, and it cautioned me the only way it knew how.

But I ignored it.

Now, as the blackness invaded my vision, the splitting ache at the crown of my head going numb, I caught one last glimpse of the man responsible for it all and I wondered how I never saw it coming.

How did I never see what he was capable of, when pushed, when threatened?

How did I ever let him hold me, kiss me, have me in every way there is to be had?

How did I fall for the lie those eyes told, for the heart within that chest, for a man so evil?

They say love is blind, and in most cases, I imagine that means you look past the faults of those you love — how they leave the cap off the toothpaste or throw their dirty clothes on the floor — or perhaps past your own inhibition telling you that maybe you could do better, that maybe you deserve more.

In this case, it meant death.

Through the fiery haze, the smoke and the flames, the broken crystal and the last fragments of my heart — I saw the smirk of victory on his face.

I tried to ask him why, but it came out as a cough instead, the blood around my mouth bubbling with the effort.

And then, everything went dark.

CHAPTER ONE

Three Months Earlier

I was going to vomit.

The reality of that unfortunate truth settled in more and more as we walked the main deck, me following behind Joel, him excitedly pointing out places on the ginormous super yacht he was going to be working on for the next few months using terms I'd never heard before while I held onto my camera and looked for places to yack.

There was a head at the back of the boat, which I learned was yacht talk for the bathroom. That would work. There were a few large plants on either side of the bar we'd just walked through. The pots they sat in wouldn't do too badly. There had to be a trashcan in there, too — perhaps behind the bar.

I supposed the easiest option would be to just lean as far overboard as I could and let the contents of my stomach feed the fish below. But I'd have to have control — if I got even one drop on this yacht, I'd die of mortification before the owner would likely kill me for real.

"Pretty sweet, right?" Joel asked me, spreading his hands out on the railing at the front of the boat — or rather, the bow, as he'd so cheerily corrected me. "It's a bitch to clean it all, though," he joked. "Especially when it's time to scrub the teak. Not looking forward to that."

I tried to smile through my nausea.

"Can you even imagine being rich enough to own one of these things?" He shook his head, turning to face me again with the same dazzling smile that had made me fall in love with him our freshman year of college.

It was hard to believe that was four years ago now.

"I've been waiting for an opportunity like this for years, Aspen... working my ass off as a deck hand, catering to horrific guests on charter after charter..." He shook his head. "And now, it's finally all paying off."

Joel's smile doubled at that, and he swept me into his arms, though my hands didn't wrap around him in return. They were too busy holding onto my camera where it hung from my damp neck, like I was afraid if I removed them I'd lose all composure and my lunch, too.

"And *you're* here to experience it with me." He kissed me hard and quick, and I did my best to meet his smile with a convincing one of my own.

I had no idea why I was sick. We hadn't eaten anything of the dicey variety, and the boat wasn't moving at all where it sat at the dock. Perhaps it was a stomach bug, coming out of nowhere.

Or perhaps I was just going to miss Joel.

That had to be it.

It wasn't like we hadn't spent summers apart in the past. Every year since I'd known him, Joel had been working out of Fort Lauderdale on whatever yacht he could get a job on. He'd worked his way up from just a deck hand on a charter yacht to finally getting what he'd always wanted — a permanent spot on a super yacht with an owner.

And this time, he'd be the lead deck hand.

I didn't really understand why that was a big deal, but from what he'd told me, it meant no more having to deal with crazy guests or difficult-to-please divas or worrying that you'd get stiffed on a tip. Apparently, the guy who owned this yacht was known for being easy to work with, for letting his crew have a little fun — in other words, he didn't care if they partied, so long as they got their work done.

And if there was anything Joel loved more than me, it was partying.

Plus, who *wouldn't* want to be on a yacht in the Mediterranean — working or not?

I was excited for him — just as excited as I was for myself to spend the next few months backpacking through Europe. Joel would work on the yacht, I would get enough photographs to build a strong portfolio, and then we'd both be back in the States and starting a new chapter of our lives together.

At least, for a while, until Joel was called back to the yacht, of course.

That was the perk he'd been working so hard for, to have a permanent spot on an owner's boat as opposed to working charters. That meant we'd be in a long-distance relationship for a while, but it wasn't like we hadn't been through that every summer, anyway. Besides, he'd have some time off now and then, and he'd either come home to Colorado, or I'd meet him wherever he was for a new adventure.

For now, I was caught up thinking about *my* adventure.

It was something I'd dreamed of, spending some time alone, wandering through the streets of foreign cities with my camera at the ready. Dating an extrovert had pulled me out of my comfort zone more times than I could count over the last four years, and in that time, I hadn't taken a single trip by myself. This was a dream of mine, to travel alone, to experience new cultures from behind the lens.

It had just always seemed so far off — graduation, traveling, the real world and the jobs it held for us in it.

But it was here. The future was now.

And apparently, my stomach was very upset at that fact.

"You okay, baby?" Joel asked, brows furrowed as he swept a strand of my dark hair back and tucked it behind my ear.

I nodded, smiling again. "Just a little nauseous," I said, tapping the railing as my cheeks flushed. "Guess I don't have my sea legs like you do."

"We aren't even moving," Joel said on a laugh, but then he kissed my nose. "Hang tight. I have something that will help."

He was gone in the next breath, and I held tighter to my camera, forcing an exhale as I leaned against the railing. When I felt a little steadier, my eyes wandered over the sea of catamarans and yachts, the sun reflecting off the water between them, glistening like diamonds. These "boats" were so massive, so luxurious that I hardly believed I was in their presence at all. They were the kind of behemoths you saw on television, the ones purchased by the rich and the famous, the ones you only ever dreamed of stepping foot on.

I hadn't even had a full tour of the yacht yet, but I'd seen enough to know there was more money in this port than in the entire country of Spain.

Barcelona was rich in culture, and I already had half a memory card filled with photographs I'd snapped during our week here together. The owner of the boat paid to fly Joel out, my parents pitched in to help me get my ticket, and at the end of the summer, we'd meet back here to fly home together. I'd already decided I'd stay a few more days on my own in Spain before I made my way to France because I was nowhere near ready to leave the food or the people — not yet.

I still had so much more left to capture.

I powered my camera on — the gently used Nikon D850 DSLR that I'd used my graduation money to buy — and smiled my first genuine smile at the sound of it coming to life. Even used, it was a massive upgrade from the old camera I'd had since my senior year of high school, the one that had somehow gotten me through undergrad. I looked through the eye of it, adjusting the focus on the lens and widening the shot. Then, I waited until the sun slipped behind a cloud, casting an almost eerie glow on the boats before I pressed my finger on the shutter trigger.

Click.

I pulled the camera away from my eye long enough to glance at the digital screen on the back, seeing what I'd just captured. Then, I held it up again, playing with the focus, waiting for the right light.

My stomach was already settling with the familiar comfort photography brought me. The way that sleek little machine felt in my hands made me feel more like myself than anything else. It was like a fifth limb, always attached to me, and without it, I'd have been handicapped. It had been like that ever since I could remember, ever since my mom handed me the little Kodak disposable camera during our family vacation to the Grand Canyon and asked me to take a picture of her, Dad, and my sister, Juniper.

From the very first time I clicked that shutter and realized I could capture a moment forever in time, I was hooked.

I frowned at the camera display after taking my next shot, turning until my back rested against the railing and sifting through the photos. Then, I lifted the camera to my eye again, searching for a new focus.

I found it more quickly than I expected.

And then I promptly lost the ability to breathe.

There was luxury all around us — riches so unfathomable to someone who grew up in a middle-class household that I didn't even try to comprehend. But none of the expensive wood or gold-plated trims or crystal chandeliers compared to the power exuding off the man framed in my camera lens.

He was tall, and lean, and dressed like he just walked off the shoot for *People* magazine's "Sexiest Man Alive" issue. The charcoal gray suit he wore was fitted and tapered to perfection, his Armani dress shoes making an expensive clicking sound each time they tapped down on the teak. I could imagine the muscles lining that broad chest of his, the narrow waist, the legs that carried him effortlessly across the main deck.

The way he walked, shoulders held back and down, head high, each step calculated and sharp told me long before anything else that he was the owner of the yacht. It was in the way the crew practically bowed as he passed them, moving out of the way so as not to be seen, not to be in his way. It was in the way his lips pressed into a flat line, in the way his dark sunglasses shielded his eyes, in the way he held a briefcase with one hand as the other swung confidently at his side.

His sturdy, square jaw was dusted with a light stubble that seemed at odds with how he was dressed, but somehow worked. If anything, it only added to the power radiating off him — as if he wanted everyone to know he was rich enough to wear a tailored suit on a casual day with a five-o-clock shadow he forgot to shave.

I felt each step he took like an anvil vibration through the deck, and it seemed all the manners I'd learned in my twenty-two years had evaporated the moment he walked onto the boat, because I still stared at him through my camera lens without a care in the world if he saw me.

His dark blond hair caught a ray of sun as it slipped through the clouds above, and my finger pushed down automatically — without thought, without the good sense to pause and decide if it was a good idea or not. The clicking shutter sound of my camera sounded more like an echoing gunshot in a cave, and as soon as the picture was taken, the man's head snapped my direction.

He stopped walking, brows furrowed above his sunglasses for a moment before they relaxed. His lips turned up, just at one side, and then he started walking again.

This time, toward me.

"Oh, God," I murmured to myself, flushing so furiously it felt like a sunburn as I turned to face the front of the boat again. I had my camera pulled into my stomach, eyes on the screen, pretending like I was studying the shots I'd taken yesterday when Joel and I had explored *La Sagrada Familia*. I didn't dare take my eyes off that screen, not when I heard those Armani shoes approach behind me, not even when the man stopped a few feet away, clearing his throat.

"Hello," he said simply, and a wave of chills ran down my spine at the sound of his voice — thick and smooth, like maple syrup.

I swallowed, pressing my eyes closed with one last internal curse at myself before I turned to face him.

I wished I had sunglasses on. I wished I was wearing something more impressive than ripped-up jean shorts and an old University of Colorado t-shirt. I wished on every star there was that I wouldn't have taken that damn photo.

I rolled my lips together, trying my best to smile. "Hello."

His lips tilted up more at the greeting, and he slipped his free hand into what I imagined was a satin-lined pocket of his dress pants.

"I don't remember hiring a photographer for this trip."

Another wave of heat flushed my cheeks, and I tore my eyes away from him, looking down at where I still held my camera in my hands as my dark hair fell around my face like a curtain. "I... I'm sorry about that. I'm just, I didn't mean—"

"May I see it?"

I glanced up at him through my lashes, confused.

"The picture you took," he clarified, and his hand came out of his pocket, reaching toward me, instead. He took a step forward that had me inching back without even thinking to. "May I see it?"

"Oh," I babbled out, shaking my head and tucking my long hair behind one ear. "It's not... it wasn't anything special. I was just taking a few shots of the marina and then I..."

My next words were cut short because his warm, strong hand covered mine where it held my camera. It wasn't even a full second, his skin on mine, but it shocked me still and silent, and I released my grip on my camera like it was never really mine to begin with.

It all happened so fast, me submitting to him. I stripped the strap from around my neck, surrendering the camera and standing there by his side like he was my professor and I was turning in my final assignment of the year.

I watched his thumb slowly tick the dial, the photos I'd taken of the dock and the boats flashing on the screen. He smiled a little more with each turn, and then the screen lit up with the picture of him, and his smile faded, his hands gripping my camera a little tighter.

I held my breath as he stared at himself, and I found myself leaning closer to him subconsciously. I wondered what he was thinking, what he saw when he looked at that photograph.

I wanted his approval, I realized idly. I wanted this powerful man to tell me he loved what he saw.

Something of a laugh came from his nose, and then his smirk was back in place, and he handed me my camera as I took a heady step back from where I'd been entirely too close to him.

The man moved slowly then, tilting his head a bit before he removed his sunglasses, revealing steel gray eyes that matched his suit. They were rimmed in navy, flecked with turquoise, an ocean of color that was utterly bewitching. Those eyes watched me for a long moment, a weighted pause that even the birds seemed to quiet for.

"What's your name?" he asked in lieu of commenting on the photograph.

But before I could answer, Joel jogged up beside us, half out of breath, his slight panting breaking the trance.

"Mr. Whitman," Joel said, taking off his ball cap before he extended his right hand for the man in the gray suit. "Wow. It is such an honor to finally meet you in person, sir. I'm Joel Woods, your lead deck hand. Thank you for having me onboard," he continued as they shook hands, and I could tell he was nervous, because his voice was a little more high pitched than usual, and his words came out a little too quickly. "I'm a hard worker, sir, I assure you. And your boat is in good hands."

The man's smile had all but disappeared, but there was a glint of it now as he dropped Joel's hand and put his sunglasses back on. "I have no doubt."

The two men couldn't have been more opposite. Where Joel was just a few inches taller than me and stocky, with dark hair and charcoal eyes and a flashy, wide smile, the man in the suit towered over him, long and lean, with light hair and eyes I knew I'd never forget as long as I lived. They were both devastatingly handsome, but in such opposing ways that it seemed ludicrous to compare them at all.

"Here, babe," Joel said, handing me a bottle of anti-nausea pills. He tossed his arm around my shoulders, kissing my temple. "A couple of these should help your stomach."

I shook my head, tearing my eyes away from the man's stare as I took the bottle and murmured something of a *thank you* to Joel. I wanted to get away from Mr. Whitman. I wanted to spend my last few moments with Joel alone and in peace.

I wanted to go back five minutes ago and remove my stupid finger from the stupid shutter button.

"Feeling sick?" Mr. Whitman asked, but my eyes stayed on the bottle of pills in my hand.

"Aspen's never been on a boat like this," Joel thankfully answered for me. "Sea sick without even leaving the dock," he added with a laugh.

"Aspen," Mr. Whitman repeated, like he was tasting my name, trying it on for size. Then, his hand reached forward, breaking into view where I stared down at the deck. "I'm Theo Whitman. A pleasure to meet you."

My eyes flicked to his, now blessedly covered by dark lenses, and I tentatively met his hand with mine. He gave nothing more than a firm, polite handshake, but I once again found my chest tight, my breath throttled.

"I hope you don't mind that I brought her aboard, sir," Joel said, as if he just realized he might be in trouble. His hand grabbed for the back of his neck. "I've been working in Fort Lauderdale for four summers now but never got to share the experience with her."

Theo smiled, flashing his teeth for the first time. "Oh, I don't mind at all." He turned to me then. "In fact, you should stay for the crew dinner."

My eyes bulged in time with Joel's.

"Really?!" he said, at the same time I murmured, "Oh, no, sir. That wouldn't be—"

"I insist."

Those two words were said with such power, in such a manner that there was nothing more to say, nothing more to do than nod and smile.

"Good," Theo said, the decision made. "I'll save a couple of seats for you two near the head of the table. I'd love to see more of your photography, Miss..."

"Dawn," I muttered.

His lips curled at that. "Miss Dawn. If you don't mind, of course," he added.

I shook my head on an uncomfortable smile, which somehow seemed to make him smile even wider.

With a nod and an *excuse me,* Theo left me and Joel alone at the bow, his shoes tapping out that same steady rhythm as he made his way inside to the main deck bar.

And Joel wrapped me up in a swinging hug of celebration that we would get a few more hours together.

CHAPTER
TWO

The afternoon blew by in a gust of Joel touring me around the yacht and introducing me to the rest of the crew. The boat was massive, with four decks and more amenities than any home or hotel I'd ever been to. There were two swimming pools, because obviously one wasn't enough, a hot tub, a sauna, a full gym, a massage room, a theatre room, two sitting areas — which Joel called *salons* — to lounge or dine in, plenty of places to sunbathe and relax, and two fully stocked bars.

Those features were just the tip of the iceberg, I wagered more and more, as Joel gave me the full tour. For everything he showed me, I knew there were dozens of things he couldn't show me — guest rooms, the owner's suite on the upper deck, the jet skis that were housed somewhere below the main deck. It was as overwhelming as it was exhilarating, being surrounded by such grand opulence.

And as if that wasn't enough, I was also meeting someone new at every turn.

Mr. Whitman's yacht, which I learned was named *Philautia,* couldn't just be taken out on the water with a few people. No, he needed a crew of *fifteen* to take care of everything that needed taking care of.

There was the Captain, of course, an older, weather-beaten gentleman with curly red hair and a matching, neatly trimmed beard. He introduced himself to me as Chuck with a wide, crooked-toothed grin and an accent I couldn't quite place. His First Officer, Wayland, was from Jamaica. He seemed as overwhelmed as I did by meeting everyone, and simply offered me a warm smile and an uptick of his chin in greeting.

I couldn't place why, but I liked him instantly.

Every turn we made there was someone new to introduce me to. There were two chefs, a purser, a chief stewardess along with two other girls who served as stewardesses under her. They seemed nice, for the most part, though there was one girl in particular who didn't seem thrilled that I was joining them for dinner. She made a comment that it was supposed to be crew only, to which Joel told her I'd been invited by Mr. Whitman.

That shut her up fast.

On the main deck, we ran into the two engineers, and in what Joel called the "crew mess" on the lower deck, I met the two deck hands who would be serving under him and his direct boss, the bosun.

By the time Joel showed me the tiny room with four bunk beds where he'd be staying for his trip, I was exhausted by all the peopling.

Just in time to get changed and ready for dinner.

I felt a little guilty each time I glanced at the watch on my wrist — the one my sister gave me as a graduation gift. Not too long ago, I had been sick at the thought of leaving Joel, of us being apart for three months. Now, I was more sick at the fact that I was about to have dinner with nearly two dozen people I didn't know.

But there was no way to deny Theo Whitman of what he wanted.

I would learn that lesson time and time again.

"The stews are already dressed and working on getting everything ready on the main deck," Joel said as he stripped his sweaty t-shirt over his head. "You can use their shower and bathroom, if you want."

He nodded across the hallway to another small room with four bunk beds, and then he was kicking his shorts off and was about to get in the shower himself when I reached for him.

His eyebrows furrowed, but when he saw my face, he must have registered my nerves. He chuckled, pulling me into his bare chest and wrapping his arms around me. I sighed in relief at the contact, resting my head just beneath his chin.

"It's going to be fine," he promised. "Trust me — this crew will talk enough that you won't have to say a word. Just enjoy the fancy, free meal."

I nodded but held him tighter when he tried to pull back. "I'm going to miss you," I whispered.

Joel squeezed me hard. "Oh, baby, I'm going to miss you, too." He tilted my chin until he could press his lips to mine — lips I'd known all through college, lips I would kiss the rest of my life.

They brought me comfort and butterflies all at once.

"Now, go get showered and let me do the same. Then we can come back here for a proper goodbye before you get off the boat." He smacked my ass and waggled his brows with that comment, and I shoved him off playfully as he disappeared into the bathroom.

I took my time across the hall, smiling to myself at the already-chaotic bathroom the girls shared. It was easy to tell the difference between it and the one Joel was sharing with the other deck hands. That one had been practically bare, save for some shaving cream and a couple of razors. In here, makeup, hair product, and styling tools spilled out of every small cabinet and took up nearly every inch of the small counter space.

I was glad now that I hadn't opted to check my bag at the front desk of the hotel we left this morning. I didn't want to carry it around with me all day, but Joel insisted that I wouldn't want to backtrack to the hotel after being on the boat, and if I had my bag with me, I could just get started on my trip as soon as we said good-bye. Thankfully, I'd listened to him.

After a long, hot shower, I ran my fingers through my hair a bit before wrapping it up in a towel on top of my head. Then, I swiped the fog off the mirror with my palm, groaning a little at the reflection that found me.

I looked as tired as I felt.

Unfortunately, I was much less prepared for a nice dinner than the other girls on the boat. When I'd packed for this trip, I'd imagined being with Joel for a week and then on my own. I had five shirts, two tank tops, one pair of jeans and two pairs of shorts to get me through my entire time here. I knew I could do laundry or re-wear a lot of this stuff, and I wanted everything I needed to fit in a carry-on sized backpack. I'd succeeded in that quest.

But there was no room in there for makeup or curling wands, that was for sure.

I chuckled to myself as I pulled out the girliest thing I had — a small bottle of moisturizer — and swathed it over my cheeks. I acted as if I'd really have done more even if I knew there was going to be a nice dinner involved, but the truth of it was I didn't know how to do a thing with makeup or my hair. That was my sister's territory, and I let her play with me like one of her dolls whenever she wanted to because I had absolutely zero desire.

I wished she was here now.

With that thought, I pulled my phone out and connected to the yacht WiFi Joel had told me about during the tour. Then, I video-chatted Juniper.

"Hey, big sis! How's life abroad?"

Juniper's smile was like a million Broadway lights. She was sitting at the kitchen table at the house we grew up in, hands wrapped around a steaming mug of tea, the tendrils of her black hair falling here and there out of a messy bun on top of her head. It was six o'clock here in Barcelona, which meant it was ten in the morning in Boulder.

We looked so much alike, Juniper and I, except she was extraordinary in every way I was average. We both had long dark hair, but hers had beautiful, natural waves that she could curl into celebrity status, where mine was flat and straight no matter what I did to it. She had flawless, pale skin, where mine was peppered with freckles and sun spots. Her body was every man's dream, curvy and soft and sexy, where mine resembled a stick of celery. She stood tall and proud and smiled like she had the world in her hands, while I cowered and hid in her shadows whenever I had the chance.

But we both had our father's eyes, cerulean blue, and seeing those irises I knew so well on the screen filled my heart with warmth.

"It's beautiful," I said. "I'm on the boat Joel's going to work on for the summer."

Juniper frowned. "In the shower?" Suddenly, her face went pale. "Ew, Aspen, if you just called me after you guys had shower sex, I'm going to throw up."

I laughed, setting the phone against the mirror as I took my hair out of the towel on top of my head. "No, he's across the hall getting ready, too." I swallowed. "The owner of the boat asked me to join them for the crew dinner."

"Ohhh," Juniper said, sipping her tea. "You fancy. What's it like?"

I told her as best I could, trying to remember everything on each deck and all the terms Joel had used. She seemed the most interested in the fact that it was Theo Whitman's boat, which apparently was big news. When I was finished, she made me promise to fill her in on how the dinner went — and to try to convince Mr. Whitman that she should be his future bride.

"I'm serious," she said, the background blurring behind her as she made her way upstairs to her bedroom. "That man is *fine*, with a capital F. I may only be nineteen now but give me a few years and I'll be Trophy Wife material."

I barked out a laugh. "How do you even know who he is?"

She scoffed. "How do you *not* know? Don't you read *Business Insider* or *Forbes*?"

"Wait," I said, pausing where I was taming my hair. "There's no way *you* read either of those."

"I do so," she defended. "Well, at least, when they do a write-up of the world's youngest billionaires, I do."

I rolled my eyes.

"What are you going to wear?" she asked.

I sighed, looking over at the only pair of jeans I had and my yellow tank top, which was the nicest of the two I'd brought with me. "Nothing you'd be proud of. I wish you were here to do my hair and makeup."

"Looks like there's plenty of stuff behind you for you to do it yourself."

"It's not mine," I said. "I'm in the stewardesses' bathroom."

"Steal a little mascara, they won't know."

I laughed. "I'll be fine. It's just dinner and then I'll say my goodbyes to Joel and be on my way to the hostel I'm staying in for the next few nights."

Juniper frowned at that. "Be careful, okay? Send me a message as soon as you get settled so I know you're alive."

"I will."

"And don't tie your hair up. Just let it air dry, you always get such beautiful, natural waves that way."

I smiled. "Love you, Juni."

"Love you more."

We ended the call and I noted that when I messaged her later, I'd ask how summer training was going. My sister was the hottest new volleyball player at the University of Colorado. She'd been a star player ever since I could remember, actually, but she was at the university-level now, and one step closer to her ultimate dream of playing professionally.

I had no doubt that she'd do it.

The mirror wasn't as foggy as I looked over my reflection one last time, tucking my hair behind one ear and letting it fall over the other. The still-wet ends of it fell just below my bra line, and I liked that it hid my face a little bit. The yellow tank top showed off the tan I'd picked up during our Barcelona adventures, and I was thankful I at least had the good sense to bring one pair of jeans to pair it with. The order was to be barefoot while on the boat unless you were wearing the approved boat shoes given to the crew — something about keeping the teak nice — so at least I didn't have to show up in my dirty old sneakers.

With one final breath, I shook off the exhaustion as best I could, knowing I would need every ounce of energy I had left to get through this dinner.

Just a while longer, and I'll be alone.

I was counting down the minutes.

Dinner was many things — most of all *loud.*

One of the benefits of dating Joel, an extrovert who could have a riveting conversation with a brick wall, was that when we attended big group events like this, he took over. He was always the animated one, telling stories, making jokes, while I could sit beside him and smile and laugh at the appropriate times and chime in now and then until the whole ordeal was over. I much preferred hanging out in groups of four or less. After that, it all became too... *much.*

It was the same tonight, Joel holding the table captive with his charm, but I learned quickly that he wasn't the only center of attention at this table. It seemed nearly every member of the crew had an outgoing personality, save for Wayland and the engineers, who were all at the far end of the table having a quiet conversation amongst themselves. But the head chef, Claude, and his partner in crime, Adeline, were loud and vivacious. Their stories were as rich as the food they'd prepared for us.

It was interesting, the way it all worked. Usually, the crew would be behind the scenes, making and serving dinner and then disappearing below deck to have their own meals. But tonight, Mr. Whitman had them all seated together as equals. I found it admirable that he would do that for his crew.

Still, the dinner had to be made and served, so the crew ate and drank and enjoyed dinner as much as they were up and down from the table, taking care of the next course or, in the stews' cases, picking up plates and serving the next.

Mr. Whitman sat at the head of the table, directly to my right, with only Joel sitting between us. He was as charming as his crew, filling the hours of dinner with stories from his own travels and experiences on boats. He took a small amount of time to go over what he expected from his crew on this trip, where they'd be going, what kind of guests would be joining from time to time — which Joel informed me was rare. Apparently, it was usually the captain who would cover all of that.

Still, for the most part, Mr. Whitman sat back and ate his food and drank his scotch quietly, smiling as he listened to the crew.

More than once, I felt the heat of his gaze on me.

Fortunately, I'd learned my lesson from earlier. Unless he was speaking, I didn't dare cast so much as a glance in Mr. Whitman's direction. I kept my focus on Joel, or whoever was speaking, or my food.

Not much longer now, and I'll be out of here...

Dessert was served, and I was already feeling lighter, more jubilant at the fact that I had nearly escaped dinner unscathed. But then, after a loud roar of laughter from a story Joel had told, Mr. Whitman dipped his spoon into the crème brûlée and asked, "And what about you, Miss Dawn?"

I paused mid-bite, a spoonful of creme and caramelized sugar floating in the air as my cheeks instantly flushed. Every head at the table had turned, all eyes focused on me, and I wanted to shrivel up and die on the spot.

I cleared my throat, putting the spoon back in the dainty dessert dish to save myself from dropping it on the table. "What about me, Mr. Whitman?"

"Please, it's Theo," he said with a smile. Then, those chromatic eyes caught a glimmer of the chandelier as they stared at me so unapologetically it unnerved me in every way. "What will you do this summer, while Joel is onboard with us?"

Joel squeezed my knee under the table encouragingly. He knew how uncomfortable it made me to have the attention on me like that, but the way he smiled at me told me it was important to him that I make a good impression.

I managed a shaky smile. "Well, I'm going to do some traveling of my own, actually. Spain, France, Italy, Switzerland, Austria, Germany, the Netherlands... I'm not exactly sure where I'll end up yet, honestly — depends on where I can find work. But I want to travel and see new cultures." I paused. "Mostly through the lens of my camera."

There was something murmured down the table, and a few soft giggles had my neck heating. I picked up my spoon again, hoping the moment was over, but Theo only grabbed his scotch and leaned in closer.

"You're good," he said, and that had everyone's heads swiveling again. "The photos you showed me today... they were stunning."

I shook my head. "I was just playing around, killing some time. The lighting wasn't the best..."

"You don't have to be modest, Miss Dawn," he said, and the way he stared at me made it impossible to look away.

Joel squeezed my knee. "I tell her that all the time," he said to Theo. "Every picture she takes is amazing, but in her eyes, they're never good enough."

Theo chuckled. "Sounds like true entrepreneurial spirit." He sipped from his glass, his eyes on me again. "You said you'll be finding work? Do you mean internships?"

"Oh, no," I said hurriedly, shaking my head. "I just mean house sitting or pet sitting, working on grape harvests or picking up a nanny gig, whatever I can to have a place to stay and not go through my savings too soon. I've already found a place to pet sit in Valence, which will be my next stop after I leave Barcelona."

Theo smiled, and there was something in his eyes I couldn't quite place... something like curiosity, or amusement, or respect. I tried to figure out which it was, but he looked away too quickly, diving into his dessert again. And when he did, the conversation shifted, one of the stewardesses taking over. It was the same one from earlier, the one who didn't seem thrilled that I was coming to the crew dinner. I learned that her name was Ivy, and that she and Joel had worked together the past two summers. In fact, she was the reason Joel was selected for this job. Apparently, her uncle did business with Theo.

She was beautiful, and charming, and sweet and kind.

And now, she was the center of attention again.

I blew out a breath of gratitude and went back to eating my dessert quietly, but then Theo interrupted, dropping his spoon suddenly before folding his hands together in front of him, elbows on the table.

"You should come with us."

The silence of the table was deafening in that moment, and I had a mouthful of crème brûlée as I glanced around the table, wondering who he was talking to.

His eyes were hard on me.

"It makes sense, after all. You want to travel, to take photographs all over Europe, and while we won't be going inland to some of the countries you mentioned, we'll be cruising along some of the most beautiful and interesting places in the world. And you wouldn't need to stay in hostels or house sit for strangers." His eyes flicked to the table before he lifted his glass toward Joel. "You'd be with your man."

I was sure my jaw was on the table. In fact, I was slightly surprised to not find a goop of creme on my chin when I dabbed it with my napkin, placing it gingerly in my lap again as I tried to process. "Mr. Whitman — er, *Theo* — that... that's unbelievably kind of you to offer. But I couldn't impose. Surely, there isn't room for—"

He laughed at that, gesturing around him with his large hands wide and open. "No room? Aspen, look around you. There is nothing *but* room."

"I believe she means in the crew cabins, sir," Captain Chuck offered.

But Theo waved him off. "There are thirteen staterooms on this yacht, and four of them are on the lower deck just above where the crew quarters are. We could easily arrange a room for you and Joel to share there."

I didn't miss the way the crew shifted uncomfortably at that, and once again there was a murmuring down the table. It didn't take a genius or yacht junkie to figure out that him offering us a stateroom was extremely rare and entirely confusing.

"I'm sorry, I just don't think that—"

"Please," he said earnestly. "I insist."

Our eyes connected in the warm light from the chandelier, and all at once I was aware of every sense — the way the linen napkin felt bunched in my fists under the table, the cool breeze off the sea, the smell of the salt and the sweet dessert, the soft sound of the water lapping the side of the boat.

"Babe," Joel said, grabbing my hand under the table as he turned to me. His dark eyes were bright and hopeful. "This is an amazing opportunity, and a very generous offer. You wouldn't have to worry about the cost of travel or accommodations, you'd get to see amazing sights and build up your portfolio, just like you wanted." He shrugged. "And we'd be together. We wouldn't have to be apart this summer."

My heart squeezed at the way he pleaded with me, and I couldn't deny that it sounded incredible — but that was part of the problem. It was too good of an offer to be true, and I had no feasible logic to guide me through *why* a billionaire yacht owner would offer such a thing to a jobless college graduate.

Theo let out another chuckle, fingers trailing the rim of his glass. "I can see it in your eyes. You're uncomfortable with having a free ride, aren't you?"

I didn't have to respond for him to gauge that was true.

"Tell you what. You can work for me, too, while you're onboard. I need some updated photographs of the boat, and I'll be entertaining clients and guests from time to time. They'd love to have their own professional photographer."

I opened my mouth to argue that I was not a professional, but he didn't give me the chance.

"You work for me when I ask you to, and the rest of the time, you're free to go ashore and explore just like you were planning. Or take photos from the boat, whichever you prefer. So, what do you say, Miss Dawn?"

I glanced around the table at the eyes staring at me, and I read every emotion from curiosity and envy to apathy and boredom. But the eyes that asked the most of me were Joel's, and I saw it clear as day that he wanted me to accept.

My stomach sank as my dream summer slipped away, along with all the fantasies I'd had of being alone. But I knew if I refused Theo, it would insult him — and worse, it would paint Joel in a bad light.

This was a big opportunity for him. And, if I were being honest, a generous offer to me. A free place to stay and free mode of transportation through the beautiful Mediterranean? Who would say no to that?

I'd get to be with Joel. I'd still get to do everything I planned on doing, just a little bit differently now. And it would be good for Joel, for his career — just as much as mine.

I reminded myself of those three important things over and over as I lifted my water glass and held it toward Theo. "I say... thank you. You're very kind, and I'm very grateful for the opportunity."

Joel clapped his hands together with an excited laugh, lifting his glass to cue the rest of the table. And Theo lifted his, too, with his eyes on me, his lips tilted at the corners.

"Here's to tall ships, and small ships, and all the ships at sea," Joel said, and the crew finished the end of the toast with him. "But the best ships are friendships, so here's to you and me."

There was a chorus of *hear, hear* and light laughter as we all clinked glasses, and then the conversation picked up slowly again, along with the sound of spoons clinking against dishes.

When I glanced up at Theo, he was listening intently to a story down the table. But his eyes flicked to mine, just for a moment, and I didn't miss the way he smiled when he looked away again.

I had a feeling Mr. Whitman was used to getting his way.

Even stranger, I had a feeling I kind of liked it, too.

CHAPTER
THREE

The rest of dinner passed uneventfully, and Theo was the first to turn in, reminding his crew to have fun but to remember there was work to be done in the morning. He was kind about it, but once he left, Captain Chuck was more severe, instructing everyone to retire for the night.

The chief stewardess, Emma, showed me and Joel to the stateroom where we'd be staying. She was a small woman, maybe five-feet tall, with curves and long brunette hair highlighted with silver streaks that was braided to the side. I audibly gasped when she opened the door, and she smiled, standing next to it while Joel and I brought our bags inside.

"It's one of the smaller rooms, but hey — compared to bunk beds, I'd say it's an upgrade." Emma smiled, and it wasn't in a way that showed envy or an opinion of any kind. When she turned to look at me, her green eyes were kind and gentle. "I'm excited for you to join us on the voyage, Aspen. And I look forward to getting to know you better."

I blushed, tucking my hair behind one ear. "That's so kind. Thank you, Emma."

"By the way, I'm from Austria. I heard you mention you'd like to visit there. I can tell you all the best places to go — the non-touristy places."

"I would love that," I said, and then we were both laughing as Joel flopped belly first onto the full-size bed.

"This is heaven," he mumbled against the pillows.

"You're washing your own bedding, Joel, just so you know," Emma warned, but it was with a smile. "I'll let you two get settled. See you in the morning," she said to me next, and then she closed the door and left us alone.

Joel and I were both exhausted by the time we brushed our teeth and changed for bed, but the excitement of the day filled us, and Joel pressed me into the sheets and kissed down my neck until I came to life again under his touch.

It didn't last long once he was inside me, but I didn't mind — just being connected to him had me overflowing with happy hormones. When we finished, he kissed my cheek and pulled my back to his chest, curling around me like the Cheshire cat, and we fell asleep.

He was already gone the next morning when I woke.

It was just past seven, but when I got dressed and made my way up to the main deck, I wondered how I'd slept in so long with all the commotion. The crew was busy rushing this way and that, the deck hands working together and calling out terms that made no sense to me — like *stern spring* and *bow spring*. Each member of the crew had earpieces in and walkie-talkies on their hips that they used to communicate with each other, and there was never a moment of silence as they got the boat ready to pull away from the marina.

I grabbed a muffin from the galley where a small continental breakfast was set up for the crew, and then I walked around, listening and watching, taking pictures of the crew as they did their various jobs. I felt that same unease niggling in my belly as I watched everyone work so hard. It didn't feel right that I was there, that I didn't have a role to play that morning. I took pictures like they mattered, like I was there for a reason, but I couldn't shake the reality that I had no place being there at all.

"Hey," Emma said when I passed where she was arranging flowers as a centerpiece in the main deck salon. "Got a second to help me?"

I dropped my camera, letting it hang from the strap on my neck. "Oh God, *please* give me something to do so I feel a little less useless."

She chuckled at that, finishing where she was arranging the flowers before she waved for me to follow her. I had a little more time to study her in the light, and what struck me was she had such feminine curves, but such a strong, square-set jaw and severe green eyes. She could have been a movie star, but at the same time, felt as comfortable as a relative.

We gathered behind the bar, and then she handed me a clipboard with a long list of liquor, wine, and beer names.

"I need to make the rounds and check on the staterooms, make sure everything is looking the way it should. Can you go through this list and take inventory of how much we have of each, and highlight any that are under the minimum amount listed beside it?" She tapped the paper to show me where I'd find that amount.

I nodded. "I'm on it."

Emma winked at me, and when she left, I instantly felt better having something to do — even though I was fairly certain Emma already went through this list and had an idea of what she was working with before we left shore. Still, she saw me wandering like a lost puppy and gave me a task.

I liked Emma.

I took my time doing the inventory, but then I was back to making my rounds, camera in my hands as I tried to be as out of the way as possible while still capturing some shots of the crew, the yacht, and the shoreline as we cruised alongside it. I didn't miss the looks I got from most of the crew — a mixture between curiosity and annoyance. They wondered why I was here just as much as I did, and I tried my best to stay out of their way and appear like I was working just as they were.

Emma had given me a copy of the cruise itinerary after I finished up at the bar, and I learned we were cruising toward Saint-Tropez first. We would take it slow and easy, and likely make landfall there around sunset the next evening. Just the casual way she'd said it to me made me laugh. How absurd that I should be on a boat this size on my way to a place I'd only ever dreamed of going before now.

I wandered up the stairs that led from the main deck to the owner's deck, bypassing that level completely and continuing on to the sun deck. It was the highest of the four, and had one of the two pools onboard, as well as the hot tub. When I made the final ascent and rounded off the staircase, I stopped mid-stride at the sight of Theo.

He was sitting on the edge of the pool, his legs in the water, sunglasses covering his eyes as he tapped away on the laptop balanced on his thighs. There was a glass of water sweating next to him and a platter of fruits and vegetables that were half-eaten.

He wore nothing but a pair of navy blue swim trunks, and just as I expected the day before when I'd first met him in that suit, his chest and arms and abdomen were lined with exquisite muscles, tanned and highlighted by a sheen of sweat or lotion, I couldn't be sure. The Spanish shoreline stretched out in a picturesque way behind him, and I found my finger itching where it hovered over the shutter button of my camera. Luckily, this time, I had the good sense not to give in to the urge.

I stood rooted in place, watching him type and the way the muscles on his arms flexed and tightened with the movement. His dark blond hair was disheveled, and something about his bad posture as he sat there rounded over his laptop made me smile.

He's human, after all.

I'd come up top to get a different view of the shore, but taking the cue from the rest of the crew, I knew I should try to be invisible when it came to Theo. So, slowly, I took a step backward, trying to be quiet as I made my way back downstairs.

I hadn't set foot on the second stair down before Theo said, "I'm not going to push you into the pool, if that's what you're afraid of."

I turned to find him smirking and still tapping away on his laptop.

After a moment, he closed the screen and set the computer aside, chuckling when he looked up to find me still gripping the stair railing. "Please," he said, gesturing to the pool. "Join me."

My eyes shifted to the pool, back to Theo, and back to the pool.

"I'm not accustomed to having to make requests twice, Miss Dawn."

His voice was deep and smooth, and he relaxed back onto his palms, stretching out and letting the sun cast its rays over his tanned, cut abdomen.

I swallowed, tucking my hair behind my ear as I shuffled across the deck. My hands left my camera only long enough to lower me down on the opposite side of the pool, then I dropped my feet into the cool water and held my camera like a lifeline once more.

"Beautiful, isn't it?" Theo said, and I glanced up at him just long enough to see his gaze tracing the shoreline.

I looked at where my hands folded over my camera again and nodded.

"Have you ever been to Europe before?"

I shook my head.

Theo was quiet for a long pause, so much so that I looked up again and found him leaning forward, elbows balanced on knees, sunglasses pulled down to the tip of his nose as his eyes assessed me. "I make you uncomfortable."

It was a statement, not a question, and it made my cheeks heat so furiously I let my hair fall in front of my face again to hide the crimson.

"I'm sorry," I said.

"Don't be," Theo replied with a chuckle. "Do I scare you?"

"No," I said with a laugh of my own. "I just... I feel a little out of place."

"Because you're on a multi-million-dollar yacht?" He frowned. "I don't understand, isn't that commonplace for everyone?"

He smirked at his joke, and I relaxed a little, loosening the grip on my camera. "That's part of it, yes."

Not to mention the way you stare at me like you want to eat me alive...

"But it's more so that I feel weird not working, especially when everyone else is." I nodded to his laptop. "You included."

"Ah, you caught me," he said, sighing as he shoved his sunglasses back up his nose and looked at the laptop. He pushed it even farther away, like that would stop him from reaching for it. "I'm trying to take an actual vacation, but I'm afraid I'm a bit of a control freak."

"Worried the building will burn down in your absence?"

He chuckled. "Something like that."

"What is it you do, anyway?"

At that, his head snapped back a little, like the question was a smack across the cheek.

Oh, God.

"I'm sorry," I rushed out, shaking my head. "I should probably know that already, shouldn't I? Oh, God. I'm sorry." I shook my head more furiously, gripping my camera tight again. "I shouldn't have asked."

"No, no," Theo said, holding his hands out toward me. "It's alright. It's refreshing, actually." He leaned back on his palms again, pausing. "What do you *think* I do?"

I shrugged. "Hedge funds?"

He barked out a laugh at that. "That's a fair guess, given the size of this yacht. Sadly, I'm terrible with investments, which is why I pay someone to handle mine for me." Theo reached for a grape on the platter next to him, popping it in his mouth. "Ever heard of Envizion?"

I balked. "You work for the biggest database management system in America?"

"Worse. I created the beast."

My jaw dropped open. I couldn't help it, and Theo laughed at me before I could clamp my teeth together again. "Wow. I feel like an idiot."

"Don't. If you're not in Silicon Valley or an avid reader of business magazines, I don't expect you to know who I am. And like I said," he added with a smile. "It's kind of refreshing." Theo furrowed his brows, looking off in the distance. "Usually, people know who I am before we've even been introduced properly. Or rather, they *think* they know who I am."

He swallowed, his Adam's apple bobbing hard in his throat. When he looked at me again, I tore my eyes away.

Silence fell between us, and I watched my feet kicking in the water, my mind racing. No wonder my sister had flipped out when I mentioned Theo. Envizion had started more than a decade ago as one of the first email marketing companies for big corporations and small businesses alike. But over time, it had grown more in the technology and database software arena. And today, it was by far the best known and most successful. Their commercials ran during the Super Bowl, boasting their latest innovations. They sponsored sporting events and business conventions. Their name was on every software imaginable.

I didn't have to be in the workforce to know that practically any company worth working for used Envizion technologies for their database management, and that there was more money in that company than I could even wrap my head around.

"You'll be pulling your weight around here," Theo said after a while, and I frowned at him in confusion. "I'll have days where I'll want you onboard taking photographs for some guests I'll be entertaining. And I've already seen you taking pictures of the crew and the boat and the shoreline."

He's been watching me?

I sighed. "I suppose."

"And you'll be doing work of your own, the same you'd have done if you were on the original trip you planned." He tilted his head. "What is your goal with the photographs you capture in your time over here?"

I kicked my feet in the water, tucking my hands under my thighs. "I want to build a travel photography portfolio to use in my job applications when I return to the States."

Theo nodded. "And in your dream scenario, who would call you and offer you a job at the end of it all?"

"Dream scenario?"

He nodded.

"*TIME Magazine*," I said on a laugh, because I knew it was ridiculous to even consider. "But really, I'd be happy with any photojournalist position that gave me free rein to travel and capture what I felt was worth capturing."

"Street photography?"

I smiled in surprise. "Ideally, yes."

Theo took his sunglasses off, leaning forward again and watching me from across the pool. The way the blue water of the sea lay out behind him and the turquoise water of the pool reflected, his eyes almost glowed, the gray replaced by a translucent blue.

"I look forward to the day your photos and name are in that magazine."

I pulled my hair over one shoulder, twirling the ends of it. "You say that like it will happen."

"It will," he said confidently. "And I'll frame it when it does."

I scoffed. "On the off chance it *did* actually happen, it would be years from now. You wouldn't even remember me."

Something sparked in his eyes, and his lips curled just a millimeter before they leveled out again. Then, he scrubbed a hand over his jaw, sliding his sunglasses back on and standing so quickly I fumbled to do the same.

"I need to make a call," he said, grabbing his laptop. "Please, help yourself to anything you'd like," he added, gesturing to the plate of fruit and the bar at the far end of the deck. Then, he paused, laptop tucked to his side, a line of sweat dripping from between his chest down the valley where his abs rippled together. "And Miss Dawn?"

"Yes?"

"You are consequential," he said, voice low and rasped. "You'd do well to realize that and use it to your advantage."

He left me with those words, and I spent the rest of the morning dissecting them in his absence.

CHAPTER FOUR

"**I** was kind of thinking we could hang out just the two of us," I said to Joel later that night as he changed out of his khakis and polo and into basketball shorts and a white t-shirt. His dark hair was a little fluffed after he pulled the shirt over his head, and I ran my fingers through the tendrils. "I'm sure you're beat after such a long day."

It was almost ten o'clock, and Joel *did* look worn out — his eyes tired, face long, shoulders slumped a little. Still, he smiled a lazy smile and pulled me into him, kissing me long and slow. "I'm a little tired, but it's important I get to know the crew outside of just working alongside them all day. I especially need to get to know my new boss, the bosun, Eric. I haven't worked with him before."

My shoulders deflated. "Oh."

"We'll have plenty of time for just the two of us, I promise," Joel said, kissing my nose. "But tonight?"

He pulled me toward the cabin door, and as soon as he opened it, the faint sounds of laughter and music drifted up from the crew mess in the lower deck. "We party."

I rolled my eyes as he tugged me under his shoulder and kissed my cheek, then he grabbed my hand and led me down to where some of the crew had gathered. The Captain was already asleep in the stateroom next to ours, First Officer Wayland was on watch up top, and I didn't see the engineers anywhere. But the chefs, stewardesses, and deck hands were all together in the crew mess, talking and laughing, each with a drink in their hand.

"You're allowed to drink on the boat?" I asked Joel on a whisper.

"Not *really*," he confessed. "It's actually a liability, legally, but Captain Chuck is pretty cool. As long as we don't miss our night watch when it's our turn and we wake up in time for work in the morning?" Joel shrugged. "He's cool with it."

I frowned, opening my mouth to ask more questions, but I didn't get the chance.

"Ah, looks like Prince Woods decided to grace us with his presence," Ivy joked as Joel and I made the final descent from the stairs. "How is it up in the palace?"

Joel narrowed his eyes at her before pulling her under his arm and rubbing her scalp with one of his knuckles like she was his little sister. She laughed and shoved him off, and at the same time, one of the other deck hands tossed him a beer.

"You want one?" he asked me next. It was hard to keep all the names straight from dinner the night before, but I was pretty sure his name was Ace. He was tall and built like a bull, with dark brown skin and muscles straining against the fabric of his t-shirt.

"I'm okay. Thank you, though."

Ace shrugged in a *suit yourself* manner before plopping down at the table where Emma, Ivy, and another stewardess whose name I couldn't recall were already seated. Joel cracked his beer open and was already in a conversation with Eric while everyone at the table got back to what they were talking about before we walked in. I stood right by the stairway, grabbing my elbow with the opposite hand and wishing I had my camera to hold onto.

Emma patted the bench next to her, scooting over a little and offering me a kind smile. "How was your first day onboard?" she asked once I was seated.

I shrugged. "To be honest, I think I'm still in shock that I'm here."

"That's fair," Emma said with a chuckle. "I'm sure you'll settle in soon enough."

"I just feel odd, meandering around while everyone is working so hard."

"Well, if you ever need something to do, come see me and I guarantee I can keep you busy for a few hours," Ivy said, tossing her long blonde hair over her shoulder with a wink to the girl sitting next to her. She really was strikingly beautiful, with emerald green eyes and lips painted a deep blush. She had a beauty mark just above her top lip like Marilyn Monroe, and the way she smiled was confident and sexy.

"And then what would you do?" Emma challenged with an arched brow. "I already have a hard enough time wrangling you and Celeste as it is."

"Hey! It's not my fault," the girl next to Ivy defended, elbowing Ivy playfully. She had beautiful brown skin and jet black hair, with eyes just as dark. Her English was perfect, but lilted with a Spanish accent. "*She's* the bad influence."

"I work harder than any other stewardess you've had and you know it," Ivy said to Emma. "That's why you wanted me for this job."

"Oh, yeah," Ace said with a roll of his eyes. "I'm sure it had *nothing* to do with the fact that your uncle works with Theo."

"Shut up," Ivy said, tossing a pretzel at him with her eyes narrowed. "I earned this spot just as well as the rest of you."

"You know I'm kidding, baby," he said, pulling her into his chest and kissing her hair.

I smiled. "How long have you two been dating?"

At that, the whole table fell silent, and then a chorus of laughter rang out. "Oh, no, we're not together," Ivy explained. "Sorry, I guess it must seem odd for an outsider. We're all a little flirtatious around here." She smiled at Ace, then at Celeste, and then — very purposefully — at Joel. She shrugged when she faced me again. "Sometimes we make out or hook up, but it's never anything serious."

I balked at her forwardness, glancing at Joel, but he was already locked back in conversation with his new boss.

Emma squeezed my leg under the table and leaned in to whisper for only me to hear. "I've worked with Joel three summers now, babe. Trust me — he only has eyes for you."

I smiled on a nod, and really, I had no reason to believe otherwise. I was more surprised at the nonchalant way Ivy had spoken about the crew hooking up. Then again, I supposed if you were stuck on a boat with the same people for a long time, it made sense that attraction would grow.

The night went on, and Joel bounced around the room the same way he did when we used to go to college parties at CU. I stayed in the same spot at the table, listening to conversations, laughing at jokes, watching with amusement as the crew danced and ragged on each other. It seemed like most of them had worked together at least once before, save for Eric, the two chefs, and one of the deck hands, Mario. Still, they seemed to fit right in.

I found myself drifting into my own little world, as I often did at parties. It was all so overwhelming for me, and I slipped into my usual state of numbing out, thinking of sleep, wondering what the rest of the trip would be like. I was lost in that daze when Ivy's gold-manicured nails tapped the wood in front of where I sat.

"Do you ever wear makeup, Aspen?"

Celeste nudged her while Emma whispered a hushed *Ivy* under her breath.

"What?" she asked innocently, shrugging. "I just haven't seen her wear any since she's been here." She shook her head, making a clicking sound with her tongue against her cheek before her hand grabbed mine. Her fingers were slim and cool. "I ask only because I'm into cosmetics. And your eyes," she said, shaking her head as she stared at me. "They're so unique. I'd *love* to give you a makeover one day, if you'd be up for it."

"Oh, yes! That would be so fun!" Celeste agreed.

They looked at me expectantly, and my eyes flicked to Joel, to Emma, to anyone who might save me, but everyone just stared and waited.

"Uh... sure," I managed with a smile. "My sister used to do my makeup and hair back home. I kind of miss it."

Ivy squealed and clapped her hands together. "Perfect! It'll be a fun project."

"You always did love a challenge, Ivy," Celeste murmured, and that made Ivy smile and elbow her friend before she stood from the table and announced it was time to do shots.

Everyone roared in approval, gathering around the small countertop where the alcohol bottles were lined as I shrank into myself overanalyzing that last comment. Emma stood, too, but stopped long enough to squeeze my shoulder. "You doing okay?"

I took a deep breath, nodding with what little smile I could manage. "Yeah. I think I just need some air. Can you tell Joel I'm going up on the main deck for a bit but I'll be back?"

"Sure thing. And hey," she said, offering me a kind smile. "I know it's all overwhelming right now, but don't worry. Everyone here is harmless — albeit a little crazy, too." She chuckled. "We get rowdy sometimes. We laugh and joke and pick on each other. We're like a big, misfit family. And you're a part of that family now."

I smiled in return, though I didn't *feel* like part of the family. I thanked her all the same, waiting until all the focus was on the shots being poured before I excused myself. I took the stairs two at a time up to the main deck, and as soon as I passed through the salon and out onto the open deck, I heaved a sigh of relief.

The salty air was cool but pleasant against my hot skin. The only sound up here was the waves, and I smiled at the peacefulness of it, making my way leisurely to the bow of the boat. Resting my arms on the railing, I let my head fall back, closing my eyes and inhaling a deep breath.

Something squeezed in my chest once I was alone, a foreign but noticeable pinch that I couldn't decipher. I'd been feeling it build ever since Joel and I left the States, like my body was trying to tell me something.

It was such a strange time in my life — an in-between state of being that left me wondering where I belonged, or if I belonged anywhere at all. I was no longer a student, defined by the university I attended or the major I declared. Yet, I wasn't an adult, either. I didn't have a job or a home of my own or a plan for what would happen next.

Like a leaf on the water, I felt adrift, floating without purpose.

A heavy exhale left my chest as I blinked my eyes open, and when I did, I found a sky full of stars above. My breath caught at the sight. Sure, there were beautiful night skies in Colorado, especially if you hiked out into the Rockies and got away from the capital. But these stars were bright and twinkling, the Spanish shores quiet and dim in comparison.

I wasn't sure how long I stood there looking up at the sky, but it was long enough for my neck to start hurting. I rolled it a few times and rubbed the back of it with one hand before I turned toward the boat, leaning my back against the railing.

Then, my eyes caught on a different light shining above.

The owner's suite was on the next deck up, the windows large and wide, offering sweeping views of the water. There was a soft, warm glow coming from the lamps inside.

And a silhouette of a man.

It was hard to make out more than a shadow, but it looked like Theo had his hands in his pockets, his shoulders relaxed, his hair a bit mussed. From this angle, I couldn't be sure where his eyes were focused.

They were probably on the sea, or perhaps the stars. Maybe he was watching the shoreline, the twinkling lights of the homes peppering the land. Maybe he was looking over his yacht, noting what his hard work had bestowed him.

But that pinch in my chest painted another scenario.

And I swore I felt those magnetic eyes on me.

CHAPTER
FIVE

I woke the next morning to Joel wrapped around me like a bear, his arms and legs tangled with mine, a thin sheen of sweat forming where our skin met. I didn't mind the warmth, though, and I snuggled into him until he groaned and peeled himself out of bed far too early for my taste. But he had work to do, and he was out of the cabin before the sun had fully risen.

I took my time, showering and trying to tame my hair before dressing for the day and making my way up to the main deck. Bagel in hand, I snuck up to the sun deck while it was still vacant and took some stunning photos of the sunrise. I played with the aperture and shutter speed, varying the focus from the yacht to the water to the shoreline in the distance.

"Enjoy the peace while you can."

I jumped, breathing a sigh of relief when I saw Wayland. He smiled and leaned his elbows on the railing next to me, sunglasses-covered eyes cast toward the shore.

"We're landing in Saint-Tropez a little earlier than we thought," he said. "And Theo just informed me we'll have our first guests onboard."

"Oh?" I asked. I liked that Wayland was talking to me. He didn't seem to talk much to anyone other than Captain Chuck, and he had a thick, unique Jamaican accent that I could listen to all day.

He nodded. "Don't get me wrong, Theo is a wonderful owner and we're all lucky to work for him. It's much better than a charter," he added with a shake of his head. "That said, he has some... *interesting* friends and business partners. So, just be prepared."

I chuckled. "Well, I can just disappear into my cabin."

Wayland smiled my way, clucking his tongue. "Ah, no such luck, I'm afraid."

I arched a brow.

"Captain asked me to inform you that you'll have your first assignment onboard this evening," he said, tapping the railing in front of me as he stood straight again. "Theo has requested you join him and his guests for dinner, drinks, and entertainment."

"To take pictures," I realized.

"Indeed." Wayland took a deep breath, eyeing the shore again. "Are you feeling sick still?"

I frowned.

"Joel mentioned you'd felt a little seasick the first day."

"Oh," I said with a flush. "I think it was just nerves. I'm fine."

"Good," Wayland said decidedly. We stood quietly next to each other for a few moments before he added, "If you really want a lifestyle worth capturing, you need to come to Jamaica."

I smiled. "Oh yeah?"

Wayland pressed his lips together with an affirmative nod, like I had no idea how amazing the island was and there was no way for him to truly convey it. "The food, the music, the people — one of a kind."

"You'll have to show me someday."

"It would be my pleasure," he said, knocking on the railing. "But first, let's see if you survive the day."

He said it as a joke, but all the humor left me with my next breath, one that made me grimace at the thought of what I was about to be thrown into.

Wayland chuckled. "Just remember to smile, do as they ask, and stay out of the way. Oh, and don't take anything too personally." He shrugged, already walking backward toward the stairs. "Remember, these people are so rich they never needed manners."

He tipped an imaginary hat in my direction, and I hummed a little laugh, shaking my head as I turned back to the shoreline with the pink sky slowly turning blue above it. And though I'd only been awake a couple of hours, I found myself thinking of a nap.

It seemed I would need all the energy I could muster.

The sand-colored buildings that sprawled the Saint-Tropez shoreline looked almost pink as we pulled into the port. Emma informed me that there weren't many ports the yacht could dock at, and that usually we would anchor a ways out and take one of the two small tenders stored in the lowest deck to shore.

As it was, we pulled up to the dock and I took photos as Joel and the other deckhands rushed about, tying lines and using what looked like giant, oversized yoga bolsters that were bigger than me to keep the yacht from scraping the dock when we fully pulled in.

There was a small group of people waiting on the dock, and when Theo made his appearance on the main deck, they all cheered in unison, hollering out various greetings and jokes as Theo smiled and held his hands out as if to say *yes, it is I, your King.*

Eric gave me a flat look, one that told me he was about as excited about having guests aboard as Wayland was. I thought I heard him whisper something like *good luck* as he passed me on his way to help Joel at the front of the boat. And I swallowed, holding tight to my camera as Ace held out his hand and helped each of the guests onboard.

There were three women and two men, and the women rushed forward first, one of them running toward Theo and flinging herself into his arms. He caught her easily and spun her around, kissing her cheek, and I snapped a photo of the moment while ignoring the pinch in my stomach at the sight.

The woman chattered on excitedly as the other two girls slipped into Theo's arms, close and familiar, sharing kisses and warm greetings. Two of the women looked like they could be twins, with long, thick blonde hair and dazzling white smiles outlined by lips painted pink. The other one had auburn hair that glowed a fiery red in the setting light of the sun. Every single one of them was dressed opulently in form-fitting dresses, oversized hats and sunglasses, high heels and designer handbags.

I guessed the *no shoes* rule didn't apply to them.

I continued taking photos from a distance as Theo greeted the men next, who were decidedly quieter and calmer, though they seemed to poke fun at each other as they shook hands. Once everyone was onboard, Theo squeezed the shoulder of the taller of the two men, as if to exert his dominance over the group with just that one gesture.

"Welcome aboard the *Philautia,*" he said with a wide grin. And right on cue, Ivy and Celeste appeared with trays of champagne, their uniforms pressed and neat, hair pulled back into tight buns.

Our new guests all clapped gleefully, and once everyone had a glass of champagne in hand, they clinked the expensive crystal together in celebration.

Click.

I'd successfully stayed hidden until the moment they each took a sip and I snapped a picture. The sound had heads turning in my direction, and one of the blonde women — the one who had thrown herself into Theo's arms — arched a perfect eyebrow over her bedazzled Gucci sunglasses. "I didn't realize we had paparazzi, Theo," she said in a thick French accent.

I flushed, holding my camera right below my chest. I opened my mouth to assure her I was far from that, but then remembered Wayland's warning to keep quiet and stay out of the way.

"This is Aspen," Theo said, crossing the deck until he was standing next to me. He seemed to suck up all the oxygen as his Tom Ford dress shoes tapped their way across the teak. He wore an all-black suit, tailored to perfection, the only pop of color being an icy-blue neck tie that made the steel gray of his eyes glow even more fiercely. His hair was gelled and styled in a Hollywood swoop, and yet a thick patch of stubble still graced his jaw, as if he looked that rich and decadent without trying at all.

I watched the women as they visibly swooned when he passed, saw how the men smiled in admiration as much as they sneered in jealousy. And then, he was beside me, and in a gesture I never could have prepared myself for, his hand met the small of my back.

I inhaled a stiff breath at the contact, at how warm and massive his palm was over the thin fabric of my tank top. He had to have felt it, the way I jolted at the touch, but he held me steady and sure, smiling wide and standing tall and confident at my side.

"Aspen is a travel photographer specializing in lifestyle and street photography," he said, and I frowned, glancing up at him. He didn't return my gaze, though, and I had no option but to roll with the elaboration of who and what I was. "She's joining us for the summer, capturing photos of the yacht, the crew, and all the guests I'll have aboard over the next few months." He tipped his glass of champagne then. "Including you lovely rascals."

A soft chorus of laughter rang out then, and much to my dismay, all eyes were on me.

I smiled at the group uncomfortably. "It's very nice to meet you all," I said softly. "I assure you, I'll be as close to invisible as I can manage."

Theo made a noise under his breath, and his hand curled where it rested on my back, as if he were biting his tongue against something he wished to say.

Just as suddenly as I'd felt it, though, his hand disappeared altogether, and he stepped closer to his guests. "Audrey," he said to the blonde who had thrown herself at him. "I'm sure you'd love some photos on the top deck before the sun sets."

"Oh, we must!" the other blonde chimed in. And then they linked arms, the redheaded woman taking up the other side, and they led the way for the rest of the group up to the top deck.

The evening passed like a desert storm from that moment on, a whirlwind of *take a photo of me here!* and *oh, let me see, let me see, no, I don't like that one, let's take another, get my good side!* and *Theo, take a picture with me!*

I snapped posed pictures and candid pictures alike, cringing more and more as the night progressed and the guests got further inebriated. It seemed the longer the champagne flowed, the more provocative the poses became — smiles turning to pouty lips, eyes glazing over with lust and booze, dresses being hiked up higher and higher.

I really didn't mind, for the most part. I wanted to work. I *wanted* to earn my stay on this incredible yacht. It felt good to have something to do, the way the rest of the crew did.

But at the same time, my soul wrinkled its nose at my memory card being filled with vanity and illustrious glamour where I usually pointed my lens at humility and quiet grace.

I learned over the course of the evening that the men were clients of Theo's — big shot bankers for the largest bank in France. It didn't surprise me that they were Envizion customers, provided that a quick Google search had shown me that Envizion worked with every large bank in America, as well as the Department of Defense, among other impressive names. If my assumptions were correct, these men were likely the heads of his largest account in France, so it was no surprise they were onboard for an evening of entertainment.

The redheaded woman was wife to the taller of the two men, and I caught their names to be Bernard and

Camille. Camille was the nicest of the group. She didn't talk to me, per se, but she did offer apologetic eyes when the other women asked for me by a snap of their fingers.

The other man, who had nearly drunk himself into a stupor before dinner was even served, was named Gilbert. He seemed to believe he and Audrey were an item, but Audrey and the other blonde, Nicolette, were anything but shy about their interest in Theo.

It was fascinating, listening to Theo and Bernard talking business while the women gossiped about their friends and compared their latest shopping trips and exotic travel. For them, a night on a super yacht was just another day in the life. They drank four-thousand-dollar bottles of champagne like it was Bud Light at a frat party, kicked their expensive shoes off their feet without a care in the world, and soaked up the evening like only the rich could.

I also got a glimpse of the crew on their best behavior. I watched Ivy and Celeste serve dinner with cheerful, accommodating smiles and flirtatious jokes aimed at Bernard and Gilbert. Joel and Ace manned the bar, flirting with Audrey and Nicolette like it was part of their job — and by the way the women reacted, it seemed like it really was. Captain Chuck joined the guests for dessert, smiling and answering the questions they peppered him with.

I'd been on the boat for forty-eight hours now, but this seemed like my first *real* experience onboard.

My memory card was nearly full, and my back ached from standing all day by the time the guests finally started to call it a night. Celeste was still behind the bar, mostly keeping an eye on the guests to make sure no one got so drunk they fell overboard. The rest of the crew had been dismissed hours ago.

I didn't have to look at the clock to know it was well after midnight.

Bernard and his wife helped Gilbert walk inside where the staterooms were, as he couldn't do it on his own, and Celeste went with them as a courtesy.

That left Audrey and Nicolette, who were running their fingers through Theo's hair, over the buttons of his dress shirt, along the inside seam of his pants. I tore my eyes from the sight, holding tight to my camera and waiting to be dismissed.

When I glanced back up again, I was met by a pair of heated blue-gray eyes.

Theo watched me like I was the next expensive bottle of champagne he would crack open, like all my efforts to be invisible throughout the night had failed miserably. I'd caught his eyes on me more than a few times throughout the night, though he never said one word to me, not since the introduction on the main deck.

Now, with the men retired inside, and two women hanging on him unabashedly, his gaze was more bold, severe in its unwavering intensity. His fingers held loosely to a half-empty glass of champagne, the other hand gripping the arm of the deck chair he sat in, his jaw ticking incessantly like he was equal parts annoyed and intrigued. Audrey and Nicolette were both piled in his lap, giggling and touching, oblivious to his lack of attention.

He cleared his throat, breaking our eye contact long enough to excuse himself and slither out from the pile of women. They tittered on in his absence, touching each other's hair and smiling tipsily as Theo crossed the deck to where I stood.

For a long moment, he just stood there in front of me, sliding his hands into his pockets. Then, his eyes scanned the shoreline behind me, and the corners of his mouth tilted up just a notch.

"Thank you," he said to the night air and to me and to no one in particular. "I know this is far from the kind of photography you wish to capture in your time abroad."

His eyes found me then, pinning me to where I stood.

I managed a shrug, tucking my hair behind my ear. "Hey, this is part of the deal, right?" I offered what little smile I had energy left to give.

"We'll get you off this boat soon," he promised, nodding toward the shore. "There are far more beautiful things waiting for you on shore."

"I captured some pretty beautiful things tonight."

The words came from me in a rushed whisper, and as soon as I'd said them, I couldn't believe I had. Theo's eyes snapped to mine, and I clamped my mouth shut for fear of saying something else equally as stupid.

Theo tilted his head, frowning, his eyes glazed a bit from the alcohol. He smirked as he took a step toward me, and then another, until he was so close the lapels of his jacket touched my chest. His eyes cast down on me like I was there for no other purpose than for him to stare at, and he took his time, gaze roaming over every inch of me until I heated like a boiling pot of water.

His body jolted suddenly, crashing into mine as Audrey threw her arms around him from behind. I was pinned between the railing and his warm body for no longer than a split second, but it was enough to scar me, to brand me like a hot iron against fresh, bare skin. He stepped away just as quickly, holding out his hands as if to steady me.

"Theo," Audrey said, dragging out the vowels of his name as she hung on his arm. "Nicolette and I want to see the owner's suite."

Nicolette giggled as she slid up on his other side, wrapping her arms around his middle. "Yes, show us the view from your bed, Theo."

They cackled in unison, hands groping, longing moans slipping from between their lips. Theo's eyes were still on me, and I let him hold my gaze until Nicolette dragged her tongue up his neck and sucked the lobe of his ear between her teeth.

I tore my eyes away then, swallowing and looking down at my camera as I waited for them to leave. And they did, by way of the women dragging Theo backward, and him watching me the entire way, until they stumbled into one of the deck chairs. That seemed to shock him back to reality, and he shook his head, turning and throwing his arms around each of the women with a comment that made them both laugh and lean into his sides. He guided them inside and up the stairs, and I stood in the same spot against the railing until the lights flicked on in the owner's suite above.

That silhouette of a man that I'd seen the night before was different tonight — his arms being stretched over head, shirt peeled off, his lips colliding with one woman and then the other. I watched the scene unfold like a voyeur until Theo stumbled backward and hit what I assumed was a button, because in the next second, the curtains suddenly began to draw, hiding the suite from prying eyes.

I hadn't even caught my breath, hadn't had time to question what the hell was wrong with me or what the hell had just happened before Joel stumbled out onto the deck, rushing to me and pinning me against the railing much like Theo had just moments before.

"Babyyy," he said, his breath sour and beer-drenched on my neck. His hands were groping me in the next instant and I pushed them away, squirming out from his touch.

"You're drunk."

For a moment, Joel seemed upset at the comment, but then he smiled lazily, pulling me into his arms and pressing a long kiss to my tightly closed lips. "I am. We went below deck once we were relieved for the night. Eric had some goooood stuff," he said, drawing out the word. He frowned then, framing my face with his hands. "I missed you."

His dark eyes searched mine, and I blew out a long breath, relieving the tension that had my muscles tied in knots. I had no reason to snap at him. I didn't mind that he'd had some drinks after working for so long. If I were the drinking kind, I was sure I'd want to do the same.

"It's been a long day," I finally said.

Joel nodded in understanding. Only he knew the way a full evening of being around strangers drained me, and with another kiss — one I accepted more willingly this time — he tucked me under his arm. "Nothing a good cuddle sesh can't fix."

I smiled, letting him guide me inside, my breath finally evening out the farther we got from Theo and his guests. When we were safely inside our own cabin, we both undressed, took a quick shower together, and climbed into bed. I was relieved yet again when Joel didn't try to have sex with me. I just wasn't in the mood — not after all that had happened. And he must have sensed it, because he just pulled my back to his chest, curling his legs with mine and wrapping his arms tightly around me.

He was snoring softly in my ear less than two minutes later.

But as exhausted as I was, I didn't sleep a wink.

CHAPTER
SIX

I stayed in the cabin the next day.

Kissing Joel on his way out the door, I settled into bed and grabbed my book, reading until I was sick of words on a page. Then, I turned on the television in our room, thankful that by Theo's insistence of me staying on the yacht and thus us being in a stateroom, we had that luxury. I watched three movies in a row before I left the bed only long enough to get myself food. Then, I was right back in the cabin.

Joel didn't question me — not when he came in to check on me just before dinner, and not when he asked if I wanted to join him and the rest of the crew below deck once they were off duty. He knew me better than anyone, and he didn't need to hear me say it to understand that the day before had drained me — physically and mentally — and the only way to refill my tank was to be alone.

Blessedly, being in my cabin all day meant I escaped Theo's guests for their second day onboard. Joel told me before he went below deck that they departed after dinner, and then we pulled away from the dock, away from Saint-Tropez, on our way to Nice.

I slept hard that night — which I was thankful for, since I didn't sleep at all the night before — and I woke the next morning abruptly to the crew bustling around docking us once again. Joel had already gone from our room, and I wondered how he survived like that — working all day every day, drinking all night every night, and somehow waking up before the sun to do it all again.

When I finally peeled myself out of bed, there was a sheet of cream card stock neatly folded on the floor of our room, as if it had been slipped under the door.

Meet me on the main deck. 8 a.m. sharp. Bring your camera.

There was no name under the neatly scripted ink, but it was easy enough to determine who it was from. I sighed, wishing upon wishes that there wouldn't be another group of people for me to cater to yet again. I had barely recovered from the first time, and still had visions I was trying to erase from my mind.

Still, it was part of the deal, part of my *free ride*.

I shook my head, wondering where I would be now, had I not taken Theo's offer. I wouldn't have had as cushy of a bed, that much was certain. And I likely wouldn't have seen such stunning sights even in these first few days.

But at least I'd have been alone.

It was already seven forty-five, so I dressed quickly, grabbing my camera and bringing my small backpack with extra memory cards and lenses just in case. I found

Theo lounging in one of the chairs by the bar, his ankle crossed over knee, *The Wall Street Journal* newspaper spread out between his hands and a tall glass of orange juice on the bar in front of him.

"Ah, good morning, Miss Dawn," he said when I approached, folding the paper and setting it aside. He looked different from the other night, though he wore a navy suit and expensive dress shoes and had his hair styled just the same. Somehow, in the morning light, he seemed a little less intense and a little more boyish.

He smiled easily, folding his hands together in his lap, like the last time I'd seen him he hadn't been mauled by two wolves disguised as French women.

"Morning," I managed with a flat smile of my own.

"Were you ill yesterday?"

I almost laughed at the question, but the fact that he'd noticed I wasn't around cut the sound short. "No, Mr. Whitman... er, Theo," I corrected. "I just..." I swallowed, looking down at my camera before my eyes met his again. "Just needed a day to myself."

The corner of his mouth crept up a bit. "That's understandable. Well, are you feeling better today?"

Everything inside of me wanted to say no, but I plastered on another smile and nodded.

"Good. I was thinking you could come ashore with me. I have some business to tend to, but you could take the day to explore. Nice is beautiful," he added, sweeping his hand toward the open side of the deck. "Much to see."

My heart skipped in my chest. "Really?"

Theo smiled wider. "I told you I'd get you off this boat."

The flat smile I'd given him was replaced by a real one, relief and excitement flooding my chest in equal measure. I did something of a little dance that I didn't mean to do, but it made Theo laugh, and then he hopped up from his chair and grabbed the briefcase next to it. "Grab whatever you'll need. I realize I didn't tell you to bring your passport when I wrote that note."

"I'll be right back!" I was already hurrying back down the stairs before the words had fully left my lips. I dashed into our room long enough to stuff my wallet in my backpack, along with a cardigan just in case.

I didn't have time to find Joel and tell him I was getting off the boat, but I told Ace, and he assured me he'd relay the message. Then, once I was back up top, Theo and I made our way down the ramp that connected the main deck to the dock.

"I was thinking we could have breakfast together, before my meeting and before you wander off on your own," Theo said when we stepped off the ramp. "I know a great little place just a few blocks from here."

I chewed my lip. "Oh, I wouldn't want to impose..."

"You wouldn't. I'm inviting you, after all. Besides, I'd like to see some of the photos you took yesterday, and I have some tips for where you could go today. If you'd be interested."

Once again, I found it impossible to say no when those eyes of his watched me like that. So I simply nodded, and he smiled, another battle won.

Theo Whitman surprised me. I didn't really understand why, provided I didn't know all that much about him. But watching him walk in the narrow streets of Nice, saying *bonjour* now and then as we passed locals and tourists alike, I wondered who he was. I wondered why he wasn't as stuck up and mannerless as the guests he entertained onboard. I wondered why he was sometimes severe and cold when this warm and friendly version of him existed. Was it a front put on for clients? Was it a way to assert his power?

I wondered about his home life, about how he grew up, about whether he wanted to get married and settle down and have children of his own. And I hated that, if I were being honest with myself, the likelihood of me ever finding out the answers to those questions was slim to none. I'd be on his yacht for the next few months, and then I'd never see him again.

My chest pinched.

I was surprised yet again when we made it to the breakfast spot Theo had mentioned. I'd expected him to lead us to a grand restaurant, one where we'd be asked what kind of water we wanted, and each plate would cost at least a small fortune. *Would you like Grey Poupon with your poached eggs, sir?* But instead, he took us to a small bakery, its doors open to the street and two kind, older women working behind the counter. One whiff of the fresh bread and pastries and my mouth was watering too much to dissect the choice further.

Theo ordered in what sounded like perfect French to me, a chocolate croissant for each of us, along with two Caffé Americanos. Then, Theo left a tip so large it made both the women nearly weep in gratitude, and we took a seat at one of the small tables in front of the store.

"So, you speak French?" I asked as Theo pulled our pastries from the paper bag and handed one to me.

"A little," he said. "A little Spanish, too. German. And about ten words in Mandarin."

"You sounded fluent," I said, nodding toward the bakery doors.

He chuckled. "Far from it, but I try." Theo bit into his croissant, the buttery flakes littering the table as he did. He groaned his approval, leaning back in his chair long enough to catch one of the woman's attention inside. He gave her a big thumbs up, pointing to the pastry, and she and the other baker laughed in tandem, the sound filling the street like a song. Their eyes were still glossy from the tip Theo had left, and I wondered if he did that often, if he realized how much it made their day.

In the same moment Theo sat up straight again, a beautiful, luxuriously dressed woman walked by our table, her high heels somehow steady even on the rutted stone. Her eyes found Theo, and she nearly broke her neck watching him even after she had passed our table. Theo smiled and arched a brow in her direction.

Bonjour, she said.

Bonjour ma belle, Theo said back.

And the woman flushed so hard it rivaled the natural red state of my cheeks.

"How do you say *heartbreaker* in French?" I teased.

"*Bourreau des cœurs,*" Theo said, the words rolling off his tongue, nasally and beautiful. But his next words were curt. "Why, is that what you think I am, Miss Dawn?"

My smile slid from my face like a blob of jelly, cheeks heating. "Oh... I'm sorry, I was just—"

Theo laughed. "It's alright. Tease away. If the shoe fits, right?" He smiled with the comment, but I couldn't help but notice the way his brows ticked together, like the joke wasn't all that funny at all.

"I'm sorry if I offended you."

He shook his head quickly, sipping his coffee. "I'm not capable of being offended."

I snorted at that. "Sure, you are. Everyone can get their feelings hurt by something."

"Not if you don't have feelings at all."

"Stone cold, are you?"

"I've found life is easier that way." He shrugged, and I hated how much I liked the smile that found his lips, how sexy it was in its nonchalance.

When did I start to notice how sexy a smile was?

"Can I see the photos you took yesterday?"

I reached into my bag, retrieving my camera and turning on the preview mode before handing it across the table. It was always uncomfortable to hand my baby to someone else, to trust them to hold onto her and care for her and not drop her. But to his credit, Theo put the strap around his neck just in case, and he held the machine steady as he scrolled the photos.

He cringed as much as I did the night I took the photos as he looked through them, and after a few silent moments, he shook his head, handing the camera back to me. "I'm sorry I put you through that."

"It was fine," I lied. "They were nice."

Theo arched a brow. "Do you always lie to make others feel better?"

"What? No, I..."

Theo took another bite of his croissant as he waited for me to defend myself.

"Okay, *fine,*" I conceded. "It wasn't my favorite way to spend an evening, but this was part of our deal."

Theo nodded. "Yes, well, it's my hope that any other jobs I have for you won't be as taxing. Once you send those to me, you can delete them forever and purge your memory," he joked, but it was followed by a pause and a lift of his brows. "Audrey and Nicolette are one of a kind."

The words by themselves made my stomach roll, visions of their tongues and hands on Theo's body flashing in my mind. But the way he said them, the subtle shake of his head and widening of his eyes told me he wasn't a huge fan of the girls.

But then why did he sleep with them?

I shook my head.

Not my business.

"They remind me of my sister in some ways," I said. "She's so naturally beautiful and charming that I think she sometimes forgets she's not the center of the universe." I chuckled. "Although, most of her ex-boyfriends treated her like she was, so maybe it's not her fault she feels that way."

"We're all the center of our own universes," Theo said. "We're told not to be selfish, not to put ourselves first, but if not us, then who?"

I shrugged. "I suppose that's one way of looking at it."

"And what's yours?"

"I don't know that I really have an opinion on it."

Theo rested his elbows on the table, eyes narrowing as he leaned in closer. "Why do you do that?"

I frowned. "Do what?"

"Shy away from saying what you believe, what you want. It's like you want to hide from anyone who shows a centimeter of interest in you, like you couldn't possibly have anything of merit to add to a conversation."

My heart stopped in my chest, the quiet skip of the beat echoing in my ears as I stared back at Theo. It was unnerving, to be pegged down that way by someone who barely knew me.

I cleared my throat. "I just prefer to listen."

Theo watched me like he didn't believe that was all there was to it, but then after a moment, he sat back again, appraising me. "A lot of people could learn to listen more. Myself included."

Theo and I drank our coffee and ate our breakfast in silence for a bit, and then he relaxed more in his chair, crossing an ankle over the opposite knee the way I'd found him earlier this morning.

"Your sister, is she older?"

I shook my head. "Younger. She's just finished her first year at CU."

"And that's where you just graduated?"

"Mm-hmm," I said. "She's there on a volleyball scholarship. I don't know if you're into that sport, but she's *incredible*. She's what they call a libero. It's a defensive position, lots of diving for the ball and stuff. It's amazing to watch her when she's really in her element."

"Do you play?"

"Oh, *God* no." I laughed at the audacity. "My mom used to, though. And my dad is a sports nut, so I think my sister was his saving grace, since he doesn't have any sons. They've been Juniper's biggest fan for as long as I can remember, putting her in summer camps, doing whatever it took to get her to all-state tournaments, buying her all the best gear."

"And what about you?"

"Oh, I'm her biggest fan, too. I love watching—"

"No, I mean, what about *you*," Theo said again. "Have your parents been big supporters of your photography?"

"Oh," I said, looking down at the table and pulling my long hair off my neck. "Yeah. I mean, they know I love photography, but I just think it's not as exciting as volleyball, you know?" I shrugged on a laugh. "Not like they can cheer me on at games or anything."

I didn't like the way Theo's eyes watched me then, his brows pinched together above them, more questions dancing in his eyes that I hoped he wouldn't ask.

"What about you?" I asked, sipping my coffee. "Where did you go to school?"

"Harvard."

I almost spit out my coffee, which earned me a chuckle from Theo as he handed me a napkin. "You went to *Harvard?*"

"Don't get too excited," he said. "I dropped out after my first year."

My eyes bulged. "What? *Why?*"

"Because it was a waste of time."

I blinked.

"I didn't need to be sitting in classrooms all day, listening to washed-up professors try to tell me how to make a career," he said. "Nor did I want to be there. I had no desire to be in honor societies or fraternities or to spend my day throwing frisbee or whatever else my friends were doing. I was too obsessed with coding and database management to care about anything else. It was the early 2000s. The Internet and all it had to offer was bursting with possibility. And *I* was wasting my time and my potential trying to follow society's suggested path." Theo shrugged. "And after one year, I was tired of it."

"What did your parents say?"

Theo chuckled at the horror in my voice. "Oh, they weren't happy. But I know my father better than anyone, and I knew the only way to get him to understand my vision was to just get it done so he could see it in actuality. He's not someone who cheers on a dream," he said. "He cheers on success."

"So you just quit school and...?"

"I started building Envizion. My roommate had the same desire I did. And while, unlike me, he stayed enrolled in school, we spent all our free time working on the business plan and coding and engineering what we had in mind for email marketing. We were especially proficient with server management, which set us apart in those early explorative years." He smirked. "I know you're too young to remember this, but there was a time when there *was* no service for email marketing. So as ancient as it sounds now, it was innovative then."

"I'm not *that* young," I deflected, but I didn't miss how young I sounded trying to defend myself. From my research on Theo after I found out who he was, I knew he was thirty-three — born on December 31st at 11:58 p.m., in 1986 at Bellevue Hospital in Manhattan. There was an old newspaper article about all the New Year's Eve and New Year babies, about the race to be the first baby born in 1987.

I wondered if the author of the article ever realized that he wrote about the birth of a baby who would become one of the youngest billionaires in the world.

"The ripe old age of twenty-one."

"Twenty-two," I corrected.

Theo smiled wider, watching me curiously. He opened his mouth to say something else, but then his phone dinged in his suit pocket, and he pulled it out with a deep frown. He texted something quickly, putting the phone away again, but the line between his brows stayed in place.

"I've got to run," he said, standing abruptly.

I stood, too, the metal of my chair grating against the stones. "Thank you," I said. "For breakfast, and for letting me off the boat."

Theo quirked a brow at that. "I didn't grant you any kind of permission you didn't already have. You're free to leave the boat any time you'd like. I'm not your master, Miss Dawn." Then, he pressed his palms on the table, leaning toward me with a wicked grin. "Though, if there was ever a time you wanted to change that, I would be happy to oblige."

All the blood drained from my face, a shiver sending a flood of goosebumps cascading down every inch of me. I was frozen from his gaze, from those words, for what felt like an eternity.

Then, Theo laughed — and it was the most confusing laugh of my life. I couldn't tell if it was because he'd been joking and the look on my face was exactly the response he was looking for, or if he was dead serious, and he was laughing because he was the only one who knew just how serious he was.

"Have fun today," he said, standing straight once more and sliding his sunglasses over those piercing eyes. "If you can, make your way to the *Château de Bellet* vineyards. It's beautiful there."

And with one last knowing smirk, he left me alone with our half-eaten breakfast.

CHAPTER
SEVEN

For many people, perhaps *most* people, a photograph is simple.

It's a moment captured in time. It's a beautiful landscape — sprawling hills or glistening ocean. It's an action shot — a ball mid-air, a player's face bent in determination. It's a milestone — a graduation, a wedding, a newborn baby. It's a click of a button, a flash-freeze, a bit of light and shadow that serve as a memory, something to be hung on a wall, something to look back on and remember.

For me, a photograph was an entire world.

If you caught the right moment, the right lighting, the right subject — a photograph wasn't just a mirror image. It was a feeling, something that struck you to your core, something that made you pause and reflect. You'd look at it just as much as it would look at you — each of you tilting your heads a bit, digesting, feeling vulnerable.

Feeling seen.

I wandered the streets of Nice with eyes wide open, taking each turn as it came, not abiding by any agenda or map. I held my camera close, nestled between my hands just below my rib cage, finger hovering over the shutter button, itching for the right moment.

When I had a day to myself like that, the hours seemed to dissipate like thick morning fog on a sunny afternoon. I didn't exist as myself. I wasn't Aspen Dawn, recent college graduate and wannabe photographer. Instead, I lived a hundred different lives, all through the lens of my camera.

I was the young girl on her brand-new bike, no training wheels, fear and excitement evident in my eyes as I took a breath, took my feet off the ground, took a chance. And I was the kind-eyed, old man behind her, cigarette dangling from my lips as I gave one final push, the wrinkles of my eyes deepening with a wide smile when the girl sped off on her own, giggling with joy.

Click.

I was the street vendor selling leather coin purses and keychains, exhausted from an early morning of setting up shop, sneaking a brief snooze at my table while I waited for a customer. My head hung heavy between my shoulders, old t-shirt pulled up over my eyes, tan and hairy arms crossed over my large belly. I could just be meditating. I could just be tired. I could just be mourning the loss of someone I loved more than myself. I could just be wondering if life is worth living at all.

Click.

I was both the young man and the old woman, sitting back to back on opposing benches by the sea, one facing the park, one facing the water. We were strangers together in our loneliness. We were strangers, and yet to someone, we were friends, lovers, a son, a daughter, a co-worker, a neighbor. We were strangers, and yet inside each of us, an entire universe of humanity — a forest of wants and needs, of dreams and desires, of past pain and scars and heartbreak and resilience. We read our newspapers. We check our phones. We smile at the passerby and tip our hat. *Bonjour, bonjour.*

Click.

I was even the blushing young girl, legs straddling the sea wall, a boy I rather liked sliding closer and closer between my open legs. I felt the heat of his hungry eyes, felt the cool dampness of his fingertips dancing under my shirt, tracing the wire of my bra. *We're invisible. No one sees us. No one in the world has been this in love, this desperate to touch, this unimaginably happy.* I knew without hesitation that I would forever be safe in that boy's arms. No matter how my heart screamed for me to be cautious, to heed its warnings, I still fell into the boy with the long, dark shaggy hair and the cool hands and the thick erection hiding beneath his jeans.

Click.

I was lost in a new city, in a new country, in a new language and corner of the world. I wandered the streets and took photos until the sun disappeared over the water's horizon, and I realized Theo and I never discussed what time to meet back on the dock.

Then I asked myself why I thought Theo would meet me *at all.*

He wasn't my caretaker. Or, as he had pointed out, *my master.*

I shivered at the memory of that comment, of the way his pupils dilated when the words rolled off his tongue. He had watched me closely for a reaction, and I wondered if the one he got was the one he desired.

I didn't understand him, and more frustrating, I didn't understand *me* when he was near.

He was scrambling me like a frying pan of eggs, and the more I tried to figure out why, the more lost I felt.

I found a café with free Wi-Fi on my way back to the boat, messaging my sister to update her on my travels. She sent a full page of emojis when I told her I was on Theo's boat for the summer instead of traipsing around on my own, and when I asked how volleyball was going, for the first time in my life, she answered with a short *it's great* before demanding that I tell her everything I knew about Theo Whitman.

I laughed, thumbing through my memory card until I found a picture of drunk Audrey and Nicolette hanging all over him from the other night. I snapped a picture of the camera display and sent it to Juniper, who answered with a long line of exclamation points.

I knew he was a dirty little playboy!

Ask him if he wants a new sugar baby.

I rolled my eyes on a laugh at that, and then with a promise to check in again soon, I shoved my phone away and walked the rest of the way to the dock.

I thought about it, though, as I walked, how Juniper would fit nicely with Theo. She was just as gorgeous as he was, and charming, and smart. She'd match him wit for wit. She'd be able to play games with girls like Nicolette and Audrey, and I knew with utmost certainty she'd beat them, too.

I frowned at the thought, shaking it away and letting my mind wander elsewhere the rest of the walk back.

I didn't know if Theo was already back on the yacht when I crossed the ramp to the main deck. If he was, he was nowhere to be found, and so I decided to turn in for the night and thank him again the next time I did see him. The photos I'd captured were strong ones. I knew without even looking. I'd felt it when I snapped them.

I could hear the crew downstairs when I got back to the cabin, likely eating their late dinner or perhaps partying already since Theo was off the boat. Either way, I ignored the note on the bed from Joel saying I could join them when I got back, and instead, gave in to my exhaustion, peeling my clothes off and flopping down face first on the bed.

I was asleep before I could even make it under the covers, but I felt Joel when he came in later that night, covering me up before he slipped under the sheets, too. He kissed my neck, slow and tender at first, but then harder, his pelvis rolling against my ass, hands groping my breasts under my shirt.

He smelled like booze, like a mix of tequila and gin, and the sloppy way he kissed me told me he'd had more than just *a* drink. Normally, it wouldn't bother me. But for some reason, this time, it soured my gut. The more aggressively he kissed, the more my heart raced in my chest as I struggled to keep my breathing even, my body limp.

I could have just opened my eyes, turned in his arms, and met his eager kisses with those of my own. I could have kissed down his navel, taken him in my mouth and done just what I know he likes until he came. I could have slid my panties to the side and let him inside me. I could have done *anything at all.*

Instead, I kept my eyes shut, my limbs heavy, completely unresponsive.

I pretended to be asleep until Joel gave up and rolled away, his soft snores filling our cabin moments later.

And I couldn't figure out why, in the quiet darkness of the bed I shared with my boyfriend who I'd just denied, I was thinking about what it would be like to be touched by Theo Whitman.

CHAPTER
EIGHT

Never in my life did I imagine I would find a "normal" routine on a multi-million-dollar yacht.

Back home, in Boulder, routine was everything for me. I ate the same thing for breakfast, read for about thirty minutes, did a quick high-intensity interval training workout to get my heart and body awake and going, and then I went to my first class. I'd spend the time between classes either taking photos around campus or town, in the mountains, perhaps taking a day trip to get away. My evenings were filled with editing photos, reading, or spending time with Joel. And though there were differences each day, I had a routine that kept me stable and steady, that brought me comfort.

It was part of what I'd been missing, what had been making me uneasy since Joel and I left the States.

But now, there I was, waking up in new waters or docked at a new port every morning, eating the same thing for breakfast, reading for a bit before I did my workout, and then busying myself throughout the day by either taking photographs for Theo or helping Emma and the other stewardesses. I found I didn't mind it, even taking photographs for Theo had become easier now that I knew what to expect.

Plus, none of the other guests on the boat were as bad as Audrey and Nicolette — at least, not yet.

I was exhausted by the time the sun set each night, though — eyes red and dry as I edited photos and worked on my portfolio. When Joel came into the cabin, it was usually only long enough to shower and change before he was dipping out for his night watch, or dragging me out of the room and down to hang out with the rest of the crew. And where I would stay for an hour or so, Joel would be down there all night.

It baffled me how he had the energy.

The crew was growing on me, and in small ways, it felt like they were starting to accept me, too. Emma would fill me in on the inside jokes when I didn't understand them, and she and I spent a lot of my time below deck talking about her life in Austria and what it was like for me growing up in Colorado. We compared our favorite hikes, exchanged pictures of lakes and mountains and valleys, and told stories of our childhood dogs. She held her stomach with a longing smile as she told me about her mom's delicious wienerschnitzel and tafelspitz, and I tried to explain why dipping pizza crust in honey was a life-changing culinary event and the *only* acceptable way to eat pizza in Colorado.

I could talk to Emma the same way I could talk to my sister or to Joel, like we had been friends for a lifetime already.

Wayland was much like me in that he didn't hang out with the crew that often, but when he did, I loved to listen to him play his guitar softly and chime in on the conversation from time to time. Ace and Eric were usually found drinking with Joel, swapping charter stories or competing in arm wrestling matches or card games.

Even Ivy and Celeste had won me over. They were two peas in a pod, gossiping and making me laugh with their own horror stories from working charters. Celeste once had a man demand a twelve-course meal for him and his family, only to have all of them drink so much they passed out and didn't even make it to dinner at all. Ivy chimed in with her own experience of being cornered in a stateroom while changing the sheets, the main charter guest begging her to let him touch and photograph her feet.

They were different from me, but after a couple weeks of me working just as much as they were, they seemed to relax around me and open up a bit more. Ivy was still foaming at the mouth for the opportunity to give me a makeover, and Celeste was fascinated by my photographs. She always asked to see the most recent ones I'd edited. When I showed her the one of the young couple embracing on the sea wall in Nice, she covered her mouth with her fingertips, eyes wide and glossy when they found me. "I'm not sure why, but this photo makes my stomach ache."

Nailed it.

Still, even though I felt comfortable in my new routine and found friendship within the crew, I longed for the days on my own. The days when Theo didn't require my services, when I could walk off the yacht, or Joel could take me on the dinghy to shore — those were what I lived for. I lost hours of daylight wandering foreign streets — listening, watching, feeling. I captured life as it happened around me, telling stories that perhaps would never have been shared otherwise.

We slowly made our way down the coast of France, hopping out to islands and then back to shore until we started to creep into Italy. As much as I loved France, I found the Italian culture to be even more tantalizing. They were one-hundred percent, all the time, no matter what they were doing. They worked tirelessly, created elaborate meals that everyone in the family stopped to gather around, loved each other as if it were their life's only purpose, and drank wine like this would be their last day on Earth. They were passionate friends, lovers, neighbors and hosts. Where most of the people I photographed in France ignored me or made some gesture to let me know they were not amused, the people of Italy were curious. They invited me closer, let me get personal with their work and their families, offered me wine and food, showed me inside their businesses and homes, and offered advice for where to go next.

As for Theo?

He might as well have been in another country.

After that morning in Nice, Theo seemed wrapped up in work. He entertained clients on the yacht most days, and when he wasn't entertaining, he was tapping away on his laptop by the pool, speaking in hushed commands on the phone in the salon, or reading something on his tablet, his brows furrowed in concentration.

On the rare occasion he wasn't working, he was trying to relax — I say *trying* because I could tell just by casting a glance in his direction from time to time that it was out of his wheelhouse to fully let go of work. Even when he stretched out on the top deck to sunbathe, his fingers would twitch, knee bouncing, head tossing from side to side with distant sighs like it was laying there doing nothing that was the real work.

He hadn't said a word to me, not since that morning he took me to breakfast.

And why would he? This billionaire on his summer vacation in the Mediterranean? I was just a girl with a camera taking a free ride on his yacht. So what, he'd talked to me a few times. So what, he'd taken me to breakfast in France.

He was just being polite.

We'd been on the yacht for two weeks the day we dropped anchor outside of Vernazza, Italy. I went ashore and spent the morning and afternoon photographing the medieval fishing village, capturing the brightly colored houses and the beautiful water lapping at the coast. It was a little more touristy than I preferred, though, and by the time I made my way back to the yacht, I was ready for a quiet night in the cabin with Joel.

When I walked into our room, my camera around my neck and backpack slung over one shoulder, I found Joel halfway under our bed.

Or should I say, *inside* our bed.

The bottom of it was solid wood, but it had a few doors with knobs that opened up for additional storage. I'd assumed they were locked, since they hadn't budged when I'd tried to store some of my belongings there. Which was why I was surprised to see Joel halfway inside the biggest storage compartment now.

"What are you doing?"

Joel jumped at my voice, knocking his head on the bed frame and cursing as he shuffled his way out. "Dammit, Aspen!"

I frowned, letting my bag drop on the dresser. "Sorry I startled you."

He was still grumbling and rubbing his head, but he forced a breath and a smile. "No, no, I'm sorry. I just didn't expect you so soon." His eyes flicked to where he'd been under the bed, and he quickly shut the storage door and locked it, dropping the key into his pocket.

"What are you hiding under there?"

"It's nothing," he said curtly. "And don't go looking, either."

I arched a brow. "A surprise for me?"

He smirked, finally standing and sweeping me into his arms. "Maybe. So no peeking."

I smiled against his first kiss, and then he stripped my camera strap over my head and set it on the dresser next to my bag. My arms were around his neck in the next instant, our kisses heated and intentional, hands roaming.

I missed him.

What a strange thing, to miss someone I slept next to each night. But though we'd been together the last couple of weeks, we hadn't spent any quality time just the two of us. Even holding him now, I found myself inhaling his cinnamon scent like I hadn't smelled it in years, tracing the muscles in his arms like I'd forgotten the shape of them. His brown eyes were warm as they watched me, his smile lazy and sweet.

"Are you done for the night?" I asked, running my fingers up his arm, over his neck, and along the line of his jaw.

"I am."

"And you're not on watch?"

He shook his head.

"Maybe we can lie in bed, watch a movie?" I asked, pressing onto my toes to kiss his neck. "Or *not* watch a movie."

Joel chuckled, kissing me back long and hard before he grabbed my hands and pulled them from around his neck. He kissed my knuckles and then held my hands at his chest. "Actually, Theo gave us a night to go to shore."

"You and me?!"

"The whole crew!" he said excitedly. "Well, except for Claude and Matthew. It's their night on watch. But everyone else is going!" Joel sighed, shaking his head like he was the luckiest guy in the world. "I told you he was one of the best owners to work for. He said we've been working hard, and since he doesn't have any guests on, we should take the night off and go see Italy. Ivy and Celeste already found a great area to bar hop."

I frowned. "Oh…"

"What?" Joel asked warily.

I shook my head. "It's nothing. I just… I feel like we haven't spent any time together. I… I miss you."

"You *miss* me?" Joel said on a laugh, kissing my fingertips. "I'm right here, silly. We've been together every day. And we're going to have an amazing night *in Italia*." He said the last two words in a phony Italian accent that almost offended me, given the fact that I'd fallen in love with the language over the last week.

"What if we ditched?" I asked, chewing my lip.

Joel pulled back a little. "Ditched? Aspen, do you know how rare this is, that the owner is letting us take a night off to go party? We don't even have to report until ten tomorrow morning."

"I know but—"

"I'm already getting so much shit for us being in this fancy room," he said. "I mean, I'm supposed to be downstairs on a bunk bed with the other deck hands. And in case you forgot, you're not a guest on this yacht, either."

I frowned at his tone, at the insinuation. "I know that, Joel," I said softly.

"Well, then, you understand what I'm saying. We need to be with the crew."

"Could we come back early, maybe? Hang for an hour and then bail?"

Joel shook his head, brows furrowed at me like I was a stranger. "Do you hear yourself? What, are you too good to hang out with the help since you've been traipsing around all these exotic places?"

"What?" I shook my head, unsure of how this got turned on me all of a sudden, unsure of the way Joel was speaking to me. He didn't seem himself. "Of course not."

"Well, you're acting kind of like a snob right now."

"A *snob?*"

"Yes! *You* don't have to work the way the rest of us do, *you* get to get off the boat whenever you want, *you* have seen a dozen different places while we've been stuck on this yacht slaving away, and on top of it, you never hang out with us. If anything, you come downstairs for like twenty minutes before you disappear. Everyone keeps asking me if you're mad, if we're fighting, or if you just always have this attitude. Here I've been talking you up to these people for years, and they finally meet you, and you act like the last thing you want to do is hang out with them."

My jaw dropped. "The only reason I'm even *here*, Joel, is because you practically begged me and said we'd have more time together," I reminded him. "And you *know* how I feel about partying and being around a bunch of people I don't know."

"You could *get* to know them."

"I just want to be with you!" I yelled, my eyes welling with tears. I glanced at the door when I heard voices passing, pulling my hands from Joel and crossing my arms over my chest. I sniffed, shaking my head, yet again questioning why I ever took Theo's offer. "This isn't me," I said, waving a hand toward the hall. "The partying. The gossip. The being with other people *all the time*." I paused, heart tightening in my chest. "I should have just said no," I whispered. "Maybe we would have been better off if I wasn't here at all."

We stood there quiet for a long while before Joel sighed, opening his arms. "Come here."

I was hesitant at first, but when Joel watched me with understanding in his eyes, I stepped into him, returning his embrace when he wrapped me in his arms.

"I want you here, okay? I'm glad you're here." He kissed my hair. "And we will have more time together, just the two of us. I promise. Okay? But tonight is a special occasion. Please, come hang out. I know it's not your favorite thing, to be with everyone, but we're in *Italy*." He paused, as if to let that sink in. "Just one night. Please."

Another zing of tightness hit my chest, this time born of guilt. I knew in his mind it wasn't asking me much, to just suck it up and go out for a night.

But I didn't *want* to go.

And for the first time, I decided that if I didn't want to, I didn't have to.

"I'm tired, Joel" I said, pressing my hands to his chest as I met his eyes. "I know it's a rare occasion, but I'm just not up for it."

Joel's next breath was steady, though the way his jaw was set, I knew he wasn't happy. I saw the disappointment in his usually warm brown eyes when he finally nodded. "Okay. We'll stay then."

"No," I said, shaking my head. "It's fine. You should go. Like you said, you're already getting shit for not being downstairs with them."

Joel frowned, eyes searching mine.

I waved him off. "Go. You should enjoy the night off, and Vernazza is beautiful. I want you to see it. You deserve to have fun."

"Are you sure?" he asked, rubbing my arms.

I smiled. "Yeah. I'm sure."

Joel kissed my forehead, holding me tight again. "Thank you. And I'm sorry for blowing up like that, it was just a stressful day." He pulled back, framing my arms with his hands. "Maybe we can have a movie night tomorrow? I'll even suffer through a chick flick, if that's what you're in the mood for," he added with a wink.

I nodded, but the smile I forced felt as fake as my insistence that I was fine with him leaving. "It's a date."

Joel kissed me again, and then he released me, rattling off things that had happened throughout the day as he showered and got dressed and ready for the evening. I leaned my back against the headboard, listening, laughing when appropriate, all while staring at my camera on the dresser, the black and silver of it coming in and out of focus the longer I did.

He looked handsome when he'd finished, wearing navy blue shorts and a white button up with embroidered navy anchors all over the fabric. The white set off his tan from working in the sun every day, and he combed and parted his usually shaggy brown hair, reminding me of nights we'd go out in Boulder with our college friends.

Just like that, Joel's mood was restored, and with a spritz of cologne, one last kiss on my cheek, and a promise to spoon me when he came home later, he was out the door.

And I sat there on our bed, alone, listening to the sound of laughter as the crew barreled up the stairs to the main deck.

CHAPTER
NINE

I couldn't sleep.

Even though I was exhausted, and even though I was warm and cozy under the sheets of our bed watching *Guinevere,* my mind wouldn't stop racing. I was restless, from where I chewed my nails to where I bounced my foot under the covers. So, about halfway through the movie, I paused it to take a walk.

It was strange, being on the boat without anyone else on it. I knew Matthew, one of the engineers, and Claude, the head chef, were somewhere on their watch. But usually, I couldn't walk more than ten feet before I ran into someone — Ivy cleaning a room, Ace rushing around the main deck, Emma and Eric discussing the day's itinerary, Captain Chuck smiling over his coffee as he tipped his hat at me. Tonight, the constant hum of work and conversation was muted, replaced by the quiet sound of the water lapping against the boat.

I wrapped my cardigan around me a little tighter, feeling the cool teak wood under my feet as I explored.

I traced the expensive marble of the main deck bar with my fingertips, watched the glimmering crystal chandelier in the salon of the owner's deck, and inhaled a deep lungful of the salty fresh air when I climbed my way up to the sun deck.

Already, my heartbeat was steadier, my breaths more even, and I stood there at the top of the stairs with my eyes cast toward the stars, inhaling deep breath after deep breath.

It was a helpful reminder, to see that I was so small, and in turn, my problems were, too.

"Ah, and here I thought I was alone."

I jumped at the deep voice, blinking over and over as I pulled my eyes from the first quarter moon above and let them adjust. Slowly, a figure came into view, a dark shadow in the hot tub on the other side of the pool. The more my eyes adjusted, the more I recognized Theo's long, slightly bent nose and square jaw.

"Oh God, I'm so sorry," I rushed out, already turning for the stairs.

Theo chuckled, and I heard the water splash behind me as he lifted both hands out of the water. "No, no, please, stay."

My cheeks were on fire as I shook my head, so embarrassed by being caught lost in space like a weirdo that I didn't even have the right words to decline. "I'm sure you want privacy, I'm sorry for interrupting."

"I've had enough privacy today to drive a person mad," he insisted, and I glanced back over my shoulder. "And obviously you're looking for something to do, no?"

I chewed my cheek.

"Go change and come back up," Theo said.

"I... I don't think that's a good idea."

"And sitting alone in your stateroom is?"

I couldn't see his eyes clearly from that distance, but I felt them like warm rays of sunshine on my skin. I'd declined going out with Joel and the rest of the crew, but there was something enticing about the offer to be with Theo.

All the more reason to decline.

A moment of pause passed between us, and then Theo stood, the steaming water cascading down his chest and abdomen, the rivulets illuminated by the moonlight.

"Go get changed and get in this hot tub, or I'll come over there and drag you in."

His voice barreled like a wave crashing over me, sending chills down my spine. And as if I had no other choice, I nodded, skipping down the stairs and back to my room. I changed more quickly than I ever had in my life, and then I was back, a towel wrapped around my swimsuit-clad body.

Theo smiled when I joined him again, gesturing with a wet hand for me to sit opposite him in the tub. He grabbed his tumbler of what looked like scotch next, sipping it, his eyes never leaving me as I tiptoed to the water's edge.

God, how I wished he would look away.

But he was unashamed, a slight smirk on his lips, an arch in his brow, hand still wrapped around the glass.

I looked left and right, as if it was the possibility of someone *else* coming up that made it hard to drop that towel. The truth was, I had to look away to find the confidence to do it.

With a deep breath I tried desperately to make seem casual, I pulled the towel away, draping it over the back of one of the nearby chairs before making my way into the tub. I kept my eyes on the water the entire time, not brave enough to look up and see if Theo was watching me. The water was perfectly warm, and when I was submerged up to my chest, I sighed, melting into it.

When I finally lifted my gaze, I was met with Theo's.

His expression was different now — smirk gone, brows furrowed instead of arched. I thought I saw the bob of his Adam's apple before he cleared his throat, setting his drink on the edge of the tub and letting his hand rest around it. "There," he said, lips curling up just a bit before they fell again. "Not so bad, is it?"

I rolled my eyes, sinking deeper into the water with a groan. "I didn't realize I was sore until this very moment."

"Too much walking on shore?"

I smiled, closing my eyes as I let my head fall back against the lip of the tub. "Definitely more than I'm used to."

"I could arrange a car for you next time," Theo offered. "If you'd like."

I shook my head, eyes fluttering open to find him across the steamy water. "It's okay. I prefer to walk — I capture more that way. I just can't help but get caught up in it, when I'm in the zone like I have been. I end up walking more miles than I've trained my body to handle."

Theo relaxed, sipping his scotch before setting it aside again. He reached behind it for his phone. "I think I should have your number."

My head rolled up in a snap from where I'd been resting, eyes wide. "What?"

"In case you get lost while you're on shore, or need a ride back to the boat," he clarified, and then he stood, the water dripping down his bare chest like it had before. Only this time, I wasn't across the deck by the stairs. This time, I was just a few feet away from him — distance that he closed slowly as he moved toward me, extending his phone in my direction. "It would make me feel better to know you had a way to contact me if you needed to, and I to contact you."

Theo paused where he towered above me, the moonlight behind him making his face nothing but a shadow. I couldn't decipher his eyes, only the valleys and ridges of his abdomen, the deep cut of the V that pointed down to the hem of his swim trunks.

I swallowed, taking the phone from his hand. I thought about pointing out that Joel had my number, and I had his, so if I really needed something, I could just call or text my boyfriend.

But I already knew that Theo didn't like to ask twice.

Besides, what if Joel was working and didn't have his phone on him when I needed something?

Maybe it *was* a good idea for him to have my number.

Just in case.

I tapped the screen until I got to the contacts app, putting my name and number in quickly and handing the phone back to him. Theo smiled, but instead of crossing back to where he'd been sitting before, he lowered into the water next to me.

"There," he said, tapping out something on the screen. "I texted you so you'll have my number, too."

Theo set his phone aside then, and he got up long enough to retrieve his glass before he was beside me once more, one arm draped over the back of the tub as he watched me.

"How's it been on shore? Have you been getting the kind of photographs you envisioned?"

"It's been…" I smiled, shaking my head as the memories of the last couple of weeks floated through my mind. "Absolutely incredible. Life changing. More than I could have imagined."

"Yeah? What's been your favorite place so far?"

"I loved Portofino," I said. "The people there were so friendly, and the bright houses, the little hidden alleyways and streets. It was like being in a movie." I paused. "And Nice," I added quietly. "I liked Nice."

Theo nodded. "Me, too."

"Oh, yeah? What did you do there, other than work?"

"Had breakfast with a pretty girl."

The blood drained from my face, but Theo just smiled, watching my discomfort over the top of his glass as he took another drink.

"Have you taken any time off, or has it been all work and no play?" I asked, ignoring his comment and the way it made my skin heat.

Theo sighed, sinking a little lower in the tub. "I think I discover more and more the older I get that, for me, work is an ever-present part of life. Time off doesn't exist."

"Sounds like you need to hire someone to be here traveling with you," I said. "A Vacation Enforcer."

He laughed at that. "Oh yeah?"

"I've seen you trying to relax," I commented. "It's like watching a fish try to fly."

"So you've been watching me, Miss Dawn?"

My smile vanished.

Theo just chuckled, sipping more of his scotch. He sucked his teeth at the burn of it. "To be honest, that's how it feels for me, too — like I'm out of my element. It's uncomfortable for me, to rest. I can't even think about trying to go enjoy a day just being a tourist without breaking into hives." He shrugged. "But it's different than what people perceive. I *like* work. I enjoy it. I worked hard to make it that way. And they say if you love what you do..."

"You'll never work a day in your life."

He tilted his glass toward me. "Exactly."

"I think I can understand," I said. "I mean, if I ever get to make a living off photography, I don't think I'll want a day off, either. It's hard enough now to put my camera down when I'm *not* being paid for it."

"You will," he said confidently. "Make a living off it, that is. But I hate to be the bearer of bad news — it'll put pressure on your creativity, once you have financial implications."

"Does it put pressure on you?"

Theo fell silent for a moment, thinking. "Yes and no. My job is a little less creative, though, and more technical. I used to love to code, but I'm so out of touch with it all now. I'm more focused on strategy, and charming clients for an afternoon and then spending an evening busying my mind with how the next software update could benefit them and us both."

"It sounds to me like you don't like to be alone with your thoughts."

Theo frowned, slowly turning until his eyes met mine. I knew by the way he watched me that no one had ever said anything like that to him before.

I wondered if I'd pegged him down the way he'd done so to me in Nice.

"And," I added, aiming to lighten the moment. "Like you need a little more fun in your life."

Theo's expression relaxed. "That so? And what should I do for fun?"

I shrugged. "Read a book for pleasure instead of work. Watch a movie. Learn an instrument. See a concert. Use your ridiculous amount of money to go shopping or eat at a cool restaurant. Jump off a cliff."

"Jump off a cliff?" he echoed on a laugh. "Well, that's one way to tell a person how you feel about them."

"I mean like cliff diving!"

"Uh-huh, sure. It's fine. See if I ever offer you an all-expenses paid trip on a yacht through the Mediterranean again."

I laughed, my head tilting back, and it felt good — the way that sound reverberated through me, the way Theo's smile widened at the sound.

Then, the laughter faded, and Theo's smile waned, and in the quiet night with nothing more than the waves washing softly against the boat, I became suddenly and breathlessly aware of the fact that I was half-naked in a hot tub with Theo Whitman.

"So," he said after a moment. "Should we address the purple elephant in the room?"

My heart stopped in my chest, kicking back to life with a sharp thud. "What elephant is that?"

"Why aren't you on shore with everyone else?"

I sank deeper into the water on my next exhale. "Oh," I said, relief flooding me, though I wasn't sure what else I thought he might have been referring to, instead. "I was just too tired to go party all night," I said with a shrug. "Honestly, I don't know how they do it — working all day like that just to hang out all night and get up early to do it all again."

"It definitely takes a special kind of person," Theo agreed. Then, he tapped his fingers absentmindedly on the side of his glass, eyes glancing at the stairs behind me. "Joel didn't stay behind with you?"

My stomach twisted at the reminder of what I'd been trying to forget all night. "No... but it's okay. He was really excited about getting off the boat and seeing Italy. I don't blame him."

"I'm sure you two have spent a lot of time together anyway."

I smiled.

At least, I *think* I smiled.

"Yeah."

Theo tilted his head. "You're doing it again."

"Doing what?"

"Biting your tongue. Denying yourself the satisfaction of saying what you really want."

I frowned. "I'm not... I wanted him to go. I wanted him to have fun, he deserves it."

"And what about you?" Theo asked, and though it was only a marginal distance, I felt the heat of him moving closer, like he was the source of the hot tub's warmth altogether. "What do *you* deserve?"

My breath caught in my chest, lips parting on a breath as Theo watched me. This close, even in the dark, those blue dusk eyes were so striking they rendered me speechless. And his gaze never wavered, not until so much time had passed that a chuckle left his lips.

"It really does make you uncomfortable, doesn't it? To think of yourself instead of others."

I didn't respond. I was too busy reminding myself how to breathe.

In and out.

Inhale.

Exhale.

"I think I know what it is," Theo mused. Then, he leaned back, giving me enough space to clear the dizziness. He finished what was left in his glass, setting it aside before he pointed at me. "You're scared of hurting someone, or of being judged. You're afraid that by saying what you actually want, you'll disturb the peace."

I frowned, opening my mouth but not sure what words to give it to speak. "I'm... I'm not..."

"It's co-dependency in its truest form," he continued. "Instead of asking yourself what you want and then doing that, you ask yourself what will make everyone else happy, what will make them feel okay."

I shook my head, but the truth of his words made the motion feel sticky and slow.

"You are. You're too scared to be honest."

"I am not!" I said, louder this time, with enough determination to make Theo tilt his head.

"Okay then," he said, and he dipped lower into the water, until it slipped over his chin and met the bottom of his lower lip. The moonlight reflected off the water and into his eyes as he inched closer to me. "Tell me something true."

I swallowed, heart racing more and more the closer he came. When I was sure I'd pass out if he came even an inch closer, he stretched back, elongating himself over the water and floating for a moment before he sat upright again, the water at his chest.

He stared at me.

Waiting.

"Go on," he said. "Tell me something so true you've never spoken it out loud."

I huffed, crossing my arms over my chest at the ridiculous request.

Theo just arched a brow.

"I don't know what you want from me."

"Oh, there are many things I want from you, Miss Dawn," he said, sliding across the water until he was so close I felt his breath on my nose. He watched me for a long moment, eyes flicking back and forth, lips curling a bit when he noticed the way my chest heaved in my next breath. "Tell me something you've never told anyone else."

And I couldn't explain it, what happened next, with his eyes on me and the steam of the water drifting between us. A chill raced up the spine of my neck, hairs standing on end, and below the water, my fingers curled under my thighs, as if I were Eve and I needed to sit on them to keep from reaching out for the forbidden fruit.

"You're right," I whispered. "I am afraid."

Theo shook his head. "Tell me something else, something I *don't* know."

"I like the way you look at me."

The words slipped from my tongue like oil, slicking my inhibitions on the way out. I couldn't believe I'd said them.

I couldn't believe I wasn't tripping over myself to take them back.

Theo inhaled a stiff breath through his nose, nostrils flaring a bit, his eyes bouncing back and forth between mine. His lips parted like he wanted to speak, but something held him back.

Around us, the night came alive.

The water seemed swept away in a storm, a sudden gust of breeze sending it crashing instead of softly lapping as it had been. I somehow heard laughter floating over the water, all the way from shore. I somehow saw every crater on the moon reflected in Theo's eyes. I suddenly felt the vibration of each star in the sky, humming through me like a bass drum.

"Your turn," I said, and I would have sworn it was someone else possessing my body when I inched toward him in return. "Tell me something true."

Theo swallowed, and it was inexplicable, what that simple notion did to me. I watched the bob of his throat, the hollow area where his neck met his collarbone as it ebbed, and something hot and bewitching slid between my legs. Every muscle tightened, a frenzy of fire and ice, and I squeezed my knees together against the ache I'd never felt before in my life.

"Something true?" he asked softly.

I nodded, lips parting of their own accord.

A breath of a laugh came from his nose, and he shook his head, almost imperceptibly, like I'd asked him an impossible task. Then, slowly, he glided through the water, closer and closer, until the confidence I'd had moments before vanished in a puff of smoke.

I swallowed at the intensity of his gaze, backing away from him like I was his prey until my shoulder blades hit the edge of the tub.

"I always get what I want," he husked, his nose skimming the tip of mine.

"Something I don't know," I said, throwing his own words back in his face.

His eyes cast down on mine, and the corner of his lips tilted up just a tick, like I was just a toy he'd dragged out of his toy box out of boredom, completely at his mercy.

Under the water, warm fingertips brushed the outside of my thigh — just above the knee, and just lightly enough that I questioned I'd felt it at all as my next breath lodged in my throat.

Suddenly, Theo pushed back, the water parting for him as if he were Moses. He turned just as my breath came back to me in a kick, and in one fluid motion, he pushed himself up out of the hot tub as the oxygen burned my lungs.

He turned to face me then, water dripping from his hair, down his chest, over his arms and the swells of his abdomen. His jaw was set, arms rigid, back straight and shoulders square.

But my eyes locked on where a large bulge strained against his wet shorts, the fabric outlining every single inch of him.

Theo had to have known where I was looking. He had to have known that I could see it now, the way I affected him, but he stood rock solid and proud and un-ashamed.

And that icy-hot ping of electricity struck me at my core again, making me squirm under the water.

Without another word, Theo swiped his towel off the back of the chair behind him, wrapped it around his waist, and let heavy, wet footsteps carry him across the deck and down the stairs, leaving me in the toy box yet again.

Later, when I was back in my room, I stared at the text he'd sent me after I'd given him my number.

Bonjour.

I stared at it until the word no longer made sense, until the letters blurred and the syllables became more foreign than the language the word was written in.

Then the phone buzzed in my hand, and a new text came through.

Goodnight, Miss Dawn.

CHAPTER
TEN

Joel kept his promise.

The next night, after his shift and after we both had a quick dinner with the rest of the crew, we crawled into bed together and turned on a movie. Joel held me close, laughing when appropriate while I let my eyes go in and out of focus and always laughed a little too late.

I was too busy chastising myself to truly watch the movie.

I felt like the scum of the earth after last night, even though I hadn't technically *done* anything wrong. In my mind, words were just as potent as actions, and I couldn't believe what I'd said to Theo. More than that, I couldn't believe what I'd seen when he got out of the hot tub. Even the simple, kind, and innocent texts from him on my phone seemed to haunt me, like they were something I should be ashamed of, like I should hastily delete them and his number altogether from my phone the next time Joel got up to go to the bathroom.

I couldn't shake the guilt I felt, the warning bells ringing shrilly inside me — not even when Joel ignored the final twenty minutes of the movie in favor of lying me down in the sheets of that bed we shared. For the first time since being onboard, he took his time, kissing me all over and driving me wild with foreplay before he finally pressed inside me.

I faked an orgasm so he would come, too.

And then we both fell asleep.

The next day, I vowed to get myself right. It wasn't a big deal. So what, I had a little crush. That was normal. Lots of people in relationships had crushes. And so what, I'd stumbled up on Theo in the hot tub. So what, I'd joined him at his insistence. He was the owner, after all — what was I supposed to do?

I chose to ignore the rest of what happened that night, and my avoidance tactics worked so well that after a few days, I wondered if I'd imagined all of it. My theory was aided by the fact that Theo didn't talk to me or text me or so much as *look* at me. He was all business again, bringing clients onboard and attending to his business on shore. He asked me to work for him when necessary — usually through instructing Wayland to tell me rather than himself — and he stayed out of sight on the days he had off.

Part of me wondered if he'd taken my advice, if he was on shore doing some stupid touristy attraction, or forcing himself to take a real day off.

The other part of me slapped my wrist that I was thinking of him at all.

Fortunately, I was able to keep busy over the next couple of weeks, exploring culture-rich spots like La Spezia and Pisa and Portoferraio on my days off, and working for Theo when called upon to do so. I'd become accustomed to his guests. I knew how to handle them, how to please them and still keep my sanity.

At least, until we made it to the coastline near Rome, and I got my first taste of the horrific experiences I'd heard the rest of the crew talk about from their past years working charters.

The group of hellish, impossibly rude and rambunctious men boarded the yacht at a dock near Fiumicino on a warm and sunny day. I never did catch what company they were with, but they became known by myself and the rest of the crew as *la sporcizia*.

Translated to: *the filth*.

Where most of the other guests had been in small groups of two to four, this one was a large and loud group of twelve Italian men. The suits they wore their first day on the yacht was about as far as their professionalism seemed to go. And after watching their behavior for just a few hours, I knew they must be an important client for Theo to put up with their antics.

He did seem to be more severe with them than with the others he'd hosted, though, and he ensured they followed a strict day-to-day itinerary that involved conferences, meetings on shore, and strategic planning. I didn't understand the nature of the business relationship, but I knew after being pulled this way and that, being asked to take some of the most ridiculous pictures of my life, and having a story of my own to tell Ivy and Celeste — thanks to one of the men getting me alone in the main deck salon and offering to pay me ten grand for any photos I had of Theo lounging topless on the sun deck — I was exhausted and beyond ready for them to disembark.

And I wasn't the only one having trouble with our guests.

They put the chefs through the ringer with their outrageous requests for exotic and pricey fare, including a specific kind of fatty tuna sushi that they demanded be flown in fresh from Japan the day of the meal. Emma was ready to tear her hair out with the men's insistence to have a themed party every night they were onboard. Ivy and Celeste looked run down and ragged after cleaning the rooms each morning, and Joel and Ace were working dawn until dusk, facilitating requests to go to shore or take out the jet skis or helping the stewardesses with hosting and serving drinks by the pool.

Even the engineers had a run of it after the air conditioning unit fritzed. Captain Chuck seemed about the only one able to keep his cool, and he was the steady rock for the rest of us through the hellish ordeal.

When *la sporcizia* finally departed, there was a universal sigh of relief onboard. And when Theo announced that we'd have a crew pool party the next evening as a thank you for handling the difficult guests, that sigh of relief turned into a cheer of celebration.

Well, for everyone but me, anyway.

"He really is the best owner *ever*," Celeste said shortly after we got the news. We were all downstairs in the crew galley, and everyone except for me had a well-earned drink in their hand. "I mean, most of the time after handling a group like that, you have one night of rest and then you get up to do it all over again. On the worst days, they get off the boat in the morning and you're welcoming the next charter that evening." She shook her head, her dark eyes more tired and worn than I'd ever seen them. "Theo is a god."

Ivy chuckled. "I don't know about all that, but he at least takes pity on us." Her smile bloomed then. "A *pool party*," she said, shaking her head. "This is going to be epic."

"Are you going?" Emma asked me with a nudge.

I shrugged. "I don't know..."

"Oh, come on," Celeste said. "You have to come! Even *you* got your fill of *la sporcizia*. You should celebrate your first real guest experience."

"Parties aren't really my thing," I said — to no one's surprise.

"Yeah, but it'll just be us!" Ivy said. "It's not like you're going to a club or something. Oh!" She perked up, her sea green eyes bright and bushy-tailed. "This is the *perfect* time to do your makeover!"

Emma and Celeste squealed and looked to me excitedly just as I tried to shrink away. "Oh... I don't know..."

"You promised!" Celeste said with a pout, which was not *exactly* true, but the way the three of them watched me like it was my decision whether the party happened or not, I felt a prickle of guilt and expectation nudge me over the edge.

"Okay," I conceded to a chorus of claps from the girls. "But," I said, holding up one finger. "Nothing too crazy, okay? It's a pool party, not a gala."

"It's a *nighttime* pool party," Ivy reminded me. "An evening of champagne and food and a night under the stars." She lifted her hands to the ceiling before pulling them to her chest. "It will be magical."

Her eyes found Joel then, and he smiled in return, and I silently wished for a case of food poisoning to get me out of this mess.

"Oh... my... *God*," Celeste said behind Ivy. They were both crowding over me in Joel's and my stateroom, Ivy brushing something on my cheeks as a final touch before she pulled back to join Celeste in admiration.

"I'm a miracle worker."

Celeste scoffed and elbowed Ivy, but then her hands were reaching for me, and she pulled me up from the bed, rushing me to the bathroom. "Just *look* at yourself."

She shoved me in front of the mirror, and then she and Ivy were behind me, waiting expectantly over each of my shoulders while I took in the reflection that I could hardly believe was me.

Celeste had taken over my hair, weaving it into a braided crown that wrapped around my head entirely before the braid continued down over my left shoulder. A few tendrils were free from the braid, curled into tiny soft waves that framed my face.

Ivy had been master of the makeup, and though I couldn't imagine ever taking as much time as she had doing my *own* makeup, the result left my lips parted, jaw hanging open. My skin looked flawless, all freckles and blemishes covered, and somehow my cheek bones were more prominent, my nose thin and long. She'd even contoured my collarbones, which I didn't even know was a thing, and painted my lips a siren red.

But what stole the show — and my breath — were my eyes.

Though I was never one to dote on myself, I had always appreciated my blue eyes. They were something that made me feel beautiful. But tonight? They weren't just blue.

They were diamonds. They were a turquoise sea washing against a private island beach. They were aqua waterfalls in a jungle. They sparkled and shone bright, framed by dark liner and long, black lashes. The lids were dusted various shades of brown and gold, which somehow gave me a natural look but with a pop of something magical and alluring.

"Oh, Ivy..." I whispered, reaching up to touch my face. She swatted my hand away before I could make contact.

"Don't mess it up!"

"I can't believe this is me," I whispered.

"Well, believe it, sister," Celeste said. "Now, what suit are you wearing?"

I frowned at her in the mirror. "I only have one."

We made our way out of the bathroom, and I pulled the suit from where it was shoved in one of the dresser drawers. It was a simple, burnt orange two-piece, with an athletic-like halter top and high-waisted bottoms that covered my hips and butt completely. The last time I'd worn it was when I'd been in the hot tub with Theo.

One look at it and I knew Ivy and Celeste were not impressed.

"Okay, no. You can't take all this," Ivy said, gesturing to my face. "And pair it with *that*."

"Not to worry," Celeste added with a wave of her finger, and she was already dashing out the door. "I have a few extras!"

She was gone before I could protest, and then for the first time, I was alone with Ivy.

She smiled, shaking her head as she touched up something above my left eyebrow. "You're stunning. Joel is going to lose his shit when he sees you."

I flushed. "Thank you for doing this."

"Of course. This is what girlfriends do. And we're friends, right?"

She smiled, and I think I managed one in return, though something rolled in my stomach like the feeling you get before driving in a thunderstorm.

"So, do you love being on the boat with Joel?" she asked, casually walking into the bathroom to check her appearance. She primped and puckered while I took a seat on the edge of the bed.

"Yes, but I'll admit, this isn't really my scene."

She arched a brow. "The long days of work?"

"More like the long nights of partying."

"Ah," she said, nodding like she understood. "Yeah, it definitely takes a certain kind of person to be a Yachty. You've got to be tough, resilient, hardworking. You know?" She shrugged, wiping at the corner of her mouth where some lipstick had smeared. "It's not for the weak."

Celeste bounded back in before I could reply that my preference to spend quality time with my boyfriend rather than party every night had nothing to do with me being *weak*, but we shared a look — one that I hoped told her I saw right through the passive-aggressive comment.

I couldn't figure Ivy out. One minute I felt like we were friends, the next, I was sure she'd shove me overboard if she thought no one was looking.

"Okay, I have others, but I saw this one and just *knew* it was the perfect fit," Celeste said, shoving something black and strappy into my hands. "Go put it on and then we should go. Everyone else is already up there partying, and as much as I love to be fashionably late, I don't want to miss out on the free booze." She lowered her voice as if anyone else was around. "I heard Theo is *serving* us tonight."

My eyes widened when I held up the swimsuit she'd brought. "Um..."

"Just put it on," she said, shoving me toward the bathroom. "Trust me."

And for some ungodly reason, I did.

CHAPTER
ELEVEN

The party was in full swing when we ascended the staircase to the sun deck.

It was evening, the sky twirling with shades of orange and pink as the summer sun stretched its last rays over the water and the coast of Italy. It stole my breath when it all came into view at the top, and I paused, soaking it in, reveling in the moment that reminded me just how insane it was to be here.

When I stopped gawking at the sunset, I realized every single pair of eyes was on me.

It was like a DJ record scratch, the way the crew stopped mid-drink to look at where the three of us had just entered. I tried to convince myself it was Ivy and Celeste who had everyone staring, but one sweep of my gaze around the boat and there was no contesting it was me their focus was on.

Claude and Adeline were fussing over the appetizers on the bar, but they'd stopped, staring at me and muttering something to each other in French. The engineers were seated on the edge of the pool with Wayland, and I heard one of them whistle under their breath while Wayland gave me a knowing grin and shook his head in awe.

Joel was in the hot tub with a drink in his hand, and Ace hooted and hollered, clapping him on the shoulders with a goofy grin while he stared at me slack-jawed. Emma was already rushing over to me, her fingers touching my hair and the thin straps of the "swimsuit" that barely covered me. It was a triangle top with a half-circle bar of silver that sat in the center of my chest. The way it fit, it pulled what little cleavage I had front and center, up and tight. The bottoms looked like they were straight out of the 80s, high-waisted with the thighs cut out just as high, so that the fabric created a deep V from my hips down to my pelvis.

Thank God I shaved, I thought when I first put it on.

Emma was going on and on, but I couldn't hear a word. Everything sounded fuzzy and distant, like Charlie Brown's teacher, because all around the pool, people I barely knew were staring at parts of me I'd never shown in public before.

And all the way across the deck, behind the bar, in the shadows, almost completely out of sight... was Theo.

Unlike everyone else, he wasn't in swim attire, but rather a perfectly fitted beige suit with a navy tie that made the dark specs of blue in his eyes pop. His blond hair curled a little where he'd gelled it, and the stubble on his chin looked freshly trimmed. He held a drink just like Joel, but where Joel's jaw was open in a goofy grin of shock, Theo's lips were flattened in a hard line, his jaw tense, and even from this far away I saw the muscles of it tick as he watched me make my entrance.

"*I told you* you'd be a showstopper," Celeste murmured under her breath, and it was the first sentence that I heard clearly. Her words snapped me into the present like a taut rubber band.

"I'll say!" Emma chimed in, still inspecting me. "Girl, I had *no idea* you had a body like this hiding under those clothes. Look at this little ab line!" she said, poking my stomach as I shied away from the touch.

"Joel, you going to come kiss your girl or let one of the other guys beat you to it?" Ivy called in a tease, and then Joel popped up out of the hot tub, padding his way over.

I wrapped my arms around myself as much as I could, wishing I had a cover up. My cheeks were on fire, and all I wanted was for everyone to go back to what they were doing before we all walked in.

"I think it's too much," I whispered to the girls.

"You look hot," Ivy argued, and then as if on cue, Joel swept me into his arms and kissed me hard and long in front of everyone to seal the sentiment.

There were distant cheers, laughter and *atta boys*, but I pressed against his chest to stop the public display of affection.

"Holy shit, babe," he breathed, holding me in his arms as he pulled back to take it all in. "You're a bombshell."

"Can I borrow your shirt?"

He chuckled like I was joking, pulling me into his chest with a kiss to my forehead before he started walking me toward the pool. "Alright, alright," he called. "Enough gawking over my girl. Let's get back to the party!"

That earned another round of cheers, and then the music blasted once again, and blessedly, all eyes were off me.

Well — all eyes except for two very intense ones behind the bar.

Joel walked me right in Theo's direction, and I felt the weight of his stare like an anvil on my chest. My feet were heavy lead, dragging behind me as I fought the dizziness a look like that brought on.

"What do you want to drink?" Joel asked me when we made it to the bar. He winked at Theo. "Boss man is actually *serving* us tonight, if you can believe it."

I didn't know how long I was quiet, how long I stood there pinned by Theo's gaze. His eyes didn't move from mine, didn't trace my body, didn't take in the swimsuit or my body.

And still, I felt naked as the day I was born.

"Babe?" Joel asked.

I shook my head, croaking out *water* as best I could.

Joel chuckled, throwing his arm around me as he faced Theo. "She doesn't drink," he explained. "Never has. My little good girl." He kissed my cheek. Then, someone called his name from the pool. "Come join us in the pool once you've got your water, yeah?"

I think I nodded, because he patted my butt below the bar where Theo couldn't see and scampered off toward the pool. I heard a big splash and a chorus of cheers a moment later, but I just stood still, watching Theo watching me.

His nose flared. "Sparkling or still, Miss Dawn?"

Those words seemed to snap me from the spell, and I shook my head a bit, dusting off the remnants. "Still," I said, surprised at how steady my voice was.

Theo reached into the cooler below the deck for a bottle of water and poured it into a cocktail glass over ice. Then, he added a sprig of mint and a couple raspberries before sliding it across the bar.

"Thank you."

He nodded, watching me as I took my first sip. I turned toward the pool, watching Joel and Ace play some sort of game that involved a lot of thrashing and wrestling. Instinctively, I positioned myself behind the corner of the bar, crossing my arms over my middle.

"I have to admit," I said after a moment, not taking my eyes off the scene in the pool. "I'm surprised by all this."

I hoped the comment landed in the easygoing, *I-totally-didn't-notice-you-had-a-hard-on-the-last-time-I-talked-to-you* zone.

"By the party?"

I nodded. "You're a billionaire, and you hired these people to work for you for the summer. Dealing with guests and difficult circumstances is part of their job. And yet, here you are, rewarding them for what they were hired to do." I arched a brow when I finally looked at him. "And serving them alcohol to boot."

The corner of Theo's lips tilted. "My father taught me a lot of things when I was younger, especially when I first started Envizion. And one thing that always stuck with me was that you should treat every employee, regardless of position, like a guest in your home."

"That's a really kind and generous way of looking at things."

Theo shrugged. "He always said running a business should be similar to being the head of the family. You work hard as a team, you go through hardships as a team, and you celebrate as a team. You have each other's backs — always."

"It sounds like you two are close."

Theo swallowed, busying his hands with one of the bottles behind the bar. "He's my role model. Always has been."

I felt the urge to inquire more, to ask question after question until he told me everything about himself. But before I could, Theo's eyes found mine, and this time, the intensity with which he watched me walk in with was back.

"You know, you aren't the only one surprised tonight."

I cocked my head.

He gestured to where I was hiding behind the corner of the bar. "You look radiant."

Theo's words were soft, subtle, his eyes genuine where they watched me. I looked away on a blush, smiling and shaking my head in disagreement. "It's just the makeup. And the suit. Neither of which are mine."

"I disagree."

I rolled my eyes, turning to face him, but when I saw the way he was watching me, my attempt at playfulness slipped.

"It's you," he said. "No matter what you wear."

I swallowed, my neck burning like a hot iron.

He made his way over to me, leaning his elbows on the bar until his face was just inches from mine. He lowered his voice, the bass of it echoing through my chest like a kick drum.

"However, if you were mine?" His eyes traced their way over my collarbones, down the line of my cleavage, to my waist, my hips, my thighs, and back up again.

"You wouldn't have even made it to that top stair before I was dragging you back to the room for my eyes only."

My lips parted of their own accord, shock buzzing low in my stomach at his forwardness. "Theo…"

"Don't say my name like that, Aspen," he warned, his eyes flicking to where I'd pinned my bottom lip with my teeth. "Not unless you want to unleash a part of me you haven't seen yet." His jaw tensed. "A part of me I can't tame once it's loose."

All those warning bells I'd silenced over the last few weeks rang in tandem, dinging and screaming inside my mind as I tried to convince myself he couldn't have possibly just said what I thought he did.

But before I could respond or digest it further, Joel called my name, and then a chorus of *Aspen, Aspen* rang out, and I had no choice but to follow the coax.

Theo leaned back with a grin, tipping an imaginary hat toward me like we'd just been having a casual, light conversation.

And with my water in hand, I joined the rest of the crew at the pool just as the sun set, ushering in a hellish night that would change everything.

The later it got, the more the alcohol flowed.

And the more the alcohol flowed, the more I wished I'd never left the stateroom.

What started out as nice cocktails by the pool turned quickly into lines of shots. The crew went from lounging around and chatting to cannonballing into the pool and playing drinking games that seemed so ridiculously out of place on a multi-million-dollar yacht that my lip visibly curled at the sight.

Theo had taken leave of his offer to serve us, but he sat at the bar, watching the antics with a curious smile permanently on his face. Every now and then, he'd even indulge the crew in taking a shot with them. Somewhere around eleven, he excused himself with Wayland to go check on Captain Chuck, who was the only one of us still working, and the crew partied on in their absence.

I'd asked Joel if we could head out over an hour ago, but he'd pretended like he didn't even hear me at all. And I wanted him to have fun, I did — but I knew him well enough to know he was teetering on the edge of cute drunk and messy drunk, and I did not want to deal with the latter.

Contrary to the fact that I wanted to leave now, I had been enjoying myself. It was fun, being in a pool on the top deck of a yacht in the Tyrrhenian Sea. I got to chat with Emma more, hear stories about Wayland's time growing up in Jamaica, and Joel was being flirty and cute and fun.

The problem was — he wasn't being flirty and cute and fun with *only* me.

I sipped my water, watching him and Ace in the pool. They were speaking in hushed tones, and then suddenly, they slid through the water quietly, depositing their drinks on the edge of the pool before they lifted themselves out.

I saw what was happening before Ivy and Celeste did.

The poor girls were dancing to the playlist Claude had put on, their hips swaying this way and that, when Ace and Joel snuck up behind them. They wrapped their arms around them, dragging them kicking and screaming toward the pool. The girls had put their feet in and gone waist deep, but had avoided getting their hair wet.

Until now.

Joel and Ace launched themselves into the pool with the girls wrapped up in their arms, and when they all emerged, it was to squeals and curses and both girls swatting at them as they laughed.

I chuckled, shaking my head at the show, but then Ivy shoved Joel over to the far edge of the pool. She muttered something for only them to hear — something that made Joel smile wickedly — and then, in front of me and God and everyone else, he grabbed both her tits in his hands and squeezed.

It wasn't a sexual advance, more like a playful boob squeeze that reminded me of something my sister would do to a friend. But it didn't matter. Regardless of intent, he'd grabbed her somewhere he never should have, and he'd done it in front of everyone.

Ivy laughed and shoved him away, and then her hands disappeared under the water, and he bit his lip at something before wiggling out of her grasp.

Another laugh left Ivy's lips as she made her way out of the pool, and Joel slapped her ass on her ascent.

That did it.

I wasn't one for confrontation. In fact, even now, as I stormed over to the pool, everything inside me was screaming for me to just walk right past all of them and go downstairs, go to my room, go to bed. It was fine. He was just drunk. They were just playing.

But something had clicked inside of me.

All summer, I'd felt it niggling, a little prickle of something tickling my chest, my throat, wiggling its way into my body and soul. I was afloat, and in that state,

I was susceptible to doing and saying things I never would normally.

Apparently, that included stomping right over to Joel and calling him out in front of the entire crew.

"Hey, babe," Joel said with a goofy smile when I hit the edge of the pool.

"Did you forget I was here?"

My words were cold and harsh, and I crossed my arms as everyone turned to look at us.

Joel frowned. "What?"

"I said, *did you forget I was here?* Or did you want me to see you fondling another girl like I don't exist?"

Joel's mouth popped open, but I saw anger slip in quickly, replacing the shock. "You're being ridiculous. We were just messing around."

"Yeah?" I asked, popping a hip. "Well, maybe I should find someone to *mess around* with, too."

I stormed off just as a chorus of *ooooh's* broke out, along with a light cloud of laughter.

Emma was coming up the stairs as I stomped toward them, and when she saw me, her eyebrows knitted together. "Hey, are you okay? What happened?"

I shook her off when she reached for me, still fuming so much I couldn't even answer her.

I was rounding the railing of the stairs when Joel's arm caught my elbow, whipping me around to face him. Emma gave him a look before her eyes met mine, and I softly nodded, letting her know I was okay. She didn't seem convinced when she left us, but she gave us the space to talk.

"What's your problem?" Joel asked.

Everyone had gone back to partying, but I wasn't stupid enough to think they weren't still watching us.

"*My* problem?" I asked incredulously. "You just grabbed Ivy's tits in front of me, Joel. In front of *every-one*. And then you smacked her ass!"

"I was *playing*. We're just friends, we joke around like that sometimes."

"So you'd be fine if I *jokingly* grabbed a guy between the legs? How about Ace, or Wayland, or Theo?"

I didn't know why I said that last name, but I held my chin high, eyes narrowed in the challenge — and Joel folded, his jaw tensing.

"I know it's hard for you to understand, but this is how it is on the boats. Okay? We're all playful with each other. Yes, sometimes it can get a little flirty, but it's innocent. It doesn't mean anything."

"It means something *to me*."

"Ivy is literally the reason I have this job, Aspen," Joel said, shaking his head as he watched me like I was the villain. "Stop being jealous."

"I'm not being *jealous*! Why are you making me feel like it's ridiculous that watching my boyfriend grope another girl made me upset?"

"You aren't even supposed to be here!"

My head snapped back at those words, and I found I had nothing to say back to them. They hung like barbed wire between us, prickly and dangerous.

Joel sighed, running his hands through his hair as he looked back at the pool and then to me again.

But he didn't take it back.

My eyes watered, nose stinging as hurt made its way past the anger in my chest. "We should go to our room and talk."

"I don't want to leave."

"Joel," I pleaded, tears welling in my eyes.

"If you want to go, go. But I'm having fun."

And with those words, he turned his back on me, leaving me at the top of the stairs while he got back to the party like everything was fine. Ivy, Celeste, and Ace welcomed him back to the pool, but Emma watched me with sad eyes. She started to get out of her chair but I shook my head, stopping her short.

Then, I dashed down the stairs like the top deck was on fire.

CHAPTER
TWELVE

"Ugh!" I huffed when I made it to the stateroom, slamming the door behind me before I let my back fall against it. As soon as I was alone in that room, the tears I'd been trying to hold back flooded, rushing down my hot cheeks as I swiped at them. I didn't want to cry. I didn't want to show any kind of pain or weakness.

I wanted to be mad.

I ripped Celeste's swimsuit off, tearing at it like it was the enemy before I threw it across the room. I thought seriously of shredding it with a pair of scissors, but then remembered I didn't have any. So, with another huff, I pulled on a pair of cotton panties and the one sleep shirt I had with me. It was light gray, soft and long, hitting me mid-thigh and the sleeves almost reaching my elbows. The moment the fabric fell over me, I found a sigh, my first real breath since I'd left the top deck.

And with it, my face contorted with another wave of tears.

"Come on, Aspen," I whispered against the pain. "Get it together."

I dragged myself into the bathroom, almost laughing at my ridiculous reflection in the mirror. I didn't have any of the miraculous makeup remover my sister had at home, so I settled on a hot, wet washcloth and soap.

I scrubbed at my makeup, watching as the black and golds and pinks swirled together in a Picasso fashion on my face. And all the while, two sides of myself battled in my heart.

He's just drunk. He doesn't mean it.

It doesn't matter if he's drunk, that was mean.

He's right, though, you're not usually around. And this is the way they all act with each other. You may not understand it, but it's the culture.

Bullshit. Your boyfriend shouldn't grab another girl's tits. Period.

Ivy is your friend. Look, she even did your makeup tonight!

You can trust Ivy about as far as you can throw her.

But Celeste...

DIDN'T STAND UP FOR YOU. No one did.

Joel loves you.

You don't even know who Joel is anymore.

Everything is fine, just go to sleep and you'll feel better in the morning.

Nothing is okay. Who even are you anymore?

With each volley, I scrubbed harder and harder, making my skin red and agitated. Most of the makeup was coming off, but the mascara was waterproof and stubborn. I scrubbed it as much as I could before I gave up and tossed the washcloth in the sink.

I stared at my reflection — at my tired, puffy eyes, my red cheeks, my disheveled hair. My eyes caught on the stupid pair of bedazzled earrings Ivy had given me to wear and I growled, fussing until I got one of them off and then the other. I accidentally dropped one of them, and I cursed, falling to my knees on the floor as I scurried around looking for it.

The girl had fondled my boyfriend under the water with me right there, and yet I didn't want to be the jerk who didn't return her earrings.

Typical.

I was on my hands and knees, padding around on the bathroom floor looking for that stupid earring as more tears flooded my eyes.

And that's how Theo found me.

I heard the door to the stateroom creak open, and I looked up, thinking maybe Joel had come to talk.

Instead, Theo walked in, his dress shoes tapping along the wood until he stood at the doorway of the bathroom. He slipped his hands in his pockets, looking down on me with bent brows. "Sorry I didn't knock," he said, but he didn't look sorry at all.

I sniffed, wiping at the tears on my face and trying to hide the mess I was from his gaze as best I could.

"I was in the salon on the main deck when you blew past," Theo said after a moment. "You looked upset."

"I'm fine."

"Oh, so we're back to lying to each other?"

I breathed a laugh, shaking my head, and all the while I was still looking on the floor for Ivy's earring.

"What happened?"

I sat back on my heels, looking up at Theo with a helpless shrug as more tears flooded my eyes.

As soon as he saw them, something washed over his face — Anger? Pain? Longing? — and then in a motion that shocked me still, Theo dropped to his knees, too.

His eyes were level with mine, now — steady and strong while mine were puffy and glossed. His gaze searched mine, and when I tried to look away, to hide my emotion from him, his fingers caught my chin, holding me so I couldn't.

I shivered at the touch.

"You wanted to know something true," he said, voice soft and low. "The other night."

My eyes flicked back and forth between his, a flash of that night in the hot tub hitting me like a subway train. Suddenly, I realized how close we were. Suddenly, I realized we were alone. Suddenly, I remembered what he'd said earlier, about what he would have done if I were his.

What would it be like to be his?

Theo let out a steady breath, his thumb brushing my jaw where he held me. "So here it is," he said. "Something true."

His eyes traced my features, taking in every inch of my face before he locked his gaze on mine once more.

"For some impossible reason I cannot fathom, I care for you," he said, and it wasn't a whisper, but a sound, steady statement. "It's kept me up at night, Aspen. I've had one question haunting me."

I swallowed.

"How could a seemingly ordinary girl from Colorado who wasn't even supposed to be on my boat at all, become the center of my focus and attention, of my every waking thought and every sleepless night?"

My throat tightened with a new wave of emotion, and my next breath was labored and hot.

"There's a truth," he whispered, moving closer, his fingers sliding up until his entire palm rested against my cheek where I leaned into the touch. "And seeing you upset like this makes me want to light this entire boat on fire, if it means destroying whoever it was who brought you this pain."

My face twisted, and the tightness in my chest let loose all at once in the form of another rush of tears. I choked on the sob, and Theo pulled me into his chest, wrapping his arms around me and holding me tight against him as I surrendered to the breakdown.

I let him hold me, let my fists twist in the fabric of his suit jacket, tugging him closer as much as I was pushing him away. I sobbed into his chest as he ran his fingers through my hair, loosening the braid it had been in and calming me with a gentle command.

Shhh, shhh. I've got you. I'm here.

I cried even harder at those words, and for the longest time, that's how we existed — me in his arms, him shielding me from the world on that tiny bathroom floor. I cried until I had no tears left to give. I sobbed until my breaths had no choice but to steady. My eyes dried up, and then they closed, and exhaustion flooded over me, taking me under.

I couldn't be sure how long we were there, how long he held me and soothed me until I fell still and silent in his arms. The fatigue that found me was all-encompassing, and I couldn't open my eyes, let alone lift my head to thank him.

In the distant haze of my awareness, I felt Theo lift me from the floor. I felt him carry me into the room, lay me on the bed, pull the sheets and comforter up and over my shoulders. I felt his hand brush away the hair from my face, and that was the last touch he gave me before the light clicked off, and the door opened and closed again with a quiet snick.

And I fell into a fever dream, one where the yacht was on fire, the flames licking the dark night sky while Theo carried me dazed and confused down the dock toward the shore.

Toward safety.

CHAPTER
THIRTEEN

I woke up alone.

My head pounded like someone had shaken me so hard it'd scrambled my brain, and I groaned against the pain, squeezing my eyes tight before I was brave enough to creak them open. It had to be early, judging by the soft little bit of light coming through our one and only window in the cabin, but Joel wasn't here.

I had no idea if he left for work already or if he ever came home at all.

Slowly, I lifted myself onto my palms, scooting back until I could rest against the headboard. After a good scrub of my hands through my hair, I steeled a breath and fought the headache long enough to make it to the bathroom.

Joel's wet swim trunks were draped over the towel rack.

I sighed as I stared at them from the toilet, wondering how I had passed out so hard. Had he slept here?

Did he come in with just enough time to change and leave again?

I needed to find him, to talk to him, and yet, when I popped an Advil and made my way back to the bed, the first thing I did was reach for my phone and pull up Theo's text thread.

There were no new messages.

Still, I stared at that thread, at those two innocent texts he'd sent after that first night I'd given him my number.

And then his words from last night filtered in through the fogginess in my head.

For some impossible reason I cannot fathom, I care for you.

I shivered at the memory of his voice, his eyes, his hand on my cheek. I'd spent the night in a mixture of dreams and nightmares, and in all of them, he was present.

My stomach tightened so fiercely I doubled over in bed, and I rolled onto one side, shaking my head as question after question assaulted me. Theo Whitman was a billionaire CEO of a Fortune 100 company. He was one of the richest men in the world. He was devastatingly handsome and could easily have any woman he wanted with just a snap of his finger.

Why was I even on his radar at all?

And *why* did I love that I was?

When he looked at me, my body reacted in a way that was foreign and exciting, fresh and new and terrifying. I wondered what it would be like, to be his, to have walked up to that party last night and been hauled up over his shoulders and back downstairs as soon as he saw me. What would he do to me if he had me to himself?

If we spent a night together?

I groaned, covering my face with my pillow to snuff the noise. "You have a boyfriend, Aspen," I reminded myself, the words muffled where they echoed back to me.

That reminder made my stomach upset for a completely different reason.

I pulled the pillow from my face, staring up at the ceiling as I replayed the scene at the pool. Joel had tossed my feelings aside so easily, and more than that, he'd chosen partying over making things right with me.

I needed to talk to him.

But I *wanted* to talk to Theo.

Everything in my body ached to go up on the main deck, seek him out, demand he explain what he meant by everything he said last night. I wanted him to tell me I imagined it. I wanted him to laugh at the audacity and call me crazy — because that's how I felt — absolutely, certifiably insane. *Silly little girl, why would I have any interest in you?*

But perhaps more than anything?

I wanted him to tell me more.

I wanted him to tell me he wanted me, he needed me, he couldn't stop thinking about me. I wanted to know his dreams were filled with me, that this wasn't all in my head, that the electricity I felt when he was near was coursing through his veins, too.

I wanted to be the source of every desire Theo Whitman had.

My body awakened to the thought, nipples hardening as I squeezed my thighs together against the ache between my legs. My breath grew shallower the more I thought about it — about his sultry eyes, his cocky smirk, his broad shoulders in his fitted suit.

I slipped a hand under my panties, shivering at the cool touch against my core.

When I closed my eyes, I saw Theo's face.

And I pretended my hand was his.

It's kept me up at night, Aspen.

I've had one question haunting me.

I couldn't bite back the moan when one finger slipped inside me, and that seemed to jolt me back to reality.

My eyes shot open, and I ripped my hand from my panties, sitting up quickly with a frustrated groan.

What is happening to me?

I didn't know if I wanted to cry or scream or give in to my desire. No one would know. Joel was at work, Theo wasn't here, of course. I was alone. Would it be so bad to get lost in a little fantasy for a few moments?

Yes, Aspen, seeing as how that fantasy is not about your BOYFRIEND.

I felt like a meteor spiraling in space, like a bottle teetering dangerously on a choppy sea, safe for now but just one wrong wave away from drowning.

So, I reached for my phone again, and this time, I called the one person I hoped could ground me.

"Hey, big sis, how's life of the rich and famous?"

As soon as Juniper's voice was on the line, my eyes welled with tears again. "It's... interesting," I answered. "How are you?"

"I'm good. Busy. Tired." She yawned, and it was then that I realized it was the middle of the night there. "I was actually sleeping, though. I think you forgot about the time difference."

"Oh God, I'm sorry sis."

"It's okay. I've got a busy day tomorrow." She paused. "Er, today now, I guess. But maybe I can call you later this week and we can catch up?"

My heart sank, and a million responses screamed at me in my head.

No, I need to talk to you now.

I need someone to tell me what to do.

I need someone to help me figure out the mess inside my head.

"Sure," I said instead, sighing with the resignation.

Juniper was silent for a moment. "Everything okay?"

God, no.

"Mm-hmm." I sighed, shaking my head as I forced a smile even though she couldn't see it. "Just needed to hear your voice."

"Aww, you big softie. I'll give you a call later this week. Okay?"

I swallowed. "Okay."

"Until then, give Joel my love, and for Pete's sake, sis, have some fun. You sound like you're wound up tighter than a virgin's asshole over there."

"Juniper!"

"Oh, get over it. I'm nineteen."

I chuckled a little at that. "I love you."

"Love you, too. I'm going back to sleep. *You* go have some *fun*," she said again, and then the line cut out, and I was alone with my thoughts again.

What a dangerous place to be.

Joel walked through the cabin door at 8:04 that evening.

I was still in bed, reading a book, which I laid flat on the comforter at the sight of him. His eyes were red and puffy, along with his nose, as if he'd been crying too. His dark hair was sticking up this way and that, his shoulders slumped as he dug into his pockets and emptied everything out of them, dumping his wallet and keys and such on the dresser.

He looked as tired and worn and sad as I felt.

"Hi," I said tentatively.

I expected him to jump into bed and throw himself on me. I expected an apology, an explanation, a promise to never do it again. I expected a flurry of kisses, his arms encompassing me, his forehead pressed to mine. That was always how it went. We were like any couple — we had our fights, but we always came around, and making up was the best part.

A night with just the two of us, connected in the most intimate way we could be — that was exactly what I needed to get my mind off my stupid Theo fantasies.

Joel's eyes were flat when they met mine. "Hi."

I swallowed. "How was your day?"

"Fine," he said on a sigh. "I'm going to take a shower."

"Can we talk first?"

"Dammit, Aspen, I'm *tired*, okay? It's been raining, I don't feel good, and I had a long day on the boat. I just want to take a shower and go to bed."

He seemed exhausted just from having said the words, the deep rumble of his voice etched with weariness.

Remorse was nowhere to be found.

I frowned, closing my book and setting it aside before I stood and rounded the bed to where he was. "Are you not even sorry about what happened last night?"

"About your overreaction to me having fun? No."

"Joel..."

"I'm sorry," he said, pinching the bridge of his nose on a sigh. "Look, I really don't feel well. I'm not myself right now."

"Hungover?"

He glared. "No, like I actually feel sick, but thanks for that." He shook his head, stripping his shirt overhead. "I'm getting in the shower. We can talk tomorrow."

"I'd rather talk tonight."

"Well, I'd rather not."

With that, he slammed the bathroom door to seal his point.

I was fuming while he was in the shower, pacing back and forth, planning out everything I would say when he got out. Except that when he actually did, I saw it — *really* saw it — how long and worn his face was, how the puffiness and redness wasn't from crying, how just the sight of him made *me* feel achy in my bones.

He really was sick, and as much as I wanted to talk, I wanted him to be okay even more.

"Do you need anything?" I asked.

"Just sleep. I'll be okay."

I nodded. "Alright. Mind if I keep my lamp on to read?"

"Do whatever you want."

He crawled into bed with a cough and a wince, then he rolled onto one side, facing away from me as he turned out the light on his side of the bed. He didn't say goodnight, didn't give me a kiss, and within minutes, he was snoring.

I sighed, crawling back into bed next to him and leaning against the headboard.

I'd spent nearly the entire day in the room, save for the few times I snuck out to get food, and I was beginning to wonder if it had even been a day at all. It was one of those weird stretches of time that could have been a dream. I felt antsy, like I needed to get out, but my body protested, keeping me firmly in bed.

I picked up my book again, but I couldn't focus. I read the same page three times before I conceded, shutting it altogether and deciding I should just get to bed early, too.

Just as I was turning out the lamp, my phone buzzed with a text...from Theo.

My heart lurched into my throat at the sight of his name on my phone.

I glanced at Joel, who was still sound asleep, and then unplugged my phone from the charger and settled into the sheets, sliding my thumb across the screen until the text opened.

How are you feeling? I didn't see you all day.

Butterflies.

A stampede of furious, stir-crazy butterflies.

I bit my lip, heart thundering a little louder in my chest.

I'm okay. It was a weird day. How are you?

I would be better if I could have seen you on deck.

I pressed the phone into my chest, rolling my eyes up to the ceiling until they closed altogether. I stifled the little squeal threatening to break loose from my throat, and after a breath, I looked back at the screen just in time for another text to come through.

I hope I didn't scare you last night.

I swallowed, replaying the scene for the one-hundredth time that day. Even in the darkness, I could picture his sterling eyes fixed on mine.

Not scared. Surprised, maybe.

Good surprise?

Joel stirred next to me, and I panicked, throwing the phone under the covers until he settled again. Guilt sank into my stomach, and when I lifted the phone again, I typed and erased, typed and erased until another text came through.

I have a terrible habit of making you uncomfortable, don't I, Miss Dawn?

He sent the text with a smirky emoji, and I rolled my eyes, but couldn't fight the smile blooming on my lips.

I have a terrible suspicion you like it.

Theo sent back a wink emoji, and then the little dots were bouncing again, letting me know he was typing.

Meet me tomorrow morning. I want to show you something.

I bit my lip, glancing at Joel with the pit growing deeper and darker in my stomach.

My phone vibrated again.

I won't take no for an answer.

I swallowed, hating the way my body betrayed me, the way it came to life like those text messages were Dr. Frankenstein's volts of electricity, and I was the monster he created.

Goodnight, Mr. Whitman.

Goodnight, Miss Dawn.

CHAPTER
FOURTEEN

Joel was sick on our first date in college.

I had no idea, of course, because that was the way Joel was — if he was sick, life went on as normal. Looking back now, I should have noticed his persistent cough at the movie, and his watery eyes in the candlelight at the little pizza joint we went to, and how red his nose was when he first grabbed my hand as we walked back to my dorm room.

But the super cute guy who ran in the same circle of friends had asked me on a date. No way was I questioning *any* of it.

He didn't tell me until almost a year into our relationship, which was the *next* time I saw him sick. And just like that first time, he insisted he was fine, that he could go to school and work and party just like he always did. *Lying on this couch isn't going to do me any good,* he'd said, and I'd marveled at his strength, because when I was sick? All I wanted was to be doted on while I whined and curled up in a ball of blankets.

So, when I woke the next morning to the sound of us dropping anchor and Joel was still asleep next to me, I knew something was wrong.

I pressed the back of my hand to his forehead, his neck, shaking my head when I felt how hot his skin was. "You're burning up," I said.

Joel groaned. "I feel like I've been run over by a truck."

"I'll be right back."

I popped out of bed, pulling on a pair of shorts, a sports bra, and a tank top before I rushed upstairs. I made some tea, rummaged around in the crew galley until I found a stash of cold medicine, and then went back to find Joel trying to get dressed for work.

"You should rest," I said, popping two of the daytime cold pills into my palm. "Here, take these."

Joel shook his head, but took the medicine, anyway. He accepted the tea and sat on the edge of the bed, one shoe on, eyelids sagging, his hair a complete mess from tossing in his sleep. "I can't rest. I have to work."

Just then, there was a knock on our door.

I frowned, glancing at Joel before I hopped up to answer it, and then nearly stumbling back when I swung the door open and found Theo on the other side.

He was already dressed and ready for the day, a robin's egg blue hugging the muscles of his arms. The top three buttons were popped, the neck hanging open just enough to see the light bit of hair that dusted his chest. He had a coffee in his hand, and he tilted it toward me with a grin.

"Good morning," he said to me first, and then his eyes settled on Joel, his smile slipping. "Jesus. You okay, Joel?"

"He's sick," I said at the same time Joel answered, "I'm fine."

Joel glared at me, and I widened my eyes on a shrug like *what? It's true.*

"You look pretty rough," Theo said.

"He's got a fever, and he was groaning all night, tossing and turning."

"Body aches," Theo said on a nod, looking at Joel again. "Why don't you take the day off?"

Joel was already shaking his head, trying to stand, when it looked as if he got dizzy from moving too fast and fell back down onto the bed.

Theo arched a brow. "I think it's probably a good idea."

"I need to work."

"The rest of the crew can handle it. We're already anchored for the day, and I won't be having any guests on board."

"See? And if you rest today, you'll feel better sooner and can get back to work when you're actually needed," I chimed in.

Joel looked defeated. "I don't want to be a burden."

"Trust me, Captain Chuck isn't giving the crew any difficult tasks today. It'll be an easy one, mostly maintenance and cleaning and getting ready for the week ahead. Don't worry, they'll save the teak-scrubbing for when you're feeling better." Theo tried to smile with the joke.

Joel hung his head even more, but started taking off his shoes. I sighed at the sight, thankful he was listening to us.

"Sir," Joel said after a moment. "Excuse me if this is rude but... why did you come to our room so early?" He paused, looking at Theo. "Or at all?"

My stomach cramped at the way Joel stared at Theo then, with his brows slowly furrowing, like he just realized there was a snake in the grass next to him.

Theo smiled as if it wasn't odd at all, and then his eyes found mine. "Actually, I came to see if Aspen would like to go to shore with me today."

A million tiny butterfly wings tickled my chest.

"I have some business to attend to, but Positano is a great picture stop."

I gasped. "We're in *Positano*?"

The soft pull at the corner of his lips was my only answer.

My heart *tha-dumped* in my chest, not just from the way Theo looked at me, but from the thought of all the amazing photographs I could capture on shore. I'd seen pictures of Positano in travel magazines and on Instagram, the colorful houses and shops nestled into the cliffs along the bright turquoise water.

But one look back at where Joel sat on the edge of the bed with his head hanging between his shoulders, and I knew it wasn't possible to leave him.

"I should stay and take care of Joel," I said, forcing a small smile. "But thank—"

"No, go," Joel interrupted, shaking his head with his eyes squeezed shut. "You should go."

I frowned. "But—"

"I look *and* feel like shit, Aspen. I'm just going to be lying here all day, probably sleeping. There's no reason for you to stay."

It was a nice gesture, insisting that I go enjoy my day, but for some reason, I felt like it was more that Joel didn't want me around. It didn't feel like a sweet, *no no, you should go.*

It felt like an *I don't want you here.*

"But what if you need something?"

"I'll be sure Emma knows to check in on you," Theo answered, nodding to Joel with a smile. Then, his eyes were on me. "Come on, Joel needs rest, and trust me when I say you can't miss out on this stop for your portfolio."

I chewed my lip, watching Theo, and then Joel, back and forth like whatever decision I made in that moment would somehow change the course of my life forever.

"*Go*, Aspen," Joel insisted again. "Please."

I sighed, not happy with the thought of leaving him, but even more unhappy at the thought of missing out on Positano.

"Are you sure you'll be okay?"

"I'll be fine," Joel grumbled, and he was already crawling back into bed, wincing against his body aches as he did so.

I nodded, deciding the choice wasn't really mine, anyway. Joel didn't want me to stay, and he *would* just be resting. If Emma was going to check on him throughout the day... he'd be fine, right?

"I'll wait for you on the main deck," Theo said, and then he told Joel to feel better and left us alone.

"Babe, are you sure—" I tried, sitting on the edge of the bed and reaching out for Joel. But he rolled away from the touch, pulling the covers up to his chin.

"Aspen, please. I just want to sleep."

My heart sank like an anchor into the deep pit of my stomach, and it stayed there as I got dressed and brushed my hair and packed a bag for the day. I tried to settle the tightness in my chest with deep inhales and full exhales, but it was no use.

Anxiety crept in like a storm cloud, low and menacing. I hated that Joel was sick, but I hated even more that he still hadn't apologized, that he was still making me feel like it was *me* who had something to be sorry for.

He was asleep — or pretending to be asleep, I wasn't sure — by the time I had my bag packed and my camera strapped around my neck. My chest was still tight as I climbed the stairs up to the main deck, but the moment I laid eyes on Theo, the anxiety faded like a pencil mark under an eraser.

Theo leaned against the railing, sunglasses in place and a smirk on his perfect lips. He stood taller when I approached, slipping his hands into the pockets of his grey Chino shorts.

"Ready?" he asked.

And I couldn't help but feel like that question held more weight than it appeared, that he wasn't just asking me if I was ready to get off the boat, but if I was ready for something else entirely. A new adventure, perhaps.

Or a new life.

I nodded on a smile, stomach fluttering again when I took in the breathtaking view behind him. The coast of Positano was peppered with sailboats and speed boats alike, colorful buildings sprawling up the cliff above the pebble-covered beach. My finger itched where it hovered over my camera.

"Ready," I whispered.

Theo smiled, gesturing for me to follow him.

Wayland was our driver in the tender, taking us safely to shore before he told us to have fun and that he'd be back thirty minutes before sunset to retrieve us. Theo and I walked the dock toward the beach in silence, both of us looking around at the sights.

"I can't believe this is real," I said, turning my camera on. I paused on the dock, adjusting the aperture and focus to get a shot of the gemstone water, the sepia-tone beach, the charming kaleidoscope of houses and stores and restaurants that stacked up from the water's edge all the way to the top of the seaside cliff.

"Just wait," Theo said. "You haven't seen anything yet."

Click.

I smiled, pulling the camera away from my eye to glance down at the playback screen at the photo I'd taken. It was going to be difficult to capture the magic I felt on that dock, the enchanting personality of Positano that was already infecting me. That was the true challenge with photography — how do you let the viewer feel exactly what you did when you took the shot?

"So, what business do you have here?" I asked when we started walking again.

"I don't have any."

I frowned, pausing at the edge of where the dock met the beach. "But you said..."

"I lied."

Theo smirked at my confusion, and my stomach somersaulted.

He lied.

He lied to get me on shore with him.

I fought the urge to lift my camera and take a photograph of him there on the edge of the beach, Positano stretching out behind him, turquoise water sparkling off to his left. I wanted to capture that moment, to store it away in a place only I could find for a lonely night when I'd long to remember what it felt like to stand on the coast of Italy with Theo Whitman smiling at me like we had nothing but possibility ahead of us.

Besides, I needed that camera as a buffer.

He was so heartbreakingly beautiful it hurt to look at him without a lens to mute his allure.

"Come on," he said, steering us toward the pebbly beach. "I told you I have something to show you."

CHAPTER
FIFTEEN

"**Y**ou're joking," I said on a laugh. "You really dressed like a baby and sucked your thumb for a college presentation?"

"It was to prove a point," Theo said, gesturing to a shop on our right. It was a small boutique with dresses and swimsuits hanging in the window. "Let's go in here."

I followed him in. "I think the point is lost on me."

"The code we were learning, the data structures..." Theo shook his head, sliding his hands in his pockets as we walked the walls of the shop. "It was all juvenile. Outdated. I mean, *none* of it would be useful in the real world. So, in lieu of doing an actual presentation on the bullshit he was teaching us, I thought I'd prove my point."

I arched a brow. "You were a little shit, weren't you?"

Theo's eyes bulged. "Wow. I think that's the first time I've heard you curse," he said as I flushed, looking from him to a flowy, orange maxi dress. I let my fingers wander over the soft fabric as he continued. "But yes, I was," he agreed with a grin. "To be fair, I dropped out the next day. So, it was kind of my fare-thee-well."

"I'm sure they never forgot you at that school."

"Oh, are you kidding? It's Harvard. They were pissed I dropped out, and even more pissed that I made something of myself *after* dropping out. It was proof that no one needs that expensive piece of paper from them to accomplish what they want." He shook his head. "College is archaic in more ways than it's relevant, unless you're in medicine, I suppose."

"I don't know," I mused. "I enjoyed my time there."

"But did you learn anything of value?"

I cocked my head. "I think so. I learned more about the craft, the rules, the theory of photography."

"And let me ask you this," Theo said, stepping into me. My breath caught in my chest at his proximity, at the way the little boutique suddenly shrank to the size of a shoebox. "Your best photographs... the ones that you're most proud of... do any of those follow *the rules*?"

I swallowed, looking up at him through my lashes. I couldn't quite decipher why, but I liked when he looked down on me like that, when he towered over me, when his power and presence was all-consuming. "Some of them, yes."

Theo narrowed his eyes like he didn't believe me, but then he tilted his head with a knowing smirk. "Rules are made to be broken — haven't you heard that old saying, Miss Dawn?"

Heat rushed over me, from where my hair fell over my shoulders all the way down to the leather straps of my sandals on my feet.

"You should try that on."

I blinked at the subject change, taking a deep inhale when Theo stepped back, giving me space to breathe again. He nodded at the clementine maxi dress I hadn't realized I'd still been touching.

"Oh..." I turned away from him, looking the dress up and down. The price tag was tucked away, nowhere to be found, which told me without even hunting for it that it was way too expensive for my measly travel budget. "No, that's okay."

But Theo reached his arm over my head, grabbing the dress from the rack. I turned back to him just in time to see him merely *look* at the young woman behind the counter. She jumped like he'd snapped his fingers, coming over immediately with a brilliant, toothy smile.

"Try this one, yes?" she asked, her English lilted with an Italian accent.

"*Sí, e quello,*" he said, pointing to an olive green one-piece swimsuit.

The woman grabbed the maxi dress from his hands, retrieving the swimsuit next before she followed him around the store. He walked slowly, appraising each item, his hand absentmindedly rubbing the scruff on his chin. Every now and then, he'd point, and the woman would scoop up the item he'd selected, draping it over her arms.

"Theo..."

"*Anche questo,*" he said, pointing to a pair of yellow sapphire stud earrings in a glass case on the back wall. "*Grazie.*"

The woman nodded, and then she deposited the clothes into one of the dressing rooms, holding back the curtain with a smile aimed at me. "Earrings last," she said simply.

I blinked at her first, and then at Theo before I looked back to the woman again.

"Please," she said, gesturing inside the dressing room. "For you."

I gave Theo a cautioning look, shaking my head. "I can't... I don't..."

"I want to see every single one of them," he said. Then, with an air of confidence I'd only seen this man possess, he took a seat on the plush couch in the middle of the boutique, smiling at me as he crossed one ankle over the other and kicked back like he owned the place.

I let out an incredulous laugh. "Just who do you think you are?"

He shrugged, making an arrogant expression that suggested I already knew the answer to my own question.

And I had no choice. I shook my head on another laugh of disbelief, and then I let the salesclerk — Evelina — guide me into the dressing room. She smiled, pointing out each of the outfits she'd arranged, and then she closed the curtain behind her, leaving me alone.

I didn't have to look at a price tag. I knew without hesitation that I was in a tiny dressing room with at least a couple thousand dollars' worth of clothing. But curiosity got the best of me, and I took down the maxi dress first, fishing the price tag out of where it had been tucked into the back.

One-thousand five-hundred and ninety euros.

I blanched, nearly dropping the hanger from my hands. "Theo," I said, pushing the curtain open to show him the price tag. "I can't—"

But he just pointed at the dressing room with a

grin, his brow arched in a way that told me I wasn't getting out of this — no matter how I tried.

"Ugh, you're incorrigible," I groaned, snapping the curtain shut.

"You have no idea," he mumbled in response.

I stripped off my tank top and shorts, kicking my sandals to the side before I slipped into the maxi dress. It was the kind of fabric I'd never had against my skin before, the kind that I had never been able to afford and never *dreamed* of affording, either. It was soft and luxuriously heavy, the way only quality fabric could be, hanging on my hips and bust in a way that made it look like I actually had a little curvature. I turned this way and that in the mirror, admiring the way the fruity orange looked against my tan skin, the way the thin straps accented my collarbones, the way the fabric flowed just below my knees before tapering down to the ground in the back, showing just a little of my legs.

I hated it.

I hated that it fit so perfectly, that the transparent top layer was so gorgeous and flowy against the slightly darker, heavier bottom one. I hated that the color set my tan ablaze, and that for the first time in my life, I was in a dress and I didn't want to cower into a corner. I hated that the deep V cut of the back somehow made me love my spine and ribcage. How was that even a thing?

I hated it because I loved it.

And there was no way I could ever take it home with me.

I sighed, giving myself one last look over before I tentatively made my way through the curtains and into the boutique.

Evelina was talking to Theo in Italian, something that made them both chuckle, but when I walked out, their eyes snapped to me.

"*Bellisima!*" Evelina said on a gasp. She shook her head, advancing on me and tugging at the fabric in a few places before she snapped her fingers and scurried off toward the shoes.

My eyes found Theo next, and he was trailing his gaze up from where my bare legs showed through the bottom of the dress, up my thighs, along the lines of my hips and waist and bust until he met my eyes.

Fiery hot coals smoldered in his irises, his pupils dilating the longer he stared at me. He was still reclining on the couch, seemingly unaffected save for the swallow I watched strain his throat.

"Do you like it?" I asked on a whisper, absentmindedly playing with the strings that tied around the waist.

His nostrils flared, but before he could answer, Evelina rushed back over, thrusting a pair of beige wedges into my hands.

"With these," she said, and then she pulled my hand into hers, opening my fingers and dropping the yellow sapphire earrings into my palm. "And these. Trust me," she insisted, and before I could argue she was ushering me back into the dressing room. "It will be perfect."

Against my persistent arguing, we left the boutique with me wearing the orange maxi dress and the earrings. Blessedly, I'd convinced Theo and Evelina that I couldn't walk in the wedges, so they'd settled on a strappy pair of leather sandals that I loved as much as the dress. In the white paper bag that swung from my arm were the clothes I *had* been wearing, along with the olive one-piece swimsuit, which was the compromise I offered to keep Theo from buying me a five-thousand-euro Italian leather jacket.

I still couldn't believe he'd bought all of it for me. I thought it would sink in as we walked the streets and hidden valleys of the town, or that I'd forget about it altogether as I got lost behind the lens of my camera. But I marveled at the way the silky-smooth dress felt against my skin every second, every minute, every hour of that day. And my fingers absentmindedly wandered up to tuck my hair behind my ear now and then, and every time, I'd brush the gemstones of those sapphire earrings and smile.

If I'd thought the places we'd hit on the coast so far had been gorgeous, they paled in comparison to the sights Positano offered.

My memory card filled with colorful shots of lemon tree farms and cobblestone streets, of the dozens and dozens of staircases around every corner, of clothes drying on a line strung from one pastel house to the other. I gasped at the sight of the water through small windows and alleyways, lost my breath at the way the ivy crawled the ancient walls of every building, and craned my neck in wonder as we walked down a street with flowers weaved together in a wondrous ceiling above us.

"Theo?" I asked as we both stared up at the floral ceiling, the soft hum of tourists buzzing around us.

"Yes?"

"Why did you name your boat *Philautia*? What does it mean?"

Theo smiled a little when I glanced at him, but his eyes were still on the flowers above. "That's an easy question with a complicated answer."

I kept silent, waiting.

After a moment, Theo nodded toward an empty staircase nestled in an alleyway. There was a man there playing a violin, and Theo pulled a one-hundred euro note from his pocket, giving it to the man and whispering something in his ear. The man's eyes bulged at the note first before he smiled and nodded at me politely, excusing himself and leaving us alone.

Theo took a seat on the third step, waiting until I sat next to him before he said, "Did you know there are seven different words for love in the Greek language?"

"Seven?" I asked, arching a brow. "Do you mean like how we have *love* and *lust*?"

Theo shook his head. "Much more than that. I'm no expert, but the way I understood it when I first heard the story, it's like... there are different levels of love. Different shades. For instance, you can love your mom, but not in the same way you love your favorite restaurant. And you can love your dog, wanting them to be safe and cared for, but it's different from the way you might love a *lover*, with passion," he said, and his eyes met mine then. "With desire."

I swallowed.

"The Greeks have understood this for a long time, so they have different words for love, depending on what kind it is. Like *Ludus*, which is kind of like our version of having a crush on someone, flirty and fun. Or *Eros*, which is passionate and consuming, sexually driven," he explained, smirking a little when my cheeks flushed. "The way a first love might be."

I nodded, tucking my hair behind my ear and glancing at the tourists passing by just to catch a breath. After a moment, I looked back at Theo again. "So, what kind of love is *Philautia* then?"

Theo smiled. "Self-love."

"Hmm," I mused, frowning a little as I tried to piece together why he'd pick that one. "Well, are you going to tell me why you chose that as the name of your boat, or do I have to guess?"

He chuckled. "Well, what I loved about this word is that it encompasses more than just a lovely concept. Sure, part of it is self-love in the way we see it in the States." He paused, folding his hands together where they rested between his knees. "Like, *oh, it's been a long work week, tonight I'll run a hot bath and read a good book* kind of love. But the *other* side of *Philautia* addresses the more selfish kind of loving yourself. Pleasure-seeking. Narcissism, if you will."

I frowned. "So, you're telling me you're a narcissist, then?"

"Aren't we all in some ways?" Theo asked. "If the answer to that is no, then, frankly, I think that needs to be addressed."

"I'm not sure I understand."

Theo sighed, watching the people pass for a moment before he elaborated. "I think it's important to love yourself — even in the selfish way — because you're the only person truly looking out for yourself. Even if someone cares about you, a friend or family member, at the end of the day?" He shook his head. "Their life goes on, regardless of how you choose to live yours."

Theo paused, chewing the inside of his cheek for a moment.

"I think it's important to put yourself first sometimes. Do what makes you happy. Say no when you don't want to do something. Say yes to whatever you love, even if others don't understand or support it. Choose yourself every now and then, because if you don't, then who else will?"

I didn't miss the way Theo's eyes darkened with that question, the way his jaw tightened.

"I chose *Philautia* because that was a lesson I learned the hard way. For a long time, I put others before me no matter what. I would say no to advancements for Envizion because I knew my partner wouldn't like them, or say yes to doing a publicity event because I knew my parents wanted me to. I would try to be whatever my current flavor of the month wanted me to be — sometimes that meant working out more than I cared to, or eating differently than I usually did, or indulging in pastimes I wasn't actually fond of all in the name of making a woman happy."

He shook his head, as if, just like I was currently thinking, he couldn't believe he'd ever been that way. I couldn't picture Theo as anything but powerful and steady as a rock in the face of anything, work or otherwise.

"And I was burned," Theo continued. "Over and over, until I finally realized that though I had good intentions, I was losing myself in the name of serving others."

Theo's eyes met mine then, and my heart stopped in my chest at the intensity of his stare.

"I think you can understand that, can't you?"

I nodded, little flashes of my own sacrifices playing out like a movie reel in my mind. "I can."

Theo smiled a little, like he understood more than I let on. Then, he leaned back on his palms. "So, *Philautia*. A self-care gift to myself as well as a constant reminder that a seemingly selfish love for yourself can be a good thing, so long as the balance is there." He looked at me then. "So long as you aren't an asshole about it."

I shook my head on a laugh. "I like it."

"Why, thank you," he said with a little bow. Then, he stood, reaching his hand out for mine to help me up. "Shall we?"

The rest of the day was spent exploring Positano through the lens of my camera.

We happened upon a wedding in the streets, and the bride and groom laughed and danced and posed for us while I clicked away. An older woman with ash-gray hair and deep wrinkles smoked a cigarette as she watered the flowerpots hanging outside her shop. A young boy whizzed by on a scooter, the wind in his hair, and he turned to smile at my camera just as he passed. Two nuns walked the streets in long, beige habits, handing out small cards with the Serenity prayer. I captured a shot I knew would be in my portfolio just as one of them extended a card toward me, her smile wide above it, eyes crinkled at the edges with a small alleyway lined with flowers stretching out behind her, and at its apex — the Tyrrhenian Sea.

I spoke with the locals who were open to me prying into their lives, holding up my camera and pointing at their shops, their homes, their restaurants. With each place we ventured, I found myself lost a little more in the culture, in this magical city on the seaside cliff. I grimaced when I tasted limoncello for the first time at the insistence of a loud and boisterous Italian man named

Giovanni. I laughed at the little girl who played tricks on her uncle while he worked their leather shop on the street. And I blushed with a quiet *thank you* when an old man who spoke no English at all offered me a lapis lazuli necklace, the blue gemstone tied onto a simple, thin, brown leather strap.

And all the while, Theo walked alongside me in silence, watching me attempt to freeze-frame the world around us.

By the time the sun started to make its descent over the water, my legs ached from all the stairs we climbed, and I longed for a hot shower. But when I suggested we start to make our way back to the dock, Theo declined.

"I have one more stop, the place I said I wanted to show you."

I laughed, gesturing to the sights around us. "You mean more than you already have?"

His smile was my only answer, and he led the way up a small winding road at the top of the town where we'd climbed.

I scurried to catch up. "Didn't Wayland say he'd be at the dock before sunset?"

"I called him earlier and told him we'd need more time. Don't worry," he said with a smirk over his shoulder. "I'll have you back before you turn into a pumpkin."

I rolled my eyes, but before I could pop off a remark, Theo gently gripped my elbow.

He held me that way for a moment, still walking, and as we climbed the steep street, his hand slowly slid down lower. His palm was warm where it traced down the inside of my forearm, over the delicate bones of my wrist, and then he interlaced his fingers with mine, grabbing my hand tightly in his own.

I felt that squeeze like a naked plunge into the icy depths of the Arctic Ocean.

It was searing hot. It was burning cold. It was as numbing as it was electrifying, a battle of sensations that left me dizzy and weak in the knees.

"Is this okay?" he asked softly, his eyes finding mine.

I swallowed, staring at where our hands met, knowing my answer should have been an easy *no*, but not able to find the will to say the word.

Instead, my traitorous body responded with a slight nod of my head, and Theo smiled, holding my hand even tighter.

We climbed the street a little farther, and then Theo tugged me over to the edge of the sidewalk where a white metal railing lined the cliff. There was a bench under a tall tree, but he leaned us against the railing in lieu of sitting.

"May I see your camera," he asked, and I felt the loss of his hand in mine like a lifejacket being ripped from the water just as I lost my last effort to swim.

I peeled the strap from around my neck, handing the camera to him, and he held the machine steady in his hands with his eyes dancing curiously between mine.

"Now, turn around."

I did as he asked, and then I gasped, covering my lips with warm fingers that were just interlaced with Theo's.

We were on the south side of the city, near the top of the cliff, and from this angle, Positano spread out before us like a red carpet of glittering lights. The sun had just set over the horizon, casting the sky in brilliant shades of orange and pink that played with the deeper hues of purple and navy as the night tried to creep in.

One by one, lights popped on over the city. Streetlights, porch lights, lights in windows high above the cliffside, and lights on boats that still littered the water below. The night came alive with a warm orange glow from that little seaside city, and it was the most beautiful sight I'd ever seen in my life.

I turned to face Theo again, and right when I did, he snapped a photo.

I knew without looking at it what would be reflected in that photo. I knew there would be wonder and adoration in my eyes, and I knew the sky would be painted brightly behind me, and I knew that the way Theo had positioned us under a streetlight, there would be a soft orange glow on my forehead and down the bridge of my nose.

I smirked, shaking my head and reaching for the camera. Theo obliged with his own grin, and when the camera strap was around my neck again, I rested my hands on it.

For a long moment I stared at that camera, then back behind me at the sunset over Positano, and then back at the camera. When I found the courage, I finally lifted my eyes to meet Theo's.

"It's breathtaking," I whispered.

He nodded, swallowing. "As are you, Miss Dawn."

I shook my head again just as he stepped closer, his hand reaching out for my cheek. I leaned into his warmth, and then closed my eyes on a wince as if the touch had scarred me for life.

Perhaps it had.

"Why do you say things like that to me?"

"Because they're true," he answered with a cock of his head, as if the answer was obvious.

"But… I'm just…" I shook my head, looking down at myself. "Me. Just a girl from Colorado with a camera in her hand. And you…"

Theo frowned when my gaze met his, and he thumbed my jaw line, rolling his lips together before he whispered, "And *I* can't get enough of you."

My next breath shuddered out of me, and Theo's hand swept back into my hair, gripping the back of my neck just slightly. He pulled me in, and my eyelids fluttered shut as I pressed onto my tip toes. I leaned into that touch like a moth to a flame, and when his heat came nearer, when I felt his breath on my lips, I wished with everything that I was for his lips to meet mine.

But inside, my stomach lurched in warning, and my body jerked back with the force.

"Uh," I said, shaking my head when I'd pulled away. I tucked my hair behind my ear, glancing up at Theo's confusion through my lashes. "We should probably get back to the boat."

For a long moment, Theo just watched me, a million indecipherable emotions surging in his eyes. I watched the muscles of his jaw tick, watched the way he slid his hands into his pockets as if that was the only way to keep them from reaching out for me. He let out a long, slow, and steady exhale, and then a small smile found his lips. "Lead the way," he said, gesturing toward the path that led down to the beach.

So I turned, and held my camera between my hands, snapping a few last photos as we made our descent.

Theo didn't try to hold my hand on the walk back.

And later that night, when Joel was fast asleep next to me, I stared at the photo Theo had taken of me at the top of Positano and wondered who that girl in the photo was. She looked fresh and young and vibrant. She looked beautiful and luxurious and confident. She looked just seconds away from a laugh, just minutes away from a kiss. She looked aglow, like only a woman newly in love can.

She looked like no one I recognized.

And everything I ever wanted to be.

CHAPTER
SIXTEEN

I spent that night wishing I could paint.

I couldn't stop thinking about the photograph Theo had taken, and for some reason, I kept comparing it to the self-portrait assignment I had my freshman year at CU. The assignment had been simple: take a photograph of yourself. But it was so much more than that. You had to capture your entire essence in a single photograph, as if that one picture would be all the world would ever know about you.

I had buried myself in books pried open at the spine, pages and pages of ink on cream paper covering me from toe to nose. The only part of me that peeked through the books were my hands wrapped around a camera and my eyes.

And at the time, that was exactly the right image to depict.

I was the shy girl, the quiet girl, the one with her nose stuck in a book or a camera covering her face. I was an observer, which was why I left only my eyes and my camera visible in the self-portrait. The rest of me didn't need to be seen. I was not the object of art — I was the creator of it, the one sent to Earth to take the photographs, not be in them.

I wondered what my self-portrait would be now.

And the more I wondered, the less I held onto hope that I would sleep.

I pictured myself on the top deck of the boat, eyes cast toward the ocean, wind whipping through my hair. There would be a storm off to my left, broody black clouds whispering of destruction. And to my right, a gorgeous sunset, with pink and orange clouds much like the ones I'd seen off the coast of Positano.

My hands would be on the railing, except to my left, toward the storm, there would be no railing at all.

My hand would be suspended, toes just off the edge of the teak, as if to show the viewer that just one tiny inch of movement would push me over the precipice and into that storm.

But I couldn't capture that with a photograph — not without manipulation in post. So, I wondered what it would be like to be a painter, to be able to just create what you saw in your mind at any given moment with a brush stroke.

My eyes were bloodshot when Joel's alarm clock went off, and I swallowed back the guilt I felt as I watched him get ready for work. He still looked miserable, but I didn't even bother to try to get him to rest another day. One day had been victory enough.

He didn't say a word to me as he dressed, but he did stop by the edge of the bed and kiss my cheek before he walked out the door. When he was gone, I pressed my fingertips to where his lips had touched my skin, and tears welled in my eyes.

I'm a monster.

It was as if that realization drained all the energy I had left, and I slumped down into the sheets, succumbing to sleep after viciously fighting it all night long.

I woke after noon, sweaty and with my head swimming like I was hungover. I groaned and kicked the covers off, reaching for my phone next and frowning when there was nothing more to look at on the screen than my background photo — one of me and Joel hanging out in his dorm room last semester. We were both wearing CU hoodies, and he sat between my legs while I draped my arms over his shoulder. Our smiles were the kind you couldn't fake, the kind only true affection can beget.

Where are those smiles now?

I wasn't sure why my stomach plummeted at the fact that Theo hadn't texted me, especially since I *knew* after yesterday that I needed to disconnect. I needed to stay away from him, because any time I made the mistake of being near him, I crossed lines so much that my feet were beginning to erase the pencil mark they were drawn in.

After lying in bed for another twenty minutes, I dragged myself into the shower and then up on deck to work. I needed something to distract me from my thoughts, and so I begged Emma to give me a task, and though she looked at me with a cocked brow like she knew something was off, she didn't press. Instead, she set me to work doing the crew laundry and polishing tableware, and I lost myself in those mundane tasks for the rest of the day, retreating to my room around dinnertime.

When I did, my sister called.

"Hey, sis, how's life of the rich and famous going?"

Just hearing her voice broke the last twig of self-control I had, and I sucked in a sob, trying to hold myself together.

"Oh, Aspen," Juniper said softly. "Are you okay?"

I laughed through the next wave of emotion that hit me, shaking my head as I leaned back against the headboard of our bed. "Just peachy."

"What happened?"

My eyes welled with tears again. "I'm afraid to tell you."

"Why would you ever be afraid of telling me anything? I'm your sister — if anyone has your back, it's me."

I sniffed. "I don't want you to hate me."

"Not possible. Now, answer my video call request and tell me everything."

My eyes blurred even more when the video chat connected, and my little sister held her coffee close to her chest, encouraging me to fill her in until I broke down and did. I told her everything — what Theo said to me in the hot tub, how I could see how I affected him when he got out, the pool party, Positano. I spilled everything until my face was hot with shame and it was all I could do not to bury my face in my hands to avoid the way my sister was looking at me now.

Like she had no idea who I was.

Join the club, sis.

"You hate me, don't you?" I asked on a sniff.

"No, no," she assured me, sighing before she took a sip of her coffee. She paused for a long moment before she spoke again. "I think we all lose our way from time to time. You know?"

I nodded, looking down at my hands in my lap.

"You held hands with another man, Aspen." She lowered her voice, looking around like she was afraid my parents might hear her where she was set up in her old bedroom at their house. "You almost *kissed* him."

"I know," I said, covering my face with my hands.

"That's... *cheating*."

"*I know*," I repeated, groaning before I dragged my hands down my face and let them fall into my lap. "I don't know what's wrong with me, Juniper. I..." I shook my head, throwing my hands up. "I'm feverish when I'm around him, and yet I'm addicted to the heat. And with Joel..." I pressed my lips together against the emotion in my throat. "I don't even know who he is anymore. I've never seen this side of him, and now that I have..."

I paused, shaking my head, not willing to finish that sentence.

"Nothing makes sense. Nothing feels right except being with Theo, which I know is the one thing that should feel *wrong*." I panicked the more I admitted, shaking my head more and more, faster and faster as every inch of me trembled. "I'm spiraling out of control."

"Listen to me," Juniper said earnestly, setting her coffee aside and leaning in toward the camera. "This is all just a weird string of coincidences, okay? You and Joel are having some issues. What couple doesn't? He's got a lot on his mind with work, you're feeling out of place, *neither* of you expected this to happen, for you to be on the yacht with him. It's just a lot of unexpected stress, that's all."

I nodded, wiping my nose with the back of my hand.

"But the ball is still in your court. Okay? You still get to decide what happens from here."

"What do I do?"

Juniper shrugged. "Nothing has actually happened yet, right? I mean, the hand holding, but it was just for a moment, and you stopped the kiss."

My gut churned at the memory, at how much I wished I *hadn't* stopped the kiss.

But I didn't tell Juniper that.

"Just take it back to friendship. Set boundaries with Theo, whether that means staying away from him or having a conversation the next time you're together."

My stomach twisted again.

"And sit Joel down tonight. Don't take no for an answer. You two need to work this out."

I sighed, nodding, my lips rolling together as I fought back the urge to tell her that staying away from Theo was the last thing I wanted to do.

She was right.

I wasn't a cheater. I wasn't the kind of girl who would betray my boyfriend of almost four years just because some rich, beautiful man messed with my head.

But what if he's not messing with you at all?

What if he actually means everything he's said?

I shook my head, denying the possibility before it could even fully bloom. "Thank you, Juni," I said, shoulders slumping on my next sigh. "I wish you were here."

"Oh, *trust me* — so do I." She smiled, but her eyes watched me with pity. "Are you going to be alright?"

"Yeah," I promised with the best smile of my own that I could manage.

"Call me if you need *anything*, okay? No matter what time it is here or there. If you need someone, or if anything happens, I'm just a call away."

I nodded again, and then we ended the call and I slunk back into bed, covering my head with the sheets.

Later that night, Joel stumbled into our cabin like a rhino in a room full of bowling pins.

The door slammed back against the wall, and he cursed, laughing at himself as he managed to shut it again. Then, he tripped over something, falling into the dresser and knocking half of what was on it off onto the floor. He laughed again as I rubbed my eyes and reached over to turn on the lamp beside the bed.

"Joel? What's going on?"

"Shhhh," he said, smiling as he held his finger to his lips. "I'm trying not to wake my girlfriend up."

I smirked at his slurred words, at how much he looked like the young boy I met at CU in that moment. His hair was mussed, his cheeks rosy, eyes a little glazed and low.

"Hmm... well, I think it's safe to say she's already awake."

Joel launched himself into bed, climbing on top of me and wrapping me up like a burrito. "Well, in that case," he said, leaning back long enough to peck my nose. "Hi."

I chuckled. "Hi, there. How are you feeling?"

"A little tipsy."

I arched a brow. "I can see that, but I meant are you still feeling sick?"

Joel shrugged. "Ah, I'm fine."

His eyes were lazy as they watched mine, and he tucked my hair behind one ear, rubbing the skin there with his thumb. For a while, we stayed like that, and I knew by the way his brows bent together as he watched me that he could tell I was upset.

"We should talk," I whispered. "About the other night at the party."

"I can think of something a lot more fun than talking," Joel replied, and then his hand slid back into my hair and gripped, arching my neck for better access. He kissed me hard, grinding his pelvis between my legs, and I felt how hard he was, his desire rolling off him in plumes.

And once again, it made me ill.

I closed my eyes, forcing a breath and kissing him back. I wanted to want it. I wanted to give in, to solve the issue with a makeup session so good that neither of us would remember why we were mad in the first place.

But then he grabbed my breast, and I remembered how he grabbed Ivy's.

And a flash of Theo struck behind my eyes, making my stomach turn violently.

"Joel," I said, pressing my hands into his chest to stop his next kiss.

"Come on, baby," he pleaded, pressing just as hard against my palms. His lips captured mine again with another roll of his hips. "I want to fuck you so bad right now."

It should have turned me on. It should have made me moan and reach for him in equal earnest, should have had me drenched with desire. Instead, it made me want to slap him so hard he'd be knocked out until the morning.

"Well, I want to talk," I said, trying and failing to keep the disdain out of my voice.

Joel pressed himself on me harder, snaking his hand under my shirt. "We can talk after."

"No, *now*," I tried, but Joel laughed like it was a joke, squeezing my breast as he sucked the skin of my neck between his teeth.

And something in me snapped.

I kneed him hard between the legs, shoving him off me when he bent over in a groan of pain. I jumped up from the bed, crossing my arms. "I said *no*, Joel!"

He was still grimacing in pain, rolling from side to side with his hands cupped over his groin. "What the hell is wrong with you!?"

"You know what's wrong!" I shook my head. "We haven't so much as *talked* since the pool party and now you're forcing yourself on me like—"

"I didn't *force* anything," he sneered. "God, when did you become so dramatic?"

"Dramatic?" I asked with a scoff.

"You kneed me in the balls, Aspen! Do you know how much that fucking hurts?"

His eyes were wild now as he watched me, like no version of him I'd ever seen before. Still, as mad as I was, I couldn't help but feel bad when I looked at him still grimacing in pain with his hands covering his groin.

I sighed, my shoulders slumping. "Look, I'm sorry if I hurt you, but you really hurt *me*. And you're still acting like I have no right to be upset."

"You can be upset and not knee your fucking boyfriend in the balls!"

"I'm sorry. Okay? I am." I reached out for him, and he relaxed marginally, though he was still wincing as he stretched out on his back and let his hands fall to his sides. "I just... I really need you right now."

Emotion washed over me like a wave of smoke, choking my next words as tears flooded my eyes. Everything I'd talked to Juniper about rang in my ears, and desperation filled me to the brim.

Joel sighed, sitting up and brushing my hand off him as he stood. "I'm going back down with the crew."

"Joel," I said, grabbing his hand and making him face me again. "Don't you see how torn up I am right now? We had this big fight, and then you were sick..." I shook my head. "I feel like... like I'm losing..." I couldn't even figure out how to say it, so instead, I said, "we need to work through this. Together."

"Work through *what*, Aspen?!" Joel screamed — and I lurched back like he'd hit me, because I'd never heard him raise his voice like that. Not at me. Not ever. "This is about you being jealous and uptight when it's *me* who has to make excuses for you every time you don't come hang out with the crew. It's *me* who defends you any time they make jokes that you're lame or stuck up. It's *me* trying to convince them how great you are. And to be honest?" His chest puffed with each breath, and he shook his head, stepping away from me and toward the door. "I'm starting to forget myself."

"Joel," I choked, frowning as I reached for him again, but he pulled away.

Then, he was out the door with a mumble of something under his breath, and I collapsed into the sheets on a sob that ripped through my chest like a rusty knife.

CHAPTER
SEVENTEEN

The next two days passed in a numb blur.

It was rainy and gray, which so perfectly matched how I felt inside that I almost laughed at the coincidence of it all. I convinced myself getting back into a routine would help me, that I was out of whack because I didn't have any semblance of normalcy.

So, I worked out in the mornings, and I washed my face at night. I wrote in my planner and I got back into reading the mystery I had bookmarked in the middle. The days were spent on shore with my camera, the nights in bed with my laptop. I edited photos until my eyes were too dry to stay open. I wrote captions for each photo before uploading them to the staging site for my web portfolio. I answered all of my sister's texts with lies telling her everything was fine.

I stayed away from Theo.

Joel stayed away from me.

It was like living in a nightmare, in an unending swirl of color and light that had no purpose. I wandered through those days like a lost soul, and the only proof I had that I was still living at all were the photos that slowly filled my memory card.

On the afternoon we anchored off the coast of Capri, I was sitting in bed editing photos when out of nowhere, I had the urge to put on the sapphire earrings Theo bought for me.

If anyone would have been there to ask me why, I never could have found the right words to explain it. It was like a sudden jolt of electricity, a force so strong that I slapped my laptop closed and popped up out of bed like I just remembered I was late for a meeting. I walked straight over to the dresser, and then I frowned, because I'd set the earrings between the cords of my headphones the night I'd first come home with them and I hadn't touched them since.

But they were gone.

Panic niggled inside me, and I turned everything on that dresser upside down, checking ridiculous places like the cap of my lip balm and the inside of Joel's shoe. I emptied my backpack completely with my heart racing faster and faster with each minute that passed and the earrings didn't show up.

Oh my God.

I lost them.

The panic I'd held at bay took over completely, and I dropped to my knees, searching the ground around the dresser as I chanted *no, no, no* over and over and over. I convinced myself it was because those earrings were expensive, and that they were pretty, and that I liked them so much that losing them would be devastating.

It was *not* because Theo bought them for me.

It was *not* because I wanted to hold them in my palms and feel a connection to the last good day I'd had.

I crawled from the dresser over to the bed, yanking on the compartment underneath. It was locked.

Cursing, I started picking up Joel's pants off the floor, checking the pockets one by one until I found the key I was looking for. I unlocked the bottom compartment, and just as I did, the door to our cabin opened.

"What are you doing?!"

Joel's voice boomed before he ripped me back from my search under the bed, slamming the compartment shut as the key went flying from my hand. I fell back on my butt, spine against the dresser, and when I looked up at Joel, his eyes were like a dark forest.

"I told you not to look in there!"

"I... I'm sorry," I said, shocked and quiet at first before I realized I didn't need to be sorry for anything. I frowned. "I was looking for my earrings."

"Earrings? What earrings? You don't ever wear any."

"I do, too," I said.

"What do they look like then?"

I opened my mouth to respond, but then remembered that Joel didn't know Theo bought me earrings in Positano. He didn't know about the dress or the swimsuit, either.

And what would he think if I told him?

I shook my head, using the edge of the bed to help me stand up before I brushed off my sweatpants. "Just forget about it."

"You're lying," Joel said, pointing his finger at my chest. "Why are you snooping on me?"

"*Snooping?*" I asked incredulously. "It's *my bed,* too. I was just looking under it for something I lost." I narrowed my eyes. "What are you hiding under there, anyway?"

"It's none of your business, and I mean it." He swiped the key from the floor and hastily tucked it in his pocket. "So just don't—"

"Then tell me what it is!"

"It's a surprise! Okay?" Joel's chest heaved, in and out, his eyes crazy as he watched me. "A surprise for you. But you're going to ruin it if you look."

My heart squeezed with something between guilt and suspicion, but in the end, guilt won out.

"Oh..." I blew out a breath, shaking my head at myself as I sat back on the bed. "I'm sorry. I swear, I wasn't trying to snoop. I just..."

I just wanted to find the earrings Theo bought for me because I can't stop thinking about him even though I know I should.

I sighed in lieu of continuing my answer, because I didn't feel like lying. I was too exhausted to lie.

"Why don't you get dressed and come downstairs," Joel said after a moment, and I thought I heard an ounce of pity in his voice. "You've been by yourself too much. You're..."

"Losing it?" I asked, but it was more of a dare when my eyes met Joel, and he was smart enough not to take it.

"Just come hang out for a while."

"And watch you hang all over Ivy?" I scoffed. "No, thanks."

Joel rolled his eyes, ripping the door open. "Fine. Sit in here alone then."

He slammed the door before I could respond, and I flopped back on the bed, covering my face with a pillow before I screamed into it. I screamed until my chest burned, until my lungs threatened to seize up if I didn't inhale a fresh breath of oxygen. Then, I pulled the pillow off, staring up at the ceiling with my chest heaving.

I really am losing it.

My nerves were alive like I'd just run a marathon, a combination of the panic I'd felt looking for the earrings and the confrontation with Joel.

He's planning a surprise for me?

He's lying.

But maybe he's not. Maybe he had something romantic planned before I blew up about the Ivy thing.

Or maybe he's being a jerk.

Did I overreact to the Ivy thing?

No, and why is he trying to make me think I did?

I couldn't sit still, couldn't stop groaning and fuming and tossing this way and that in the bed. I was entirely restless.

I laid there for a long time, forcing calming breaths, placing my hands on my stomach to ground me. I felt the breaths there, followed the inhales and exhales as my heart steadied. Time slipped away again, and I relaxed, drawing circles on my belly and listening to the hum of the yacht.

The more my fingers brushed against my skin, the more it tickled to life.

Goosebumps spread out over my navel, up my chest and down my thighs. I sighed at the way it felt to be touched, and when I flattened my warm palm against my stomach, everything in my core reacted.

Joel and I hadn't had sex in weeks, and alone in that bed with my body buzzing to life with every small wisp of my fingers, I didn't think about the last time he touched me. I didn't think about the last time he slid inside me, about the familiar way he filled me or any of my favorite times we'd been together.

Instead, I thought of Theo.

I thought of the way his hand touched my thigh in the hot tub, how soft it had been, so tender I wasn't sure it had happened at all. I thought of the way he stared at me across the pool when I wore Celeste's swimsuit, and the way his eyes devoured me when I modeled the orange dress for him in Positano. I thought of all the words he said, his promises of what he would do if he had me alone.

I told myself to stop, but then I thought about our conversation in Positano.

Philautia.

And then in the name of self-love, I let my imagination take over.

I saw Theo there at the cabin door, throwing it open and staring down at me, his chest heaving as he took in the sight of me spread out on the bed.

Why have you been hiding from me?

I let my knees drop open, my hand sliding between my thighs.

I'm not hiding anymore.

With a growl of need, he descended upon me, and I felt the vision like it was the realest thing I'd experienced in days. I could smell his skin, the citrus and the smoke. I could feel his hands wrapping around my rib cage, pinning me to the bed, his weight descending on me. A pang shot between my legs and I chased the sensation with my fingers, running them through my wetness before I circled my clit.

I moaned, arching into the touch, imagining Theo covering my mouth with his palm and urging me to be quiet.

Someone might hear.

My fingers circled faster, hips gyrating as my breath hitched in my throat and my heart rate climbed higher and higher with each touch. I could see his eyes. I could feel his breath hot on my lips, his mouth just centimeters from mine, just like they had been that night in Positano.

Kiss me.

I thought the words so loud I swore I heard them rolling off my tongue in real life. Maybe they had. Maybe I was begging Theo in the quiet of the room where I was alone to take me and tell me nothing else mattered.

Maybe I was summoning him like a spirit on a cold night.

The faster I circled, the more my imagination ran wild. I twisted in the sheets, thrashing this way and that, like I was chasing the feeling as much as I was trying to escape it. Everything about it felt wrong. I shouldn't be thinking of Theo as I slipped two fingers deep inside me and rubbed my clit hard with my free hand, but he was all I saw.

Just then, three hard knocks pounded on the door.

My eyes shot open and I nearly fell off the bed with how fast I ripped my hands from under my panties. Reality crashed over me like an avalanche of snow, my breaths labored as I stared at the door.

Did I imagine it?

There were three more knocks, and then I wondered if I'd been unknowingly performing a seance, because Theo's deep voice came muffled through the wood.

"Aspen? Are you in there?"

Oh, God.

I jumped up out of the bed, running over to the dresser mirror. "Just a minute!" I called, and then I ran my hands through my tussled hair, pulling it over one shoulder. My cheeks were too flushed for him to believe I was just lying around, so I ripped off my sweatpants quickly and pulled on a pair of track shorts.

Then, stupidly, I took my shirt off and answered the door in my sports bra.

Theo stood outside the door, just like I'd imagined moments before, only he looked even better than in my fantasy. His emerald eyes sparked in the chandelier light from the salon, and he smirked, letting those eyes trail over my chest, my stomach, my legs.

My body hummed under his gaze like a universe being born from nothing.

"What were you doing?" he asked with an arched brow. "I thought I heard some... noises."

"Yoga," I said quickly, hoping my smile was convincing. The fact that I had a light sheen of sweat on my neck and chest would surely help the case. "Just needed to unwind a little."

Theo grinned wider, but something in that smirk made me feel as transparent as wax paper. "I know the feeling."

My cheeks burned hotter, and I leaned a hip against the doorframe, looking behind him before I let my eyes settle on his again. "Why are you down here, anyway?"

He shrugged. "Was just taking a walk."

"Just taking a walk," I echoed, crossing my arms. I waited for him to tell me the truth, but he just smiled back at me like I already knew it.

A loud chorus of laughter came from downstairs, and Theo cleared his throat, nodding in the direction of the crew mess.

"Why aren't you with them?"

I fought the urge to scream again like I had into my pillow when I thought of Joel, of our fight, of the way we seemed to *always* be fighting lately. He was down there now.

With Ivy.

"I'm just over partying," I finally answered, and the way the words left me was like just saying them was so exhausting I needed to sleep for a decade.

Theo nodded like he knew everything I *wasn't* saying, then he took a tiny, minuscule step toward me that felt more like a shift of the entire world. "Want to sneak onto the island with me?"

I blanched. "What?"

Theo smiled. He knew he didn't need to repeat himself for me to know what he'd said.

My heart hammered harder in my chest, warning me as if my sister had taken over the organ.

You have to stay away from him.

You cannot be alone with him.

You still have a boyfriend.

You need to talk to Joel.

But the more my sister's voice came into my head, the angrier I became.

I'd *tried* talking to Joel. I'd *tried* working things out. All he wanted to do was party and be with the girl he'd groped right in front of me.

He didn't care that he'd hurt me.

If anything, he was trying to make me feel crazy for being upset at all.

"They'll be busy for hours," Theo said on a shrug when I didn't say anything else, casting a glance behind him before his eyes were on me again. He stepped even closer, his voice just above a whisper. "And from what I heard," he said, biting the inside of his lower lip, "it sounds like maybe you need to blow off a little steam."

All the blood drained from my face.

Oh, God.

Theo chuckled, stepping back and allowing my next breath. "Come on," he said.

Then he turned with the confidence of a man who knew I'd follow.

And follow him I did.

Theo didn't tell a soul we were leaving the boat — not even Captain Chuck. Instead, he motioned for me to follow him quietly as he led us down to where the jet skis and tenders were in the water. Next to them was a rowboat, one I'd seen Theo take out a few times in the early morning. He was the only one I'd ever seen in it.

Until now.

He helped me climb inside the small boat, handing me a few bags before he climbed in, too. Then, he fixed the two oars to the sides and started paddling us away from the yacht.

The sun was beginning to set over the small island of Capri, though it seemed to be taking its time now that Theo and I were on the water. The sky was a brilliant orange, the water a stunning aqua blue, and the white limestone crags of the coast seemed to glow a color somewhere between the two. I longed for my camera that I'd left behind, but took mental snapshots, instead.

Theo watched me as he paddled us toward the coast, his brows furrowed, the muscles of his arms ebbing and flowing with each row. I wore the same shorts and sports bra I'd answered the door in, but I'd taken enough time to throw a t-shirt on before we left, and it was as if that fabric caused him physical pain.

"You're pretty good at that," I commented as we made our way toward the limestone.

"Rowing?"

I nodded.

"I try to keep some semblance of my routine when I'm on vacation. Back home in New York, I row every morning," he explained, leaning forward before he pulled back again. I found myself mesmerized by the way his abdomen flexed with the shift, the way the setting sun played on every rise and fall of his muscles. "Five a.m. sharp."

"*Five?*" I asked incredulously. "Why so early?"

"Why not?" He shrugged. "There's only so much time in each day. I want to seize as much of it as I can."

"*Carpe diem*," I said with a smile. "How very Roman of you." I paused. "What's it like living in the city?"

"Loud. And boisterous. And dirty and bright and chaotic," Theo said, the corner of his mouth tilting. "So, absolutely perfect."

I laughed at that. "It sounds like a nightmare for me."

"Why, because of the people?"

I nodded. "I'm much more at home in the mountains of Colorado."

Theo shrugged. "I think it's just because you've never been to the city."

"How do you know I haven't?"

"If you had, you wouldn't be so quick to write it off. Trust me. There's something magical about Manhattan. And as much as I love the mountains the same as you, I think you'd find more of a home in New York than you think."

I shook my head. "I haven't found much of a home anywhere at all, to be honest."

Theo watched me curiously. "I get that. I feel the same way sometimes."

"You?" I laughed. "You seem at home no matter where you are. I mean, you speak a dozen different languages and make every stranger feel like your best friend."

"Maybe," he answered. "But you make every stranger feel human. Seen. Understood."

"When I have my camera, maybe."

"Even without it." Theo paused rowing. "You don't see it, do you? The way people feel stripped by your gaze."

I wanted to laugh, but the gesture was stuck inside me in the form of a large lump in my throat.

"Don't look at me like it couldn't possibly be true," he continued. "So many people love to hear themselves talk, or are desperate to tell you what they want you to know about them. They want to paint this beautiful picture. But you? You don't let them. *You're* the creator. In the quiet way you observe others and truly listen to them, you know more about them than even their closest friends within twenty minutes of meeting them."

My chest tightened. "That's a lovely way to be thought of."

Theo smirked, but the smile fell quickly, and he frowned again with his next row. "I haven't seen you at all since Positano," he said. "Did you end up sick like Joel was?"

I sighed, casting my gaze out over the water. "No," I said. "I just... I've had some family stuff going on."

"Your sister?"

I nodded, and as if mentioning her brought her to life in my head again, I heard her voice whispering warnings.

You are playing with fire.

"Is she okay?"

"Yes."

"Are *you* okay?" Theo asked.

I laughed, because the answer to that question should have been simple, but it was so far from it. "I don't want to talk about it. Let's talk about you, instead."

"Me?" Theo asked with a grin. "Okay. What do you want to know?"

"Hmm," I mused, tapping my chin. "What's your family like?"

"Boring."

I chuckled. "That's not very nice."

"I'm not talking about my family. I'm talking about your question."

I frowned.

Theo looked out over the water, thinking for a moment before he said, "My parents are English. They both grew up in London but migrated to the United States in their twenties, so I grew up on the Upper East Side in New York. My four times great grandfather was in the railroad business, so I guess you could say we come from *old money*. Dad loves to golf. Mom loves to shop. Both of them love to drink red wine and dote on their one and only son."

I smiled.

"Now," Theo said, heaving another row of the boat. "Ask me something more exciting."

"Exciting?" I chuckled, tucking my hands under my thighs. "Um... I don't know..."

"Sure, you do. Ask me something you actually want to know."

"But I did want to know about your family."

"What else?"

I frowned, and for a long moment, it was just the sound of the water lapping against the boat, and the oars dipping into the sea, and the birds flying overhead.

"Let me give you an example," Theo said, and he paused rowing long enough to lock his eyes on mine. "Were you touching yourself this evening, before I came to your door?"

My eyes popped out of my head, and that was answer enough for Theo's lips to spread into a wide grin.

"You were," he said, leaning back and letting the oars rest. He swallowed. "What were you thinking about?"

My lips parted in shock. *Was he really asking me this?*

"Or should the question be *who* were you thinking about?"

This time, my jaw hinged open. "Theo!"

"Oh, that's right," he said as he began rowing again. "You wanted to talk about *me*, huh?"

Theo winked, and I rolled my eyes, playfully splashing him with water as he steered us toward a small opening in the limestone cliffside. Part of me wanted to cover my red face with my hands or leap into the water to get away from his gaze, but he somehow made me feel... comfortable. I couldn't explain it. He'd just asked me the most personal question anyone ever had, but it didn't make me angry and I didn't feel embarrassed, either.

If anything, I was starting to get turned on again.

What is wrong with you, Aspen!?

The closer we got to the island, the more I craned my neck to take it all in. There were stairs that led down to the water from what appeared to be a restaurant above, and Theo tied our boat to the railing before digging into one of the bags.

"Here," he said, tossing me a pair of swim fins. "Put these on."

"What is this place?" I asked as I strapped the fins to each foot.

"The Blue Grotto."

"Really?!" I asked excitedly, eyeing the small cave opening in the side of the cliff. "Don't we have to pay for a tour boat or something? I was reading up on it because I wanted to take some photos."

"They run tours all day until about five or so," Theo said, strapping on his last fin. "After that, everyone leaves, and the only real way to get here is if you have a boat." He waved a hand over our little rowboat with a grin.

"Sounds like we could get in trouble," I mused. Then, I held up one of my fin-covered feet. "Isn't it also illegal to swim in the Grotto?"

His smile widened, but he didn't answer. Instead, he stood, his eyes cast down on me as he stripped his white t-shirt overhead and let it drop into the boat at his feet. He arched a brow at me, something of a challenge sparkling in his irises, and then he dove over my head and into the water.

The splash of cold water made me gasp, but then laughter bubbled out of me, and before I could even think better of it, I had my t-shirt peeled off and I was jumping in the water, too.

"Ah!" I said when my head emerged again. "It's f-f-freezing."

"You'll warm up," Theo said, and there was mischief in his eyes when he added. "I promise."

He nodded toward the small cave opening in the limestone, and then we swam that direction, and I was thankful for the fins because there was nothing to hold onto and no hope of possibly touching the bottom. I followed behind Theo with him checking over his shoulder now and then to make sure I was alright, and when we got to the cave opening, he paused, reaching back to grab my hand.

"Hold onto me," he said, pulling my hand to rest on his shoulder. "Stay low in the water and watch your head."

The opening was so small I couldn't imagine sitting on one of the row boats I read tour guides brought people in with. And once we made it inside the cave, there was a split second where I wondered how more than just a few people fit inside.

Of course, that thought vanished in the next second, because I lost my breath at the grand wonder of it all.

The closer we got to the cave opening, the bluer the water seemed to get, and once we passed through and inside, it was as if the water was glowing from underneath us. It was crystal clear, a shade of blue so illustrious I couldn't quite put a name to it. It was turquoise, but also robin's egg, and perhaps a sky at dawn or a fresh fountain in the sun. The limestone stretched up and over us, and it was as if the ceiling was dripping down but had been frozen, the jagged edges caught mid-drip.

"Oh my God," I whispered, because speaking at a normal level inside that beautiful cave seemed rude and uncalled for. "This is... I can't believe this is *real.*"

Theo smiled, swimming deeper into the cave and pulling me along with him. "It's even brighter when it's midday and the sun comes in full force, but of course, you have to battle row boats full of tourists if you come then," he said. He paused when we were in the middle of the cave, turning to face me. "I've always come here after hours. Shhh... don't tell on me."

I smirked, but something in my chest tightened at the thought. "I'm sure every girl you bring here just swoons right into your arms."

Theo cocked a brow. "I wouldn't know," he said, smiling at my confused expression. "I've always come alone."

My heart *tha-dumped* in my chest, a quick beat and then pitter-patters that left me feeling dizzy and short of breath.

"Does that surprise you?"

"Yes," I confessed.

Theo smiled, leaning back to float in the water. "Oh, that's right. You think I'm a big playboy, huh?"

"Are you not? I mean, I saw you with those French girls that first night I worked for you on the boat."

Theo arched a brow. "You were watching me?"

"No," I said quickly, cheeks hot again. "Well... I mean, I just saw you with them all night, the way they were hanging all over you. And then you all went up to your room…"

"And were you in there, to see what happened after?"

I looked away, not willing to admit that I *had* seen them through the windows before he drew the curtains closed.

Then again… what had I seen, exactly?

"Audrey and Nicolette were both very drunk that evening, as was I," Theo said, floating on his back with his eyes cast toward the cave ceiling. "I kissed them both, sure, but then I put them to bed and I slept in a different room."

"You did?"

Theo smiled. "I did."

"You didn't want to… to…"

"Have sex with two beautiful women?" Theo answered for me, glancing at me with a grin. "On a normal occasion, yes. But let's just say my mind was a little… pre-occupied."

I frowned, tilting my head to the side. Theo waited for me to connect the dots, but I didn't see the dots at all. And so he sighed, blowing out all the air in his chest until he slipped under the water. When he re-emerged, he swam toward me with his mouth under the water, his nose and eyes over it, gliding through the blue mirror like a predator.

My breath hitched in my throat, and he didn't stop until the warmth of his body struck me through the icy cold water. He didn't touch me, but was close enough that everything inside me buzzed to life with the desire that he would.

"I'm growing tired of this game, Aspen."

"What game?" I asked on a breath, one that was met with his, and the cave seemed to quiet, as if it was closing its doors to all others and locking us inside.

"The one where you pretend like you don't want me," he husked, and under the water, a warm palm wrapped around my waist.

I inhaled a stiff breath, shaking violently at the touch, my eyelids fluttering as he slipped that hand around to my lower back and pulled me closer, into him, until we were flush against each other and I could feel his desire pressed against my core that ached for him in return.

"And I pretend like you're not already mine."

My next breath shuddered out of me, and I clung to his arms. "But I'm not yours," I reminded him, but the whisper was so faint, so shaky from the cold and my nerves that I wondered if I truly believed what I'd said at all.

Theo swallowed, and I traced the water as it dripped from his hair and down the bridge of his nose, down the edges of his jaw, over his lips that were rolling together as he watched me in return.

"Is that so?" he asked. He pulled me closer with one hand just as his other slicked up my chest in a way so possessive I felt my soul gravitate toward it like a magnet.

My entire body trembled at the warmth of his palm running over my breasts, up my collarbone, until his fingers wrapped around my neck. He squeezed just a pinch, and then released the grip, trailing his hand up more. His thumb and pinky fingers stayed fixed at my neck, but his index finger skated over my wet bottom lip.

And I opened it as if he'd entered some secret code.

His finger slipped inside my mouth, and I tasted the salt of the sea on his warm skin as a pang of desire shot between my legs. My eyes connected with his, and his nose flared, his erection flexing against me where our bodies met under the water.

"I call that bluff," he whispered as he pulled his finger free, and I would have sworn it was someone else in my body, because I sucked it on the way out, like I didn't want to let it go.

Like it was a different part of him entirely.

Theo groaned, his next breath nothing but a hiss, and I yelped when he yanked me toward him in the way a wild beast might ravage its prey. His lips were on track for mine, and I leaned my head back, closing my eyes, opening my mouth, surrendering.

Until suddenly, a flashlight blinded us both, along with a deep voice screaming at us in Italian.

I panicked, shoving away from Theo and shielding my eyes from the light as the man yelled and yelled. His booming voice echoed in the cave, disorienting me even more than the light.

Theo held up his hands, and when the flashlight swung to him, my eyes cleared enough for me to see the man had rowed in on a small boat labeled *Carabinieri*. He was wearing a uniform and had a baton attached to his hip.

Theo hollered back something in Italian to the man, who continued yelling back and shining the light between the two of us.

"What's going on?!" I whisper-screamed at Theo.

"It's the police," Theo said, but there was no panic in his voice. In fact, he smiled when he looked over at me. "Guess we aren't supposed to be here, after all."

My eyes widened. "Oh my *God!* Are we being arrested? I told you it was illegal to swim in here!"

Theo laughed then, shaking his head and reaching for my hand under the water. "It's just a little fine. But, sadly, I do believe we have to leave now."

The police officer continued yelling, and the way he was moving his flashlight, I knew he was saying we needed to swim out of the cave now.

Theo swallowed, not bothering to fight back his smile as his thumb traced my wrist under the water. "What a pity," he whispered. "Just when things were getting interesting."

And I couldn't help it then.

I laughed, too.

CHAPTER
EIGHTEEN

Theo was slapped with a fine equivalent to something around six-thousand U.S. dollars.

It was enough to make my eyes pop out of my head, but so little for Theo that he almost laughed at it when the police officer had him sign the paperwork. Then, we were escorted back to the yacht, and warned that should we try to swim in the Grotto again, we would be thrown in jail.

Wayland was on the lower deck when we pulled the boat in.

He watched us both curiously, his eyes holding mine with about a dozen questions swimming in those warm brown irises. But he didn't question either of us, just helped us secure the rowboat back on the yacht, and then Theo quietly wished for me to have a pleasant evening and I muttered something about needing a shower before we both disappeared — Theo going one way, me going the other, and Wayland pretending not to watch us leave.

When I rounded the corner on my way back to the cabin, I nearly ran over Ivy, who tilted her head with a satisfied smirk at the guilty look on my face.

"Have a nice swim?" she asked, eyeing my wet clothes. Her eyes flicked behind me to where Theo and I had just been with Wayland.

When I finally calmed down, the first thought I had was to smack that smirk off her stupid face. But the second thought I had was that she'd just seen me with Theo, and I didn't know exactly *how much* she had seen.

"Don't worry," she said, not bothering to wait for me to answer her question. Instead, she brushed right past me, turning and walking away backwards with her finger pressed against puckered lips. "Your secret is safe with me."

She laughed to herself as she turned, and I thought about stopping her, asking her what the hell was wrong with her, confronting her about the pool party.

But honestly?

I had more pressing things on my mind.

I rushed back to the stateroom, thankful to find it empty as I peeled off my wet clothes.

In the shower, I finally brought myself to climax.

I was so worked up from the evening — from my time alone in bed and then the cave with Theo — it only took about sixty seconds for me to fly apart.

So much for staying away from him, I thought, as I guiltily got dressed for bed. But the guilt was so over-shadowed by want that I wondered if I really felt guilty at all.

Mostly, I just felt excited.

And desperate for more.

The next morning, I woke up in an empty bed. Joel clearly hadn't slept beside me, and he either didn't realize I'd been off the boat or didn't care.

I reached for my phone, wondering if I'd have a missed text from him, but instead, there was one waiting from Theo.

Come to the top deck when you're ready. I need you to "work" today.

There was a winking smiley face next to the text, and my stomach did a little flip as I stared at the words.

As I got dressed, thoughts of Joel hammered me with the annoyance of a dentist's drill. I wondered what he'd done all night, where he'd been, who he was with. Then, I thought of our fight, of our *string* of fights lately, and how he seemed in no rush to make things right.

My eyes washed over the dresser, and sitting right there on top was the key to the storage under our bed.

And I didn't care that he didn't want me to find what he was hiding there.

I'd had enough of the lying, the avoiding, and if I couldn't get answers from him, maybe I'd find them under our mattress.

But when I popped the compartment open, there was nothing to be found.

In the days that followed that evening in the Blue Grotto, I slipped into Wonderland.

It happened slowly and suddenly, as unseen as water shaping mountains into valleys and as obvious as a forest fire. In the tumble down that rabbit hole, I lost any semblance of who I was before, and I found myself only half-interested in finding out who I would be next.

I just wanted to be me.

Now.

And I wanted to be with Theo.

It was too easy to pretend like he was working on shore and just taking me along so I could work on my photography. Or that he needed me to take photographs of the boat or of him *on* the boat. We were in a place where time didn't exist, where other people didn't matter, where we could do what we wanted without repercussions.

No one questioned us, no one cared.

Well, except for maybe Wayland, who had pulled back from talking to me as much as he had before and often cautioned Theo and I both with a hard glance or two.

Emma would sometimes ask me why Theo needed so many photographs of himself on his giant yacht, but she'd make a joke of it and I'd laugh along, pretending like I was as clueless as she was on the matter.

I didn't miss Ivy and Celeste murmuring under their breath every time I walked by. Our niceties had ended the night of the pool party. But where I used to cower away from them, duck my head down and scurry by, I now looked them head on with a smirk that I hoped told them I couldn't care less what they thought of me.

Everyone else was caught up in their own jobs, or perhaps their own drama, and they didn't seem to notice how much time I started spending with Theo.

Joel most of all.

I didn't question him when I found the space beneath our bed to be empty after him making such a big deal of it. Maybe it was because deep down I knew I didn't want to know, or because I simply didn't care anymore. And he didn't question where I went each day that I was gone, or why he would sometimes come back from partying with the crew before I came back from my adventures with Theo.

The communication between us was as broken down as an old highway billboard.

If anything, the only thing Joel seemed to care about was getting his next high.

He'd been a drinker ever since I met him, but I had a feeling there was more involved now. I saw it in the dilation of his eyes, in the graying of his skin, in the way he seemed to shake if he went even one day without partying.

We seemed to have both given up on trying to work through what had happened that night at the pool party. In his head, he didn't have anything to apologize for. It was *me* who was being crazy.

And I was too caught up in Theo to care if Joel was right or not.

I avoided my sister's texts and calls like the plague, as well as the gnawing pit in my stomach each time I skipped off with Theo.

I began to live for the moments we stole together.

Most of the time, Theo had to work and I had to keep myself busy to keep from wishing he *didn't* have to work. But on the days when he could get away, we would walk the streets of Italy as I took photographs, talking about everything and nothing at all.

He would ask me about why I chose a certain subject, or what books I liked to read, or sometimes just be silent and watch me work. One day, as he drank a cold lemonade and watched me photographing a small child playing in the rocky pebbles that made up the beach, he asked me what I felt when I clicked the shutter button.

I'd frowned at first, glancing down at the photo I'd just taken before playing with a few settings and trying again. I was struggling to find the right words, searching through my vocabulary for something impressive, something with enough magnitude to capture the truth of my answer.

In the end, I simply said, *"I feel free."*

Theo enjoyed taking me to restaurants with appetizers more expensive than a four-course meal at the places I went when I was back home. There was always some new place to go at the end of the days we did get to spend together. And while he drank his scotch or wine and chuckled as I tasted each foreign bite with either a grimace of disgust or a squeal of delight, he'd tell me about Envizion, and his beach house in Miami, and all the crazy things he did for fun like bungee jumping and sky diving and free solo climbing and skiing every black diamond slope he could find.

I teased him about being an adrenaline junky and he teased me about my love for the herbs I'd started growing in my dorm room and how brokenhearted I was to leave them in my sister's hands while I was away.

Through all of this, to both my relief and my dismay, Theo kept our relationship completely PG-13.

Gone was the hunger in his eyes that night at the Grotto, as well as any attempt to kiss me. Sometimes, he would grab my hand from across the table at dinner, or sweep my hair behind my ear, or gently guide me with his palm at the small of my back when we weaved in and out of crowded alleyways. Each time he came even close to me, my body would tremble with delight, with anticipation, with hope and dread swirling inside me in equal measure.

Please, touch me.

Please, don't touch me and make me tell you to stop.

Please, tell me again how crazy you are for me.

Please, let me pretend this is all innocent.

We lounged side by side on his friend's private beach in Praiano, and as the waves crashed gently on the shore, Theo slid his sunglasses down and looked at me over the bridge of his nose. *"I have spent my whole life devoted to work,"* he'd said. *"It's all I've known. But now that I know you, I wish to never work again."*

He would say things like this — the kind that shook the very foundations of which I was built on — in the most magical of times. The more it happened, the more I started thinking that I really *was* in Wonderland, in a place where dreams and reality dance together.

And if I was lucid dreaming, I would make the most of it.

Theo made me feel more confident in my own skin. Everywhere we stopped, he would take me into a new boutique and tell me to pick something out. And each time, I went for something new and exciting that I never would have tried before — thin straps, bright colors, silky fabrics and exotic patterns. He had awakened a side of me I didn't even realize was asleep. I thought it didn't exist *at all.*

But I found I rather loved putting on a pretty dress and seeing the way Theo smirked in approval.

I liked to think I brought out something new in him, too. Not that he was a stranger to adventure, but I wondered if his entire trip would have been filled with work if not for me. Instead, we hiked the breathtaking Path of the Gods trail near San Michele, lounging in a hammock under a shade tree at the top with the turquoise water spreading out beneath us. Theo fed me lemon cake after we toured a farm in Amalfi, and I photographed him among the ruins in Minori. Theo ignored his phone when it buzzed in his pocket and I left mine on the boat altogether.

And all the while, he was the perfect gentleman.

Until he could no longer stand it.

It was exactly one week since the night we'd escaped to the Grotto, and Theo had given the crew the night off. We were anchored in Salerno, and we needed provisions, so Theo instructed the crew to get everything on the boat taken care of and then they could reward themselves with an evening in the city.

And he instructed *me* not to go with them.

I sat in bed while Joel got dressed and ready, pretending to read my book and focusing hard on not bouncing my knee too much.

I couldn't wait for him to leave.

I couldn't wait to be with Theo.

I couldn't wait to see what was in store for the night.

"Are you sure you don't want to come with us to shore?" Joel asked, sitting on the edge of the bed beside me.

I was almost shocked that he'd addressed me at all after the last week. We'd been more like roommates than anything else, and with him staying out all night, even *that* title was a stretch.

"Mm-hmm," I answered, not even looking away from my book.

Joel sighed, gently placing his fingertips on the top of the pages until I lowered the book into my lap. "Hey, I know we haven't... I know things have been..."

He paused, his mouth pulling to one side. He couldn't even find the words to explain what we were.

Or what we weren't.

Joel shook his head. "I just... maybe we could use a night out. Me and you. Together."

My heart stopped. "What?"

"I know you've been wanting to for a while, and I've been..." Again, he stopped, looking out the window of our cabin with a strange look in his eyes. His brows were pinned together, corner of his lips turned down in a frown.

I reached for his arm. "Are you okay?"

He didn't look at me for a long while, and when he did, it was like staring into the eyes of a stranger. "Do you ever feel like you've lost your way?"

I swallowed.

"I know it sounds..." He waved his hand. "I don't know. It's just, we go along with all these things, and we think we know who we are and what we're doing but then..."

He didn't finish the thought, but my stomach was knotted up more and more with each word he spoke. Even when I was angry with him, I couldn't help but love him — it was all I'd done since I was a freshman in college. For four years I'd loved that boy through every up and down life handed us. And in that moment, I saw Joel sitting on the edge of my bed in my college dorm. I saw the same worry in his face that I'd seen before a big final, or before we said goodbye to each other for a summer, or before he went home to visit his addict parents for a holiday.

Say something.

Hold him.

Tell him you understand.

Tell him you love him.

My heart screamed at me, but every time it did, my body would refuse the request. I was torn between seeing Joel as the boy I'd loved since I was nineteen and the man who had so casually tossed my feelings aside.

They were one in the same, and I couldn't see one without the other.

"It sounds like *you* need the night out," I said with a laugh, hoping the comment would lighten the mood. "Go have fun with your friends. Okay? I do understand what you're saying," I confessed, rubbing his arm. "And... I think we should talk. But not tonight. Tonight, I've got a date with a Duke," I said, holding up my book. "And you should enjoy Italy with your friends."

"But not with you," he said dryly. "You'd rather sit here and read a book than spend a night in Italy with your boyfriend."

My defenses rose at the accusation in his eyes. "You've had all summer to spend time with me, Joel. Why are you only now choosing to do so?"

At that, he scoffed, shaking his head as he stood abruptly and shook my grip off his arm. "Good question."

He left me without another word.

For a while, I just sat there, staring at the door Joel had passed through and wondering what was wrong with me. Not because I had declined his offer to go ashore and spend the evening together, but because I didn't feel bad about it.

In fact, I knew if I could rewind time, I would do it again.

Something about that killed me.

CHAPTER
NINETEEN

"**I**'m not sure what I expected when you said you were making us dinner," I said, popping another fry into my mouth. "But this was *definitely* not it."

Theo chuckled, using his fork and knife to cut into the fried fish cutlet on his plate. His blond hair looked a bit lighter against his freshly tanned skin from our time in the sun, and his gray eyes glowed under the chandelier light. He wore white jeans that hugged him in ways that should have been illegal in *any* country, paired with a baby blue button down and a navy sports jacket that he'd tossed over the back of his chair when we sat down.

I was wearing the orange dress he bought me in Positano, along with the yellow sapphire earrings — they'd shown back up on top of mine and Joel's dresser, and I figured one of the stewardesses found them when they were cleaning. I had also braided my hair over one shoulder, leaving my neck exposed.

When Theo saw me, it was the first time all week that I saw his bravado falter, his eyes dipping down to my chest, to the slit where my leg peeked through each time I walked.

"I grew up on fish and chips," he said. "My mom's favorite when she was little. Dad *hates* the dish," he added with a laugh. "But he's a smart man and knows making Mum happy is what matters most."

"Mum," I repeated with a chuckle.

"Yes, *mum*," he said, tossing a French fry across the table at me.

I batted it away on another laugh. "Your English heritage sneaks up on you every now and then, doesn't it?"

"Oh, you should hear me when I'm watching a game of football." He held up his finger, swallowing his next bite before he added. "*Not* American football, but the real thing." Theo shook his head. "I get an accent and everything. Completely absurd."

He said the last two words with a terrible English accent that had me bending over in a fit of laughter, and when it settled, I took a sip of water while Theo watched me across the candlelit table.

"Has anyone ever told you that you have this air about you?" I asked.

"How so?"

I shrugged. "You just... you have this sort of... *power* that radiates off you. Confidence. Swagger. Like a king."

"A king, huh?" Theo said, kicking back in his chair and crossing his ankle over the opposite knee. "I kind of like that image."

"I thought that the first time I saw you," I said.

"Oh, when you took a picture of me before even introducing yourself?"

I flushed. "I couldn't help it, okay?" I gestured to him, waving my hand up toward his hair and then down to his Italian leather dress shoes. "I mean, *look* at you."

"I can't," Theo said, his eyes glimmering. "I'm too busy looking at you."

My cheeks burned even more, and I looked down at my finger tracing the rim of my water glass, speechless.

"Come," Theo said, standing and folding his napkin in half before he abandoned it on the table. "I wanted to wait until after dessert, but patience has never been a virtue of mine, and I'd like to show you something."

"Should we clean up first?" I asked, gesturing to the table.

"Wayland will handle it."

I frowned at the mess we left behind, mostly because I didn't realize we weren't alone. It made sense, of course. I imagined Captain Chuck was onboard, too. You couldn't just leave a giant mega yacht unmanned.

Still, I wondered what the captain and first mate thought of me staying behind and having dinner with the owner instead of going to shore with my boyfriend...

The thought slipped away as Theo took my hand, though, and I followed him through the cool night air up the stairs. I waited for him to take me to the next set of stairs that would lead to the sun deck, but instead, he steered me around the corner.

Toward the owner's suite.

Theo smirked at me over his shoulder. "Thought you might like to see where the king rests his head at night."

He opened the door, and when we stepped inside, I lost my breath.

The owner's suite was four times the size of the room I shared with Joel, and it was grand opulence embodied. Soft, warm light outlined the edges of the ceiling and the baseboards, playing with the different shades of wood and marble that danced in tandem throughout the room. Luxurious gold and navy curtains framed the floor-to-ceiling windows, which looked out over the glittering shoreline and dark water. Cream push-pin couches trimmed with gold made up a sitting area in the center of the room, along with a stocked bar and record player, all underlined by a lush navy, cream, and gold Persian rug.

Theo walked over to select a record from the metallic, geometric bookshelf while I continued taking in the room. Its art deco style surprised me because it was so different from the rest of the boat and yet it fit so perfectly.

And it suited him.

I didn't know what I imagined his room would look like — perhaps because I assumed it would be a mixture of the elements that dusted the rest of the yacht. I expected the teak, and the warm wood, and the low light and grandeur. But I hadn't expected to find the pops of color, the mixed metals, the old Hollywood movie posters that hung in gold frames on the far wall.

And directly across from the windows was the king's bed.

I swallowed, walking over to touch the soft, velvet-like fabric of the comforter as Duke Ellington began to play. The comforter was a deep sea green, the bed so massive I was sure Theo could roll over six times and still not hit the edge of it. It was piled high with pillows, the four posts draped with floor-length, steel gray curtains that matched the color of Theo's eyes.

"I must admit, I'm a bit surprised," I said, still marveling at how soft the comforter was under my fingers.

"Didn't expect me to have a four-post bed?"

I chuckled, turning to find him by the record player with his hands in his pockets. "I didn't expect you to be such a fan of the 20s."

"Ah," he said, leaning forward on his toes as he looked around the room with me. The upbeat jazz coming from the record player made me feel even more like I was in a dream or a movie, far removed from reality. "Well, you'll be even more surprised when you see my penthouse in New York, then. It's like traveling back in time — well, other than the state-of-the-art appliances, of course."

I smiled, letting my eyes sweep the room until I found three framed photographs on the bookshelf. I walked directly to them, picking up the first as my grin grew wider. "Are these your parents?"

"Mr. and Mrs. Whitman in the flesh," Theo said, sidling up to my left. He pointed at the man first, an older gentleman with a full head of dark blond hair and a mischievous smirk much like Theo's. He wore a black suit and thin black tie, the edges of his eyes crinkled with his smile. "That's Dad. He's wearing that proud grin because this was taken on the day Envizion was named number one on Fortune's list of Most Admired Companies."

"Makes sense why he's got the *proud father* hand on your shoulder," I remarked, tapping the middle of the picture where a slightly younger Theo stood. "Nice suit, by the way. Is that burgundy velvet?"

"You bet your ass it is. I was going for jazz meets royalty. What do you think?"

"I think you already know what I think."

Theo smirked. "I still like hearing it."

I rolled my eyes, nudging him before I pointed at his mother in favor of stroking his ego. "And this is Mum?"

Theo chuckled. "Yes, that angel of a human next to me is my mother."

She was quite a bit shorter than Theo and his father, with light brown hair styled in a wavy swoop that made her look like she was still in her twenties. She wore a floor-length, cream gown with elaborate gold beading and a halter neckline, and even though the photo was just a five by seven, I could see the ginormous diamond on her ring finger.

"She always made it seem effortless, going to events like that," Theo said. "She would charm the pants off every man in the room and make every woman wish to be her best friend."

"Well, now I know where you get it from," I remarked, smiling as I looked over my shoulder at him. "And your eyes, too."

Theo smiled. "And who do you get your eyes from?"

"My dad," I said. "Mom likes to tell the story of when they first met. It was a camping trip, they were both in their late twenties, and her group of friends couldn't figure out how to set up their tents. My dad offered his help, and Mom says when he finished putting the tent up, he grinned at her from where he was hammering a stake into the ground, and the Colorado sky reflected in his eyes." I shook my head. "I swear. She talks about rolling clouds of white and green leaves and all this romantic flowery stuff and Dad just blushes and shakes his head." I shrugged. "It is one of my favorite stories, though."

Theo smiled, following me along the edge of the bookcase as I picked up the next two photographs — one of him and his Envizion partner in their Harvard days, and one of him skydiving in New Zealand. He made a comment about how one day, he'd have my first *TIME Magazine*-featured photograph framed there, too, and I just laughed him off the same way I had the first day we met.

I let my fingers wander the records next, leaning into every word as Theo told me about his favorite jazz musicians. Finally, I picked up a very worn copy of *The Waste Land* by T.S. Elliot, a first edition that looked so mangled I was certain he wouldn't have purchased it that way.

"I think these things are supposed to be kept in a glass case with protective film," I remarked, carefully paging through the book.

"Not in my eyes. What are books for, if not to be read?" He paused, watching me as I flipped through before he said softly. "*The awful daring of a moment's surrender which an age of prudence can never retract. By this, and only this, we have existed.*"

My stomach fluttered with the wings of a million butterflies, and I smiled, closing the book again before running my palm over the worn dust jacket. I gently placed the book back on the shelf, and then followed the edge of the room over to the vast windows.

It was curious, the way I could see so clearly through them. I saw every sparkling light on the shore, and every white cap of the waves that gently rolled by, and every detail of the yacht's bow that spread out below. And yet, the windows were dark, and I knew from experience that if someone were to look up from the deck under us, they'd see only a silhouette.

"Quite a breathtaking view," I said.

"Yes," Theo agreed, and I shuddered when I felt his hot breath on my neck with the words. His hands found my waist, and I sucked in a breath at the contact I'd been so desperate for all week long. "It really is."

My next breath shook through my parted lips, and I let my eyes flutter closed, leaning back into Theo's chest. I reveled in the warmth of him connecting with the warmth of me, at the way his arms so easily wrapped around me from behind, holding me tight to him, completely encompassed.

"You said the first time you saw me, you thought I looked like a king," he mused, nuzzling my neck with the tip of his nose. I felt every word vibrating under my ear. "Do you want to know what I thought the first time I saw you?"

His hands fisted in my dress at my hips, hiking the fabric just an inch higher, but I felt the cool air of the room sweep in like a whispered warning.

"*Mine.*"

I sucked in a breath at the word, and then Theo's lips brushed my neck, his hands fisting again and again as he reeled the fabric of my dress up higher and higher. My legs shook so violently from the touch that I had to lean all my weight into him, and he held me steady, pressing a soft kiss under my ear that made me whimper with need.

"I heard you in your room that night we went to the Grotto," he whispered as he pulled my dress all the way up to my hips. The lower half of me was bare but for the simple cotton thong I wore beneath it — one I'd felt silly putting on under such a beautiful dress. "You were begging for someone to kiss you."

Theo held my dress up with one hand while the fingertips of his other slipped under the band of my thong at my hip.

"Who did you want to kiss you, Aspen?" he whispered, sliding his fingertips over my hot skin.

I tried to answer — truly, I did. But my words were lodged in my throat, and every breath strangled to make its way in or out around the response I couldn't set free.

Theo dragged the tip of his nose up my neck, sucking my ear lobe between his teeth as a full body tremor rocked me from head to toe. "Tell me," he commanded.

"You," I said in a rush of breath. "I wanted you."

"And do you still?"

I spun in his arms, yanking my dress from his grip in the process. The skirt plummeted down over my legs in a curtain of silky fabric, covering me once again, but Theo held firm to my waist. I pressed up onto my toes, locking my eyes on his before I answered.

But not with words.

Confidence and desire took me under their spell, and I pressed my lips to his, taking what I'd wanted for longer than I'd ever admit.

Theo groaned at the contact, wrapping me in his arms tighter and pulling me so fiercely into him that I swore he wanted to completely consume me. His lips met mine in a hot, fervent kiss, and I knew from that first shocking touch that I'd never been kissed before. Not really. I'd never been so wanted, never wanted so badly myself. I'd never had a man devour me with all the reverence of his dying breath and I'd never surrendered to the punishing pleasure of a king's deepest desire.

Every cell in my body zinged to life like a million stars burning out at once, like the brightest night becoming one giant black hole. I no longer existed but as the woman in Theo Whitman's arms. I no longer cared to be anything but the source of every pleasure he would feel for the rest of his life.

With his hands gripping my hips hard enough to bruise, Theo pressed my back into the cool windows, meeting my pelvis with his own. He gripped my wrists in his hands, guiding them up the glass until they were pinned above my head, and then he kissed me harder, biting my lower lip, sucking the sensitive skin of my neck between his teeth before he ran his tongue along the small swell of my cleavage showing through the deep V of my dress.

"Is this what you imagined as you touched yourself that night," Theo husked, kissing me hard again as I moaned my answer into his mouth. He took over where he had my wrists pinned with one hand, letting the other trail down through my hair, over my neck, his palm flattening against my collarbone before he palmed my breast. "Is this how I kissed you in your fantasy?"

I didn't have to respond for him to know it was more. It was all *so much more* than I ever could have imagined. The way his masterful tongue played with mine, sending little jolts of fire sparking through my core. The way his massive hands restrained me and pleasured me all at once, one gripping my wrists above my head while the other skated beneath the fabric of my dress, brushing my tender, hard nipple.

I gasped, arching into the touch, eyes popping open to find his hooded with desire where they watched me in return.

"Where is it that you like to be touched, Aspen?" he asked between bruising kisses, pressing his body into mine. "Is it here?"

He twisted my nipple between his fingers, sending a shocking cocktail of electric pleasure and ripping pain through me. Then, he spread my legs wider with his knee, kissing the swell of my breast with his eyes locked on mine as he blindly felt for the hem of my dress and dragged it up, up, up, until he could get his hand beneath it.

"Or is it here," he breathed, and without warning, his warm finger slipped beneath my panties, running a line through my wet desire as my entire body convulsed with the touch.

I mumbled something, though I wasn't sure what because it took all my focus just to keep myself upright. I wanted to fall into him. I wanted to give him everything I was and take everything he had to give. I wanted his finger inside me and his mouth on mine and I couldn't find the words to ask him for it, so I showed him, instead.

I arched off the glass, reaching for him with my mouth before he met my request with another hot, all-consuming kiss. Then I bucked my hips against his palm, crying out with an earthquake of a tremble when his warm skin brushed my clit and his finger slid deeper into my folds, teasing my entrance.

"You're so fucking wet, Aspen," he hissed, slicking his finger before circling my clit. My knees buckled, but he caught me, pressing his weight into mine to sandwich me between himself and the window. "Do you understand how badly I wish to be inside you?"

"Please," I begged, sucking his lip between my teeth.

"Only when you're mine," he breathed against my kiss. "Are you mine?"

My body screamed *yes!* My heart and soul and every cell of my being launched into his arms, branded his name into my skin, and vowed complete and utter belonging. *Of course, I'm yours*, I wanted to say. *Take me. Claim me. You already own it all.*

But my conscience whispered a hushed *no*, and for a reason I couldn't understand, it spoke louder than the rest.

I stilled under Theo's touch, panting as I broke our kiss. Our chests heaved in tandem, my wrists still pinned above my head, his finger paused between my slick folds. Those steel eyes flicked between mine, hungry at first, but slowly, recognition fell over them, and all at once, Theo released me.

My hands fell from the window, my shaking legs barely caught me to stand on my own, and every part of me longed to throw myself at him to gain the warmth he'd taken with the retreat.

"You're still with him."

I swallowed. "I..." I shook my head, the words I needed completely lost. "It's complicated."

"It's *complicated*?" Theo asked incredulously, laughing as he threw his hands up over his head and threaded them there. "Are you sleeping with him?"

"No!" I answered quickly. "Of course not. Not anymore." I swallowed. "Not for a long time now."

Theo looked out the window behind me for a long moment, tongue in his cheek, before he met my gaze again. "Then why do you deny me? Deny *us*? Why are we still under this pretense of you being with Joel?"

"I've loved him since I was nineteen," I whispered, and already, I felt Wonderland begin to crumble, the walls melting like candle wax, time stretching and snapping like a rubber band. "I can't just... I can't—"

"Leave him? Call him on his bullshit? Point out the fact that he treats you like you're nothing to him when I'm dying to treat you like you're *everything* to me?"

My heart surged in my chest, so powerful that I pushed off the window and toward Theo, but he backed away in equal measure.

"You drive me absolutely *mad*, do you know that? Every waking thought, every restless night, every fevered dream I have is consumed by you."

"And I am consumed by you!" Tears flooded my eyes, my throat thick with emotion I couldn't swallow down. "Can't you see that? I mean, you *must* know it already. I want you, more than anyone or anything I have ever wanted in my entire life," I confessed, and my body shook with the admission, trembling violently as I longed for Theo to wrap me in his warm embrace. "I just... I am confused, and lost, and torn between emotions I never knew I could feel." That admission seemed to sting more than the first, and two tears slipped free with the words, rolling down my hot cheeks in quick little rivers. "I don't know what to do."

Theo's brows bent together, his Adam's apple bobbing hard in his throat. He leaned just marginally toward me, like he wanted to reach for me, too, but something stopped him. Slowly, his face leveled, his lips flattening, jaw hardening into stone.

"Let me know when you figure it out," he said.

And then he turned, and he left me there, and I fell into a pile of rubble on the floor as Wonderland came crashing down.

CHAPTER
TWENTY

I spent the night thinking of my self-portrait again.

I thought of how I envisioned myself standing *on* the ship, with a storm to one side and a clear sky to the other. As if I had a choice. As if I could steer the ship and turn it toward the sunset and ride away safely over peaceful waters.

How naïve.

The reality was that I *was* the ship, completely at the mercy of the captain, except there *was* no captain and I'd been pulled straight into a storm that devoured me and left me wrecked on a rocky shoreline.

I waited a long while for Theo to come back to his room, but he never did, and so I found myself wandering around the boat a little lost. It didn't feel right to go to the room I'd been sharing with Joel. In fact, that room had felt off-kilter since the day Theo and I went to the Grotto.

I didn't want to be in the same bed with Joel.

I didn't want to share space with him *at all*.

And yet, I couldn't deny him, the way Theo had asked, and proclaim myself Theo's to take.

My heart shredded itself inside my chest, self-inflicted knife slits leaving the organ in ribbons as I sat awake on the edge of the bed in our stateroom waiting for Joel to come home. I heard the ruckus when the crew made their way back onboard, but the noise carried downstairs, and even when it died down, Joel never did come back.

We were done.

I knew it. He knew it. And yet, neither of us could admit it. Neither of us wanted to be the first to say the words.

It was impossible to separate who we were now from who we'd been. I wondered if Joel felt the same way, if every time he went to say the words he saw me riding on the front of his bicycle around the CU campus, or remembered the way we fit together watching movies in his dorm room bed.

Our hearts hold onto history, to comfort, to safety. Even when we know those things have died, our hearts will tell us there is hope to revive them.

But my hope wilted like a flower without water the more the hours stretched on that night, the black sky giving way to the soft blues of dawn, and I knew whether I felt ready or not, whether I wanted to or not, I had to face the truth.

I was still sitting on the edge of the bed, back rounded, legs sore, eyes dry and weary when Joel finally snuck in. He opened the door quietly, tip-toeing inside, but when he saw me on the bed, his shoulders deflated, and he closed the door behind him without care to how loud it was.

I could see it then, that he'd been wrestling with the same thoughts I had all night. That truth was reflected in the sad smile he offered me, in the sigh that left his chest as he abandoned his jacket on the back of the statement chair in the corner, and in his tired, red eyes as he quietly sat down next to me on the bed.

For a long time, we sat side by side, not touching or saying a single word. I listened to him breathe, going over the words in my head, wondering where to start. My chest was tight, stomach turning, and already, I could feel tears building along with a knot in my throat.

"Joel..." I started, at the same time Joel said, "We need to talk."

I laughed a little under my breath, and Joel gave me a sheepish smile.

"You first," I said.

He nodded, steeling a breath before he turned to face me. "I want to break up."

I blinked, letting the words settle over me, waiting for them to feel as expected as they should have been, waiting for them to feel *okay* — but they never did. Even though I was ready to say the same thing to him, hearing it come from his mouth first surprised me.

Why did it surprise me?

I expected Joel to want to talk, to apologize for the pool, for what happened with Ivy, to ask me where I thought we should go next.

I thought it would be *me* doing the breaking up.

I was sick over being the one to break *his* heart.

And now...

"You want to break up," I repeated, testing the words on my tongue.

"I know it may feel... sudden," he admitted, grabbing the back of his neck. He wouldn't look at me when he added, "I just feel like we're stuck. I want to find myself, you know? I want to see the world, and go out, make new friends and make memories with the ones I already have. I *love* this lifestyle," he added, gesturing a hand around him before his eyes landed on me. "And after the way this summer has gone so far, I can tell you very clearly do not."

I blinked again, several times, trying to digest his words. I could have just said *okay* and left it at that. But unwarranted as it may have been, I was offended by his reasoning.

"Because I don't want to party?" I asked.

"Look at you," he said exasperated. "You're miserable. And I feel responsible for that, I do, but at the same time... I'm not sorry."

"You're not sorry," I repeated, beginning to feel like a parrot. But I was having a hard time wrapping my head around it, the fact that Joel *still* didn't see his role in any of our demise. "After everything that's happened, all the breakdown of communication and the pool party—"

"I don't want to pretend to be someone I'm not," Joel interrupted, his voice strained. "And I don't want you to have to pretend either."

I swallowed, thinking about who I'd become over the last couple of months, trying to remember the girl I'd been that first day I walked onto the boat.

She seemed like a stranger now.

After a while, Joel shrugged, reaching over to grab my hand. "We've grown apart."

I frowned, staring at where his hand gripped mine as I traced back through the summer, at what was happening in my mind versus what was happening in Joel's. I was still trying to process it when he dropped another bomb.

"I talked to Theo already."

My eyes snapped to his and my heart leapt into my throat. "You did?"

Oh God.

Did Theo tell him what happened?

Joel nodded with an apologetic smile. "He understands, and he agrees that we shouldn't be together on the boat any longer. It just wouldn't be professional."

I frowned. "Okay…"

"So, we've arranged for you to fly back to the States this evening."

"You *what?!*"

"Theo's already taken care of everything," Joel said as I ripped my hand from his. "He's got a car coming later this afternoon and a first-class ticket home — which is *very* nice, all things considered."

"So, let me get this straight," I said, standing, pacing with my heart beating like a war drum in my chest. "Not only are you breaking up with me, but you're kicking me off the boat?" My heart sank like an anvil. "And *Theo* agreed with you that this was the right thing to do?"

"Aspen," Joel said sympathetically, the way you would try to soothe an upset child. "Surely, you knew this was co—"

"And I'm sure this has *nothing* to do with Ivy, right? And the fact that you've been fucking her every summer that you worked together — this one included?"

Joel's lips flattened, and he looked away from me with a shake of his head instead of a response.

It was irrational. I *knew*, deep down in my gut, that it was. How could I be upset with Joel for breaking up with me when I was ready to do the very same thing? How could I accuse him of fooling around with Ivy, of her being the reason for this decision, when I had been far from innocent with Theo?

I had no right to be upset, and yet I'd never been angrier in my life.

"You can't do this!" I screamed, tears flooding my eyes.

"I can call your sister, if you'd like," he said, ignoring my plea. "Have her pick you up at the airport."

"Don't you *dare*," I said on a sniff, pointing my finger directly at his nose. "Don't ever speak to *any* of my family ever again. Or to me, for that matter."

"Aspen, this is for the best."

I shook my head, ripping my backpack from where I'd stored it in our closet and tossing it onto the bed. I unzipped the top open and started grabbing anything of mine that I saw, throwing it inside the bag without care.

Tears blurred my vision the more I stormed around the room gathering my things, mind racing with denial as I tried to piece it all together. Joel watched me pitifully, and I thought I heard him saying my name, but I was too angry to hear a single word. Eventually, he left me alone, and when the door closed behind him, I fell to the ground in a sob that wracked my chest.

I hugged my knees, rocking back and forth, shaking my head over and over as if I could just close my eyes and wake up in another reality — one that didn't mean I was getting off this boat.

One that didn't mean I was leaving Theo. Forever.

I quieted with that thought, my sobs cut off mid-tantrum as the realization settled in.

I wasn't upset because Joel broke up with me. I wasn't even upset because I knew he'd been cheating on me with Ivy for God knows how long.

I was upset because he wanted me off the boat.

And I was *devastated* that Theo did, too.

My face contorted with emotion, and another wave of tears assaulted me. My rib cage squeezed so tightly together I thought it would crush my lungs, and I hugged my knees tighter, shaking my head as I cried.

I'd lost him.

I'd lost *everything*.

Before I even truly had the chance to have him at all, I'd let Theo think he didn't matter to me, that I hadn't been wrapped up in him from the moment I first saw him. I let my confusion and desperation to be loyal to Joel disconcert me and keep me from falling into the man who saw me so clearly I could never hide from him, even if I tried.

Theo knew it. He knew I was his.

But he wouldn't take me until I knew it, too.

And I didn't realize it until it was too late.

Another tear slid down my cheek, and I brushed it away silently, staring at the floor. It was all so cruel, how your own heart, your own *mind* could keep you from something so good. Now, in the broad daylight of the truth, I couldn't even figure out what my original reasoning had been. Why had I stopped last night? Why hadn't I agreed that I was Theo's to have, that Joel meant nothing to me anymore?

Suddenly, another thought hit me.

What if Theo didn't care about me at all?

What if all he'd wanted was to get in my pants?

The thought struck me so hard that I jolted upright, tracing back through our time together, wondering if everything he'd said had been a lie, a ruse to get me to fall into him, to trust him, to give myself to him. I thought of what he'd said about being my master that morning in Nice. I thought of the hungry look in his eyes when we were in the hot tub, the way he wanted me so fiercely he couldn't hide it. I thought of the pool party, and the Grotto, and then he'd kept his hands to himself until...

Last night.

When I'd denied him.

And Joel went to him the very next morning with a proposal to send me home.

Why *wouldn't* he want me gone after last night?

Theo isn't a liar.

He had no reason to lie.

He wouldn't do that... my brain tried to argue.

But he had.

He *had* agreed with Joel. He'd booked a car and a flight before even *speaking* to me, and now I was leaving and there was nothing I could do about any of it.

I was a fool.

A silly, impressionable fool.

I meant nothing to him.

I let my head fall back against the dresser, but no more tears came. Instead, I blinked my dry eyes up at the ceiling, wondering how I could have been so stupid, how I could have messed my life up so royally in just one summer.

But it didn't matter now.

It didn't matter that Joel broke up with me. It didn't matter that Theo no longer wanted me either.

It was done. It was decided.

In a matter of hours, I'd be off the yacht and en route back to Colorado.

Summer was over.

It felt like my life was, too.

After I packed, I went to the bar on the main deck and poured myself a drink.

I had no idea what I was doing. I never drank. But I'd also never been broken up with or felt so numb I wondered if I was even still human.

I'd heard my parents say throughout certain times in their life that *they needed a drink.*

Suddenly, I understood that feeling.

I selected a vodka and mixed it with cranberry juice, a cocktail I knew my mom enjoyed. Then, I sat down in one of the bar stools with my backpack propped next to me and took my first sip.

I grimaced. It was awful.

"Try adding a little lime juice," a voice said, and I looked over my shoulder just in time to see Emma yawning and sidling up next to me. The silver in her hair reflected the late morning light as she eyed the drink in my hand. "Or just give it to me since I need a little hair of the dog." She winked. "You don't drink, anyway, and today doesn't seem like a good time to start."

I sighed, sliding the glass toward her. "Feels like the perfect day to start, actually."

"Trust me, you don't want to lean on alcohol to try to fix things. That's how you end up vomiting and crying to a stranger in the bathroom of a bar at two in the morning." She laughed a little, but her smile fell when I couldn't return the gesture. "I heard about you and Joel. I'm sorry."

That got a laugh out of me. "Don't be."

"Are you okay? I know you really loved him."

My heart twisted in my chest, but it wasn't Joel who came to mind when Emma said those words. "I'll be okay."

"That's the spirit," she said, taking a sip of my drink. Then, she grimaced just as I had. "Ugh, Aspen, this thing is like seventy-five percent vodka. No wonder you hated it."

"I figured go big or go home," I said, then I gestured to my bag. "Looks like it's the latter for me."

Emma frowned, reaching over to squeeze my arm. "Hey, my offer to visit Austria still stands. Any time you want, okay? I'll show you around. My mom will be over the moon when I tell her I have an American coming to visit. She'll fatten you up in just two weeks, mark my words."

I nodded, trying to smile, but tears flooded my eyes. I thought they were all gone, that I was dried up, but my numbness was beginning to fade into despair again.

"Oh, sweetie," Emma said, opening her arms. "It'll be alright."

Emma held me as I fought back the urge to cry, her hand rubbing my back tenderly. For someone who'd never married or had kids, she had the touch of a mother, and I leaned into the comfort she provided.

She was still holding me like that when someone cleared their throat, and Emma released me, both of us turning to find Theo in the salon.

"Might I have a word?" he asked, his eyes on me.

Just the sight of him made more tears prick my eyes — his mussed hair, the bags under his eyes, the frown line etched deep between his brows. I wanted to launch myself into his arms, wrap myself around him, hold on tight and beg him not to make me go.

He slid his hands in his pockets, and Emma stood, patting my arm.

"I'll be working on the laundry if you need me," she said, offering me a sympathetic smile. Then, she nodded at Theo and excused herself.

We were alone then, and with Theo's eyes on me, I couldn't help but remember the first time I saw them. I couldn't help but think of how they'd rendered me speechless, rendered me stupid, rendered me weak. I blinked and saw his smirk as he took my camera, looking at the photo I'd taken of him. Another blink, and I saw the moonlight reflected in his irises that night in the hot tub. Blink, and we were in the cave in Capri.

Blink blink blink.

A dozen little memories I hoped I'd never forget.

"How are you?" he finally asked, and I scoffed, swiping my tears away before they could fully fall as I looked away from him and out onto the deck.

I felt him watching me, and I wanted to scream at him to just leave me alone as much as I wanted to beg him to hold me and tell me it was all a dream.

When I glanced back at him, his eyes were on my bag, but they flicked to meet my gaze. There was so much pain in those blue chrome pools that I felt it radiate through me as my own.

"Please, don't look at me like that," I whispered.

"Like what?"

"Like you're upset I'm leaving. Like it isn't you who's sending me away." I sniffed, shaking my head.

His nose flared, and he tore his gaze from me and out toward the deck. We'd been anchored a ways off shore last night, but this morning, Captain Chuck had docked us at the port in Salerno, and a long, black car had just pulled up at the end of it.

Theo nodded when the car flashed its lights, turning back to face me once more. I waited for him to say his goodbye, but before he could, there was a rumble of footsteps coming up the stairs, and then we were no longer alone.

Joel, Ivy, Celeste, and Ace jogged up together, looking as tired and worn out as I felt. They were dressed in their crew uniform, the red polos and khaki shorts, Ace with his sunglasses on and Ivy with her visor.

It was easy to see they'd all had a long night, too, though I had no doubt theirs was more fun than my own.

I crossed my arms over my chest, somewhat to soothe myself and somewhat to keep my right hand from reaching out and slapping the satisfied smirk right off Ivy's face. She looked at my packed bag like it was the best sight she'd seen in the Mediterranean, and I didn't miss the way she leaned into Joel's side, cocking her head at me like *what are you going to do about it?*

"Wayland said you needed us in the salon, sir?" Joel asked, eyeing me warily before he focused on Theo. He took a small step to the side, away from where Ivy leaned against him.

Theo nodded, taking a deep breath before he let it

go slowly. He was still looking out at the car, but slowly, his gaze trailed over to me.

There was something strange about the way he looked at me then, like he knew something I didn't. I couldn't explain why, but there was a whisper of comfort in his eyes, as if he were assuring me without saying anything that it would all be okay.

And where I wanted to break into another fit of sobs, Theo did the exact opposite.

He smiled.

The man *smiled* as if we had some sort of inside joke, as if we'd had a jolly old time and he was bidding me a pleasant farewell. *Thank you for visiting, Miss Dawn! See you in the Hamptons!*

I waited for him to tell Joel and his posse to escort me to the black car at the end of the dock, but when he finally faced them, he said the absolute last thing I ever expected.

"Joel, Ace, Celeste, Ivy," he said, addressing each of them. "I want to thank you for your... *hospitality* while aboard my yacht. However, at this time, your services are no longer required."

I gaped at Theo, along with the rest of the crew, but he just smiled and stood tall like there was nothing outrageous about what he'd just said.

"Sir?" Celeste asked, the bravest of the four.

It seemed to be that word that stripped Theo of his niceties, and I saw a cold demeanor unlike anything I'd ever witnessed slip over him like a cape. His smile flattened, jaw hardening as he took two menacing steps toward the crew, and he seemed to grow six extra inches, towering over them.

"Are you all naïve enough to believe I don't know *everything* that happens on my own boat?"

At that, all their faces went white.

I frowned.

What is going on?

Joel blew out a breath, fists clenching at his sides. "I don't know what she told you, sir, but she's just upset because I broke up with her. She doesn't know what she's talking about."

I scoffed, neck burning as the rest of the crew turned on me with fierce glares. "*Me?* What do I have to do with any of this?"

"Don't concern yourself, Aspen. He's just mad he got caught," Theo answered for me, his eyes still on Joel. "These four have been stealing from me."

At that, my jaw hinged open. "They *what*?"

Just then, I noticed Captain Chuck and the other deck hands carrying suitcases down the dock and throwing them into the trunk of the waiting black car.

And it wasn't my bag they were throwing in there.

It was *theirs*.

I only knew because I recognized Joel's in the heap.

My heart accelerated, and I was thankful I was sitting, because my head was already spinning as I tried to follow what was happening.

"I didn't want to believe Wayland when he first told me," Theo said to the four of them, pacing in front of them like a warden. "He'd noticed things missing — *small* things. Things maybe you thought no one would notice. A piece of china. A Rolex watch I don't wear often. A pair of earrings Nicolette left behind. A tablet in the guest stateroom that no one was staying in." Theo shrugged. "So, I threw the crew a pool party, and Wayland and I went on a little scavenger hunt."

Ace groaned, shaking his head as he gave Joel a look that gave me the impression he was the one leading the whole thing.

I just stood there with my mouth open like a guppy.

"We found everything we knew was missing and *then some* stuffed in the compartment under your bed," he said, looking at Joel. "And yours," he added, his eyes on Ivy now. "Quite unimaginative, if I do say so myself. Still, I didn't want to assume it was you. I thought perhaps someone else was doing the grand theft and framing it up to make themselves look innocent. So, I left it alone, knowing nothing was leaving the ship just yet anyway." His gaze hardened. "Instead, we set up cameras."

"Sir, let me just say I wanted nothing to—" Celeste tried, but Theo held up a hand to silence her.

"You know, honestly? I didn't care at first. You want to take back a few watches and some tech gear to make a few thousand bucks back home?" He shrugged. "Not the end of the world. You all work hard, and I guess I don't blame you for thinking a billionaire wouldn't miss a few valuable things. I clearly have the means to replace them." He paused. "But that wasn't enough, was it?" He pinned Ace with his glare then. "You wanted more."

"I *told* you not to go for the fucking safe, Ace!" Celeste hissed, and Ivy elbowed her in the ribs, giving her a look to shut up as if her being quiet would save them at this point.

"Really, this is a reflection of me. I was too trusting of you, and I didn't safeguard myself against the attack. But last night, when I sent you all to shore, Chuck and Wayland recovered everything that had been taken and returned the items to me. I can only assume that you were planning when, how, and *what* you would take from my safe, but unfortunately for you, that day will never come."

Celeste began crying, but Ivy, Ace, and Joel stood with their shoulders straight, not denying, not confirming, just taking their lashing without so much as a flinch.

"Your bags are in the car."

"Sir, *please*," Ivy tried, but Theo cut her off in the next breath.

"You're lucky I'm not getting you tossed into a foreign jail where I could easily pay off an officer to show you how I *really* feel right now," he said, and his nostrils flared with the anger I knew he was restraining. "Consider this your first and *only* warning, and don't even think about trying to get another job in this industry. You have all been blackballed from this moment forward. I suggest you go home, lick your wounds, and consider your next life choice carefully." He paused, stepping an inch closer, which I knew from experience was enough to suck all the air out of the room. "Cross me again, and you will wish you had my mercy, as you have it today."

He held their gazes for a moment to hammer that point home, then he made a little wave in the air with his finger, signaling Wayland, Captain Chuck, Eric, and one of the engineers to come in from where they'd been on the deck. They each grabbed a thief by the arm and steered them toward the dock.

Celeste struggled, still crying, screaming out that she was innocent. The other three remained silent, though I didn't miss the look Joel gave me as Wayland forcefully moved him past me, as if this were all my fault.

It sent a chill of terror down my spine, because in that precise moment, I realized I didn't know the man behind those eyes. Not even a little bit. Not at all.

I watched them go in shock, their heads ducking into the black car with Celeste still carrying on. As soon as they were all inside, Wayland hit the top of the car twice, and it sped off.

"All set, sir," Captain Chuck said when he was back on the boat with us. He glanced at me with a regretful smile. "Sorry you had to see all that, Miss Dawn."

I shook my head, but words were lost for me at the moment. I didn't know what to say about any of it.

Joel, a thief?

And Theo had known?

"I'd like confirmation when they're all on the flight," Theo said to Captain Chuck. "Their replacements should be here within the hour. Brief them as quickly as you can to get us moving again, then you can have more of a thorough break down this evening."

Captain Chuck nodded, tipping his hat at me once more before he left us. Wayland said something under his breath in Theo's ear, which Theo addressed with a curt nod, and then Wayland left us, too.

We were alone.

"Are you okay?" Theo asked, stepping closer. He slid his hands into his pockets again.

"I..." I swallowed, looking down the dock at where the car had been. "I don't know. I just... I can't believe..." I shook my head, finally looking back at Theo. "What does this mean?"

"For who?"

"For all of us."

Theo inhaled, letting the breath leave him slowly before he said, "Well, for them, it means a free flight home that I feel is a gracious sign of mercy after what they've done. For the rest of the crew, it means picking up some slack while the replacements settle in." He paused, his eyes flicking between mine. "And for us, it's a new start. At least, I hope it is. If you want it to be."

I frowned. "So you don't still want me to leave?"

Theo shook his head, stepping into me, and this time his hands came from his pockets and reached up to frame my face. "I *never* wanted you to leave."

Tears pricked my eyes again, those words like a salvation.

"I'm sorry I ever let you believe that I did. But I hope you can see the truth now."

"The truth?"

Theo smiled, though his brows were still pinched together as he watched me. "I want you to stay."

My next breath blew out of me, the tears I'd been trying to hold back falling silently down my cheeks. Theo thumbed them away easily, his eyes searching mine.

"I'm sorry for what I said last night, for the position I put you in," he said. "It was unfair. I wanted you so badly that I didn't consider your feelings for Joel, or your loyalty to him, and I respect and admire both." He paused. "It's just, I knew things about him that you didn't. I had this... *aching* need to keep you safe, to protect you from him, to show you that you were better and deserved better. That, coupled with my feelings for you, and, well..." He shrugged. "I was blinded. I wanted to save you. I wanted to steal you away. I wanted you all for myself."

My throat tightened more and more with every new word he spoke.

"It was wrong," he whispered. "And I apologize for it, the way I handled it all. But I am not sorry for the way I feel about you, only the timing in which those feelings developed."

I shook my head, because I didn't want him to be sorry. For *any* of it.

Theo pressed his forehead to mine, and the moment he did, we both closed our eyes on a relieved sigh.

"Stay," he whispered. "Be with me now, without anyone else in the way." He lifted his gaze to meet mine again. "Let me show you the way you deserve to be treated."

I choked on a sob, throwing my arms around his neck and squeezing him tight. Theo held me steadfast, wrapping me up in his arms completely as if to reassure me that it was all okay, that I was safe, that he didn't want me to go. And when I pulled back to look at him again, he met my lips with a strong, promising kiss — one I felt like a tattoo on my soul.

"You haven't slept," he said, still holding me tight.

"How do you know that?"

"Because I haven't either." He shrugged, sweeping my hair out of my eyes. "I couldn't rest, knowing what I'd said to you, what you must have been thinking of me. And then when Joel came to me this morning..."

I shook my head, burying my face in his chest. "It was the worst night of my life."

Theo kissed my hair. "I hope to make up for it by giving you the best night of your life, over and over again. But for now," he said, pulling back and sliding his hand down my arm to grab my hand in his. "We need rest."

He pulled me toward the stairs, and I followed, my body suddenly drained. I left my bag behind without a second thought, and Theo led us up to the owner's suite.

It was cool and dark, the curtains drawn over the large windows, and Theo walked me to the bed, pulling back the covers and helping me crawl under them.

I kicked my shoes off, and Theo did the same, climbing over me to slip under the sheets, too.

I sighed at the way the mattress took my weight, as if it was wrapping me up in a big hug. It was the softest, most comfortable bed I'd ever been in, and the pillow seemed to shape itself to the exact way my neck and head needed to be supported.

Theo wrapped his arm around my waist, pulling my back into his chest, his legs tangling up with mine. His warmth enveloped me like a cocoon, and I sighed again, snuggling in closer.

There was so much to think about, so much to digest. I had a million questions for Theo but not the strength or alertness to ask a single one.

I succumbed to the exhaustion as it pulled me under, knowing that with Theo's arms wrapped around me, nothing else mattered.

"Everything is okay now," he promised with a kiss to the back of my neck.

And then I slipped into a dreamless rest.

CHAPTER
TWENTY-ONE

When I woke, it was late. Or early, I couldn't be sure. There was a strong smell of coffee and bacon and something sweet, like maple syrup. I creaked one eye open first, then the next, looking around a little confused.

I was in Theo's suite.

It all came back to me then, as I took in the view of his bookshelf, his albums, the geometric design of the tables in the sitting area. There was a tray of food on said tables, and the sun was just barely peeking through where the curtains had been drawn back.

My heart thumped hard in my chest, first in excitement and then in discomfort. The memory of what had happened surfaced like oil in salt water, slick and unwelcome. But before I could digest it too much, a warm hand wrapped around my hip from behind.

"Good morning," Theo said.

I jumped a little at the touch, which made him chuckle before he pressed a gentle kiss to my cheek, his lips soft and warm. I leaned into the gesture with a relieved sigh.

"So it *was* all real."

"Did you think it was a dream?"

I laughed a little, turning to face him as I ran a hand back through my tangled hair. "I feel like this whole summer has been a dream."

I smiled lazily at the sight of him beside me, propped up on one elbow, his hand on my hip and the soft light filtering in through the windows playing with the grays and blues in his eyes.

"What time is it?"

"A little after six."

"I slept all day?"

Theo chuckled. "And all night, too."

I balked. "It's six in the *morning*?"

With that thought, I realized how bad my breath was, and how I hadn't brushed my teeth or hair or done *anything* to myself since I left Theo's room more than twenty-four hours ago now.

I covered my face. "Oh, gosh. Don't look at me. I bet I look terrible right now."

Theo peeled my fingers back from my face, kissing my nose before his eyes settled on mine. "You look beautiful."

I flushed, shaking my head and trying to melt into the sheets. Theo just watched me squirm under his gaze, drawing little circles on my hip. "Hungry?"

My stomach growled in response, and Theo let out a breathy laugh through his nose, hopping out of bed long enough to bring the food tray over. He set it between us, then poured us each a cup of coffee from the carafe on the table and handed me that first.

I inhaled the rich, chocolatey scent, leaning back against the headboard. "Thank you. I feel like a princess."

Theo smiled. "We're almost to San Marco, should be anchoring soon. I was thinking we could go to shore." He paused long enough to take a big bite out of a piece of bacon. "I'd like to take you shopping."

I giggled, grabbing a piece of bacon for myself. I pointed it at him before taking a bite. "I feel like that's more fun for *you* than for me."

"Humor me," he said on a shrug. "Besides, San Marco is beautiful. Lots of photo opportunities. And... I thought maybe..." He paused, rolling over in the giant bed until he could reach the bedside table. He opened the drawer and faced me again with a box in his hand. "You could use this."

I took a sip of my coffee before setting it aside, taking the box from Theo's hands. It was a simple but heavy white box wrapped with a navy blue ribbon. When I opened it, I nearly had a heart attack from shock.

"Theo..." I whispered, just staring at the beautiful camera inside the box. I was too afraid to touch it, because I knew just by the model number on top that it cost more than four times what I'd paid for the camera I already had.

"I know it's probably going to take some getting used to," he said hurriedly, pulling the Sony a7 IV from the box since I was too afraid to touch it. He turned it on, placing it in my shaking hands. "And I think it's more of a landscape-focused camera, but I read that it's stunning for street photography once you figure out the settings. Oh, I got a few lenses for it, too, and the best memory card I could find." He frowned as he watched me tilt the camera in my hands. "Do you like it? If not, I can send it back, it's okay if it's not the—"

"Theo, it has sixty-one megapixels and a Bionz X image processor," I said, as if that should have been answer enough to the question. "I don't like it. I *love* it. I am floored by it. I am... *dazzled* by it. I am scared of it," I added with a laugh, letting the machine rest in my lap as my eyes found his. "And I am completely blown away that you got this for me."

Theo smirked. "Well, I know you'll do brilliant things with it."

He leaned in to kiss me before I could blush properly, and I abandoned the camera altogether, wrapping my arms around his neck and holding him to me.

Once again I found it felt like a dream having Theo in my grasp. It was both foreign and the most natural thing I'd ever done, to have my lips pressed to his, to have his body flush against my own.

Something niggled at my gut, like a warning or a reminder, but it was so faint I ignored it in favor of the sensations that flooded me when Theo kissed me the way he did.

He groaned when my tongue swept inside his mouth, hot and eager, and I arched into the touch as a humming vibration spiraled down my spine.

"Eat breakfast and then get dressed," Theo said, breaking the kiss with a stiff inhale. "Before I keep you in this room all day, instead."

My thighs clenched. "That doesn't sound so bad..."

Theo thumbed my jaw with a knowing smile. "Don't worry, Aspen," he whispered. "There will be plenty of time for me to fuck you properly."

Another zing ripped through my stomach, and I held my breath, closing my eyes at the feel of his warm thumb against my skin.

"But for now, let me spoil you," he said, popping my butt as he hopped out of bed. "After the last forty-eight hours you've had, you deserve it. Eat. Get dressed. Meet me downstairs." He paused at the door, nodding to the closet at the far end of the suite. "Emma unpacked your bag for you. I hope you don't mind."

Then he left me, and I gaped at the camera next to me, at the luxurious bed I was in, at the vast and stunning room and the equally impressive view out the windows.

What is even happening right now?

How is this real life?

I closed my eyes on a squeal, allowing myself sixty seconds to flop around in the bed in a fit of giggles before I sat up, still breathing hard, still shaking my head in disbelief.

Then, I scarfed down some food, quickly got dressed, and ran downstairs with my new camera in tow.

Theo was right — San Marco di Castellabate *was* stunning.

With its golden beaches, turquoise water, and sea cliffs that seemed to extend up into the heavens themselves, I found myself lost in wonder as we made our way through the little villages that made up the area they called San Marco. I toyed with the settings on my new camera, completely wrapped up in the experimentation of getting to know it. Theo had outdone himself with the various lenses he'd paired with the gift — each of which

I knew cost over a thousand dollars — and never in my life had I held so much expensive, elegant camera equipment in my backpack.

I felt like a little kid again, wide-eyed and all smiles as we weaved through the sights.

And when my hand wasn't on my camera, it was in Theo's grasp.

We held hands in public like it was a completely normal thing. He would even pull me into his side from time to time, pressing a sweet kiss in my hair.

We were walking inside a small boutique when he pulled me into the corner of the shop, kissing me breathless until I pressed against his chest with a furious blush, looking to make sure the shop owner hadn't seen us.

And suddenly, that little feeling that had tugged at the corners of my heart earlier that morning was back.

"I'd like to jump inside that head of yours," Theo mused, brushing my hair back from my face as his eyes searched mine.

"Not a whole lot going on at the moment."

He laughed. "I think that's a lie." His arms wrapped fully around my waist, and he leaned against the shelf behind him, settling in. "Talk to me."

I blew out a breath, looking around at all the luxurious clothing that surrounded us. Just like in Positano, I knew without looking that every item in here was well out of my budget, but nothing more than pocket change to Theo. When I brought my gaze back to his, I struggled to find the right words to explain what I was feeling.

"Everything happened so... suddenly," I started. "But then again, I feel like it's been happening for years, like I've been staring at a tree and watching it grow from a seedling to a giant oak."

Theo didn't interrupt. He just nodded, letting me know he was following.

"I just..." I swallowed. "I feel... *guilty.* I feel wrong."

At that, Theo's brows tugged together, and he tightened his grip on my waist. "What on Earth do you have to feel guilty about?"

I gave him a look. "Come on, you know the answer to that as much as I do. You and I... the other night... before everything went down with Joel." I swallowed, uncomfortable even saying his name. "I shouldn't have let myself get so close to you," I said softer, and this time, my eyes locked on his. "And yet I couldn't stay away."

Theo inhaled a long, steady breath before he let it go. "I know the feeling well." He paused. "Is this... am I doing too much, too quickly? Do you want me to back off?"

"No," I said immediately, before I could even really digest the question. It was like my body and heart and soul answered for me before I could say something stupid. I clung to him more, gripping his shirt in my fists. "That's the last thing I want." I shook my head, staring at my hands on his chest. "Does that make me the worst human being to ever live?"

"What?" Theo shook his head on a laugh. "No. It makes you honest."

I swallowed, still staring at my hands, still feeling the guilt raging inside me. "It's just, I was just in a relationship with Joel, for *years*, and now he's God knows where... and I..."

I stopped again before I could say the awful words swimming in my gut.

And I don't even care that he's gone.

"Hey," Theo said, tilting my chin until I looked at him. "Let me ask you this — during this trip, the last few months… hell, even *before* this trip… were you *really* with Joel?"

I frowned, tilting my head in confusion.

"How long has it been since he took you on a date? Or since you two had a nice evening alone together? Or even a real conversation, for that matter? When is the last time he made you laugh, or feel safe, or loved?"

My stomach tightened more with every question he asked, because I couldn't tell him a single answer.

"Aspen, it is okay to be happy," he said, lowering his head to meet my gaze when I tried to tear it away. "I think maybe you've forgotten that, or surrendered it in the name of putting others around you first, or minimizing yourself so as to not be someone else's problem. But trust me when I say it is a privilege to be around you, to soak up the sun you provide," he said with a smile. "And unlike him, I will cherish every moment that I have you."

I bit back a smile, hating that my eyes were once again glossing with tears. I had been more emotional in the past month than I had my entire life.

"You don't have to defend your happiness — ever. Not to him, not to your friends or family or strangers, certainly not to me. And not to yourself, either, okay?" He leaned in closer, sliding his hands up to frame my face. "You are not only allowed to be happy, you *should* be happy. And I hope to be a part of what makes you that way."

I shook my head, mostly in disbelief that a man like Theo Whitman would say such beautiful things to me. "And what about you," I asked, peeling his hands off my face and kissing each palm before I wrapped my fingers around his. "What would make you happy?"

He looked around behind me for a moment, frowning until something caught his eye. Then, he lit up, smiling at the sight and then down at me. He kissed my knuckles, walking past me to grab something off the wall. He held it out of my view until he turned to face me again, and when he did, his smile was grand.

"Seeing you in this," he said simply.

I gaped at the floor-length golden dress in his hand, the whole of it salted with crystals that glimmered in the boutique light. It had thin, delicate straps and a deep V-neck, the top a deep gold where the chiffon skirt was more of a cream. It sparkled with every slight move as Theo moved toward me, holding it gently over one arm as he held the hanger in the opposite hand.

I reached out to touch the fabric with my mouth still hanging open. It was like something straight out of a Disney movie, or something a member of the Royal Family might wear to a ball, or perhaps more like a celebrity attending the Met Gala.

The more my fingers explored, the more I discovered just how lush and rich the fabric was, how heavy the crystals were against the thin overlay, how high the slit was up the left side, how exposed my back would be, how the V would dip so deep it would reveal the string of freckles above my navel, the ones that lined my chest between my breasts.

"It's... *stunning,* Theo," I whispered, still shaking my head and touching each inch of the dress. "But I have nothing to wear this to."

"Wear it for me," he said. "Tonight."

CHAPTER
TWENTY-TWO

If a piece of clothing could shape shift into something magical, that dress would have been a Cloak of Possibility.

When I slipped into its dazzling clasp later that evening, pulling my hair off my neck and to the side before I dared a look in the mirror, I wasn't prepared for what the evening would hold. I wasn't prepared for the way my breath would catch when I saw my reflection, when I let my eyes trail the length of a woman who couldn't have possibly been me but who was also the most *me* I'd ever felt in my life.

The gold and cream fabric draped elegantly over my bust, hugging my waist just slightly before the skirt flowed like a waterfall down the length of my legs. I turned slightly and the skirt followed with a soft *whoosh*, and once again I found myself silenced in awe as I took in the view of the straps framing my back, the crystals on the dress catching every glimmer of light in Theo's massive, walk-in closet.

I wasn't prepared for the way I'd feel slipping my feet into a pair of high heels, shoes that once scared me but suddenly felt so powerful and *right*. I wasn't prepared for the way I'd feel when Theo saw me for the first time, his eyes dancing over the length of me, from where I'd asked Emma to help me curl my long brown hair and do my makeup to where my freshly painted toes showed through the beige straps of my heels.

I wasn't prepared for the way my stomach would lurch at the sight of *him*, Theo Whitman, one of the youngest billionaires in the world all dressed up to take *me* on a date.

He wore a smoke gray suit, tailored to perfection, each thread hugging him in a way that proved that suit was made only for him to wear. He'd paired it with a classic white dress shirt and all-black tie, and everything from his slicked hair to his polished dress shoes screamed power and affluence.

I wasn't prepared for *any* of it — the way my arm fit so perfectly in his as we walked the streets of San Marco, or the way his eyes seemed to strip me bare over the candlelight of our dinner. I wasn't ready for the onslaught of questions he would ask me as we ate, how he wanted to know everything about me — even though I felt like the most boring human in the world next to him.

That was another thing I hadn't prepared for, how special I could feel as the center of Theo's focus, or the way just a brush of his warm fingertips on my exposed back could jolt me to another time and place, like I could see where the night would lead and the rest of our lives, too.

It was terrifying, the possibilities that dress revealed to me.

And it was addicting in the way only the best drugs are.

"What are you thinking about?" Theo asked me after dinner as we strolled arm in arm through the town.

I smiled, leaning into him. "How much of my life has changed in what feels like a millisecond."

"A good change, I hope."

I let out a long exhale, letting my eyes wander the length of the stone walls that surrounded us, the ivy growing up the side of those ancient buildings. "I feel like there have been two of me my entire life," I said. "The me stuck in this body, going through the motions, doing what I thought I should be doing. And the me who watched from the outside, silently walking behind me, hoping I'd take a moment just to turn back and remember there was more to me than I realized."

"Wow," Theo said, his eyebrows shooting up. "That's deep."

"And ridiculous," I added, shaking my head.

"No," he said quickly. "I... relate, actually. It's easy to get caught up in taking the steps we think we're supposed to take. And there is joy along the way, sure, but there's also this ache that something is missing."

"Exactly," I said, pausing our steps. "Although, I'm not sure what could possibly be missing in *your* life," I added with a chuckle.

Theo smiled, but it fell short, his eyes crawling up the alley that stretched out behind me. "Everyone thinks that. They look at me and see the company I built, the success I've had, the money in my bank account. But they miss how excruciatingly lonely all that can be."

I frowned, squeezing his hand.

"I've spent most of my life feeling like every conversation I have is forced, every friendship is fake, every person I involve myself with is just waiting to ask me for something. It's been that way since I was at Harvard. Before that, I knew my relationships were real. But after…" He paused, his eyes finding mine again. "You know, that was one of the first things that drew me to you."

"What was?"

"The way you looked at me." He smiled, like he was remembering the first day we met. "You didn't look at me with opportunity in your eyes. You looked at me and found something worth capturing — so much so that you took a picture," he added with a smirk. "But when I approached you, I expected you to rattle off questions. I assumed you were a reporter or someone eager to tell me about your million-dollar idea."

Theo stopped a moment, considering his words.

"But you hid from me," he said softly. "It was like you were the first one to look at me and *see* me, and then I'd caught you, and you'd shied away like you weren't worthy of the view. And I found a new purpose, right then and there."

"To kick the crazy girl off your boat?"

Theo shook his head. "To show the crazy girl that she *was* worthy. Of everything."

As sweet as it was, I laughed, arching a brow at Theo. "You really are a smooth talker."

"I mean it," he said earnestly. "I watched you at dinner that night, the way you listened to everyone else speak, the way you observed every behavior unfolding around you. I'd never been around someone like you before — someone not eager for the spotlight, someone who would rather disappear than have a moment of attention. It was… refreshing, I admit. But it also fueled me. Because for the first time, I saw someone *deserving* of the spotlight, and she wanted nothing to do with it."

I chuckled. "I'm just me."

"You're the most talented photographer I've ever had the pleasure of knowing, and I am friends with men who frequent the pages of *The New York Times* and *Vogue* magazine."

"Theo..."

"I'm serious. You see the world in the most real, raw way. You don't have a desire to filter it, or embellish it, to make it more or less than exactly what it is. Instead, you strive to capture the beauty in the everyday, the extraordinary in the mundane. And what's more impressive, you achieve it."

I was speechless, and Theo seemed to know the way he smirked down at me.

"More than all that, you are kind. And humble. You're completely unaware of how powerful your presence is, how breathtakingly beautiful you are, and how you have this light about you that shines so bright you can only have one of two reactions from those around you. Either they want to bathe in your light, or they want to dim it so it doesn't outshine their own."

My lips parted, heart pounding in my chest from being so seen.

"I was drawn to you from the start, Aspen, but when we went to breakfast that morning in Nice? When you talked to me like you knew nothing about me, like you wanted nothing from me, like I was just a man you were intrigued by? It flipped my world upside down. It showed me something I hadn't realized I'd been starving for." He shrugged. "And dammit if I haven't been able to let go of you since."

I shook my head, resting my hands on his chest as I watched the soft lamp posts from above us twinkle in his eyes. "You are the voice I've always been afraid to have."

Theo held me closer. "And you are the life I've been waiting to live."

Emotion surged in my chest, and Theo pressed his lips to mine, inhaling a deep breath as he did so. It was as if he were breathing *me* in, the whole of who I had been up until that moment and everything I would be thereafter.

I pressed onto my tip toes, deepening the kiss, begging for more, when suddenly, music started playing.

It was soft at first, and Theo paused our kiss, both of us searching for the source of the sound.

"It sounds like a band," I said.

Theo grabbed my hand, already starting to walk toward the music. "Let's find out."

We walked at first, but the more we weaved in and out of the alleyways and streets in search of the music, the quicker our steps became. Before long, we were running and laughing, dodging this way and that, finding ourselves in a maze of cobblestone and ivy until we stumbled into a square full of life.

Lights hung crisscrossed above us, their orange glow filtering down like star dust over the fountain in the middle of the square. Every side of it was protected by tall buildings, as if it was a secret oasis that we created ourselves. There was a band of three women by the fountain — one playing a guitar and singing, one playing a cajón, and the other tapping a tambourine against her palm. They looked like sisters, all dark blonde hair and olive skin and warm brown eyes. They smiled a little wider when we bounced into the square, giving each other a knowing look before the song they were playing slowly faded into a softer, more romantic tune.

"Are we in a fairy tale?" I asked, still catching my breath as I clung onto Theo's arm. "There's no one else here."

Theo looked around at the empty square, his smile growing more and more as his eyes trailed the scene. "Perhaps the Roman gods carved out this little crumb of paradise just for us."

I grinned, holding onto Theo's arm as I lifted one foot and then the other, peeling off the straps of my high heels. "Then we better make the most of it."

I pulled back from Theo's grasp, watching the confusion on his face as I backed up more and more toward the fountain. An arch of my brow and a head nod toward the water was all he needed to understand, and he smirked, shaking his head before he started following me. I watched him pause each step long enough to take his own shoes off, and then I turned, sprinting the rest of the way.

Theo chased after me, catching my hips just as I launched myself into the fountain. The water was absolutely freezing, and I squealed as Theo picked me up and spun me around, sending a magical spray of water from the hem of my crystal-covered dress over the marble and stone that surrounded us.

When he lowered me back down, easing my feet into the water once more, we were chest to chest, face to face, our laughter fading into heavy breaths as we took each other in. Theo's silver eyes flicked between mine, one hand wrapping around my waist, and then he swallowed, taking my hand in his other and waltzing me around in the fountain.

Our moves were sloppy and slow, the water resisting the dance, but still we moved and laughed and splashed around as the band of women played on. The singer elevated her voice, winking at me as Theo twirled me past, and I let my head fall back in a full fit of laughter as the moment settled in on me.

I was dancing with Theo Whitman.

I was dancing with Theo Whitman in a fountain in Italy on the most magical night of my life.

It was too good to be true, too beautiful to be real, and yet it was. My heart pumped blood faster, as if to whisper to me *yes, this is life, this is what it's all about.* Every inch of my body was alive with nerves, as if I'd never felt water before, or a warm hand on my hip, or a breezy summer night, or the eyes of a man who wanted me.

Everything was new. Everything was grand. Everything was in its place, like all the stars in the universe had aligned themselves for this very moment.

Theo spun me around twice, and I lost my footing, slipping and nearly tumbling out of the fountain before Theo caught me in his steady arms. He made the dip dramatic, as if we'd planned it, and I laughed so hard tears pricked the corners of my eyes.

But when the laughter faded and I looked up into those soul-searing eyes, the music faded, and the lights dimmed, and everything that existed seemed to evaporate like steam into the night air.

Theo lowered his lips to mine, the kiss tender and punishing in tandem. It sent chills cascading over the skin of my neck, down my spine, all the way to my toes. I gripped his arms tight where they held me, and when his tongue danced with mine, I couldn't help the little moan that escaped the back of my throat.

"Theo..." I begged, and it was all I needed to say. No demand or desire that I could give words to would have compared to the power of just breathing his name.

Theo fished his wallet out of his pocket, leaving a generous tip for the band before he swooped me into his arms effortlessly, carrying me out of the fountain with his eyes cast down on me. They seemed to transport me through time and space, because everything around us blacked out like the beginning of a dream until the moment he sat my feet down on the plush carpet in his suite.

I didn't know how we'd gotten back, couldn't remember walking the streets or riding in the tender back to the boat. All I knew was that it didn't matter now, and I dropped the heels I didn't realize I'd been carrying in my fingertips, the sound of them hitting the floor like the gun shot that kicked off a high-stakes race.

Theo met me in a crash of limbs and moans, our hands seeking, roaming, gripping and clawing. He met every desperate touch of mine with one even more anguished of his own. It was like finally being together killed us as much as it brought us both to life, like we were breathing our last sip of air and our first gulp all at once.

Theo bruised my lips with his, slipping his fingertips under the straps of my dress and gently pulling them over each shoulder. My naked breasts flowered under his eyes, nipples hardening, goosebumps pebbling every centimeter of my skin. He palmed me first, feeling the weight of each breast in his hand before he groaned and bent to lower his mouth to my left peak.

I gasped at the sensation of his hot mouth covering the cool skin, my back arching of its own accord as

I chased the feeling. My hands tangled in his hair, destroying the gel that held each strand perfectly in place.

I wanted him messy. I wanted him to unravel just like me.

"If you only knew," Theo breathed against my chest, sucking my nipple hard between his teeth before letting it go with a pop. "The things I have done to you in my dreams."

"Show me," I begged, tugging back on his hair until his mouth was turned up toward mine. I kissed him hard, sealing the plea.

Theo groaned, gripping my waist so hard I winced as he backed me up to his bookshelf. We slammed into it hard enough to steal my breath and knock a few books and knick knacks to the floor, but Theo stayed on course, shoving my arms up over my head and locking my wrists together with one hand.

"You have been the source of my madness for months now," he husked, dragging his tongue along my arched neck as his free hand trailed down my body. The only thing holding the bottom of my dress to me now was the elastic at my waist, and Theo slipped his fingertips under it, easily dragging it down until it pooled at my feet. "And I'll be the source of yours tonight."

I whimpered, chills racing down my spine again just from his promise. Now that the dress was gone, nothing but a scrap of lace shielded me from his view — but not for long. Theo kept me pinned as he ripped my panties down to my knees, then he backed up just enough to take in the scenery.

"*Fuck me*, Aspen," he breathed, the hand that held my wrists gripping even tighter. I hissed in a breath, but Theo was too busy raking his eyes over every inch of me to let up. "You're a masterpiece."

His eyes met mine, and he moved in again, his mouth catching my next exhale. His free hand swept over each of my breasts, twisting my left nipple and then my right, as if he were testing which one was more sensitive.

"I want to touch you," I said, fighting against his restraint.

"In time."

That was the only answer he gave before he separated my thighs with his knee, pressing his whole body against mine. My already throbbing clit met the fabric of his dress pants, his thigh giving me just the right friction and just where I wanted it. I moaned at the sensation, and Theo dropped his grip on my wrists to grab my ass, instead. He pulled me to him, rocking my hips so that I dragged my clit up his thigh.

My entire body trembled so fiercely I thought I might fall, and I gripped onto his shoulders to steady myself.

"I'm not even inside you yet," Theo mused with a smirk, and he used his hands on my ass to pull me back before rolling me against him once again. Then, he sucked my ear lobe between his teeth, biting gently before he whispered, "Do you want me to be?"

I choked on my next breath of air, stars circling my vision as I let my eyelids flutter closed.

Theo kissed my neck with a knowing grin before dragging my hands up and over my head again. This time, instead of pinning my wrists, he turned my palms until they were on the bookshelf behind me. My fingers clamped down over the wood automatically, holding on for dear life.

"Keep these here," he commanded. "Understand?"

I think I nodded. I think I wet my lips and sold my soul to the devil just to see what would happen next.

Theo grinned at my compliance, kissing me hard before his voice rumbled against my lips. "Good girl."

Those words sent another chill down my spine, and then Theo descended upon me, his hands sliding down the length of my rib cage to grip my hips. He kissed a trail across my collarbone, sucking each pebbled nipple between his teeth, tracing a line with his tongue from the three freckles on my chest down my navel until he was on his knees with his eyes cast up at me.

He grinned, devilish and sexy as hell, and then he hiked my leg up to rest on his shoulder.

My breaths accelerated, and I gripped the bookshelf harder, praying it would keep me steady now that I was balanced on one leg. Even so, Theo seemed to hold all my weight, and he kept his eyes on me as he dragged his tongue over my mound and down to my clit.

"Oh, *God*," I cried, body shaking so violently I thought my knee would give out.

Theo answered by holding me even more steady, then he buried his face between my thighs, sucking and licking my clit in a rhythm set to kill.

It was unlike anything I'd ever felt before, the expert way his tongue lashed against the most sensitive part of me. It was as if he'd crawled inside my head, as if he could hear every thought. *A little softer, a little harder, down more, yes, yes, right there.*

Theo took his time discovering every part of me, what drove me crazy and what made my legs quake around him. When it was too much to bear and I was on the edge of coming, I let go of the shelf behind me, reaching down to run my hands through his hair and pull his mouth closer.

As soon as I did, Theo pulled back, letting a cool sweep of air wash over my hot clit.

I hissed, convulsing at the loss, and Theo stood abruptly, grabbing my hands in his. He spun me until I faced the shelf, slamming me into it again as more books fell to the floor.

"I told you to keep these here," he said, peeling my arms up overhead until my fingers wrapped around the shelf again.

I whimpered, and Theo grinned against my neck, kissing me soft at first as his hands trailed down my back. Those kisses became harder and harder, little nips and bites between tender licks and sucks, and then his hand slipped between my butt cheeks, index finger swiping through the wet desire he'd created.

My orgasm rushed back to me, ready to ignite, just with that one brush of skin.

"Please," I begged, and Theo sucked my ear, sliding his fingers a little farther up to brush my clit.

"Please what?"

"Touch me."

"I already am."

"Inside," I breathed. "Finger me, Theo. Show me what you've wanted to do to me all summer."

Theo growled at my confidence, biting my neck so hard I winced, but he immediately plunged a finger inside me in the next breath and all the pain was replaced by a hot, searing pleasure.

I gasped, sucking in what I didn't realize was my last full breath of oxygen. Theo wrapped his free hand around my waist, reaching down and flattening his palm against my clit. He didn't circle it, didn't rub it — he just placed his warm palm there so that every time he thrust his finger into me from behind, my pelvis rocked, rubbing my clit against his hand.

"Theo," I cried, panting, meeting his finger thrust for thrust where he penetrated me.

"Yes."

It was one simple word, permission and a command all at once. My body obliged the request, and in a trembling siege of fire, stars blacking out my vision as I let go.

I moaned so loud I knew the whole crew could hear, but I didn't care. It was like every ounce of pent-up desire I'd been holding onto since the moment I laid eyes on Theo erupted out of me in a violent volcano. I gripped the shelf hard, trying to hold myself up while my hips rocked, Theo's hand rubbing my clit while the other fingered me mercilessly.

And in the next breath, I fell still, collapsing in his arms.

Theo chuckled, kissing my messy hair. "That's my girl," he whispered.

I wanted to laugh, too, but Theo turned me quickly, finally releasing my hands as he met my eager kisses. My orgasm was still floating through me, like earthquake tremors warning of another impending danger, and I used the adrenaline to hold my hands steady as I tugged at his tie, the buttons of his dress shirt, shoving his jacket over his shoulders and hastily ripping at the belt around his waist as he shrugged the jacket the rest of the way off.

We were all hands and mouths and moans as I stripped him, and the only time we broke contact was for him to kick out of his shoes and step out of the pants and briefs I'd stripped down to his ankles.

Then, he stood before me, all mountains of muscles and valleys of hard, toned, tanned skin. He stood tall and powerful, shoulders square and back, those steel eyes watching me over the slightly crooked bridge of his nose as he stroked his thick, pulsing cock.

It was the wrong time to be thinking of Joel. I knew it, but I couldn't help it when I saw the beast Theo unleashed. I'd seen one penis in real life before, and it was Joel's.

And compared to Theo's, Joel's member was a joke.

Theo Whitman might as well have walked off a porn set, the way the veins lined his beautiful, perfectly shaped cock. The mushroom head was thick and beaded with pre-cum, and he swiped his thumb over the drop, moaning as he coated himself with it.

I was still staring, still trying to comprehend how it would fit inside me when he quickly made his way to the bedside table. He pulled out a condom and rolled it over himself before making his way back to me at the bookshelf.

"You look scared," he mused with an arched brow.

I shook my head, even though he wasn't far from the truth. "I just want you."

"How?" he asked, palming my breasts and pushing my back against the shelves again. I hissed at the bruising kiss he gave me next, gasping as his tongue massaged mine.

"Here," I said, grabbing his muscular ass and pulling him closer. "Now."

Theo growled, hiking my thigh up just like he had when he went down on me. Only this time, he lifted my ass until it sat mostly in his hands and half on one of the bookshelves. Then, he lowered his hips, reached down between us, and positioned himself at my entrance.

One look. One breath. One fiery, all-consuming kiss.

And he filled me.

A shocked moan left my mouth, but it was quickly silenced by Theo's kiss. He groaned with me as he withdrew and slipped in again, stretching me open, his body trembling just as mine had.

"Jesus *Christ*, Aspen," he breathed, pressing his forehead to mine as he looked down to watch himself entering me. He pulled back slowly, flexing even deeper, and I held onto his shoulders for dear life.

Theo pressed my hips into the bookshelf, pinning me there as he picked up the pace. Every new thrust went deeper and deeper until I was certain he was penetrating the very depths of my soul. I clawed at his back, moaning and crying out at the rush of sensations overcoming me.

I didn't even realize it was possible, but another orgasm quickly snaked its way through my bloodstream, and I locked eyes with Theo just in time to tell him I was coming before my head dropped back, body shaking in Theo's grasp.

That seemed to be the catalyst for his own release.

Theo growled, biting my neck and squeezing my hips so tight I knew they'd actually bruise as he fucked me harder, faster, slamming me against the bookshelf over and over again. Books flew off onto the floor. A vase of flowers broke and sent glass and water everywhere, but Theo didn't relent. He kissed me hard, one hand coming up to wrap around my neck as the other held my hips to his. A shudder of a groan ripped through him, and I felt him pulsing inside me, the condom filling just as I started to get warmed up for another orgasm myself.

For a long moment, Theo just held me there, his damp forehead pressed against mine, breath labored, body stiff until a wave of chills rushed over him.

"Fuck," he groaned, smirking when his eyes found mine again. "You," he said, kissing my lips. "Are." Another kiss. "*Sensational.*"

I blushed, shaking my head and laughing as he peppered me with kisses all over my neck, my chest, until his lips were on mine again.

"How do you feel?" he asked, gently lowering me to the ground. He swept my hair out of my face, cupping my jaw in his massive hands.

I bit my lip. "Like I want to do that again."

Theo's brow arched, and then he let his head fall back with a booming laugh erupting from his chest. When he looked at me again, his eyes glazed, hair mussed, body slick with sweat — he just shook his head.

"Oh, baby. Trust me," he said, sweeping me into his arms and carrying me over to the bed. "We're not getting any sleep tonight."

CHAPTER
TWENTY-THREE

Theo kept his promise — neither of us slept that night. In fact, I found myself lacking sleep *every* night after that, too, as we crawled the rest of the way down the Italian coast and crossed over to Greece.

Effortlessly, I slipped into a new way of life with Theo Whitman.

We spent our days relaxing in the sun or exploring the foreign shores that *Philautia* took us to. We ate pasta and tasted fresh olive oil, dug our toes into golden sand, fell in love with Italian hospitality, splashed around in turquoise waters, and lost many afternoons where we couldn't leave the bed at all.

It was all so new, discovering each other, and we both seemed content to spend hours upon hours trailing fingertips over each other's skin, touching and feeling, kissing and tasting.

In the evenings, Theo spoiled me with luxurious dinners onboard or by taking me to the nicest restaurants on shore. Sometimes we would read together, side by side in bed, or Theo would work while I edited photos.

Most times, not much reading or work got done at all.

I spent time with Emma, too, as the weeks passed, and she started to feel like a friend I would have for life. Wayland and Captain Chuck joined us for dinner a few evenings, and I even got acquainted with the four crew members who had replaced Joel and his band of thieves. It seemed with them gone, the partying downstairs in the crew mess was less and less rambunctious.

No one seemed to mind.

One of Theo's goals was to make his crew feel like family rather than employees, and there was no question in my mind that they felt that way. Theo gave them numerous days and evenings off to enjoy themselves, and I particularly loved those nights when we were alone on the boat.

I found inexplicable joy in the smallest things as the August mornings turned to dusk, day after day, night after night, carrying us through the tail end of summer. I reveled in moments like when I found out Theo's favorite color was black, which I told him wasn't really a color, but rather a shade, and he pinned me down in the bed tickling and kissing me until I relented and said it could be a color, too.

Or like when Theo didn't believe me that my favorite movie was *Pulp Fiction* until he put it on one night and laughed uncontrollably as I quoted it word for word, even acting out the action scenes with air guns. I then found out that *his* favorite movie was *Casablanca*, so we watched that next, and ended the night with him between my legs whispering, *"Of all the yachts, in all the seas, in all the world, she walks onto mine."*

I even got a taste of Theo's adrenaline-addicted side when he booked a parasailing trip for us. Whereas I was toying with the thin line between *this is exciting* and *I'm going to have a heart attack* with my legs dangling below me and the kite-like contraption carrying us over the water along the Grecian coast, Theo was hooting and hollering and throwing his hands up in the air, demanding the tour guide dip us in the water over and over.

"We're like shark bait!" I screamed over the wind.

"We're *alive!*" Theo argued back.

He tried to get me to go skydiving after that, to which I responded with a hearty laugh and an offer to watch him from the safety of land, thank you very much.

I loved peeling back the layers that made Theo Whitman who he was, like the nickname 'Cap' his friends had given him in sailing club because his last name was Whitman, just like the poet who wrote *O Captain, My Captain!* Or like how he was an uneasy, grumpy version of himself if he didn't get out for his morning row, or at the very least get a strenuous workout in before the sun came up. And Theo could spend entire nights awake with me, drawing circles on my skin while I told him about my studies in college and my childhood memories growing up in Colorado, like how Mom and Dad had taken Juniper and me to the Telluride Bluegrass Festival every summer since we were born.

My head fit perfectly into the crook of his arm, and I became addicted to being the first thing Theo thought of in the morning and the last thing he saw at night. No matter the exotic things we saw on shore, or the intriguing guests he brought aboard, nothing compared to staring into his eyes as we fought sleep — all in the name of talking until our throats were hoarse and our eyes could no longer stay open.

I was in the calmest, most content state of being.

Until the night we anchored off the shore of Santorini.

"Don't tease, okay? I've only been with one man before you," I reminded Theo as he fought back laughter. "I didn't know a penis could *be* pretty."

Theo barked out another loud laugh, curling over like his stomach hurt. I smacked his chest, but laughed, too, simply because I loved the way Theo looked when he was filled with so much joy.

"I'm sorry," he said, holding up his hands before he pulled me back into his chest. It was after midnight, and we were curled up in the sheets, trying to recover from the three rounds of fun that had kept us in the bedroom since dinner. "But come on, you've got to let me indulge in at least a *little* jest over the fact that your ex-boyfriend and the asshole little thief I kicked off my boat has a funny-looking dick."

I pinched his side. "I didn't say funny-looking!"

"You didn't have to."

I rolled my eyes, but settled into his chest with a smile. "And what about you, mister? I'm sure you've seen some odd-shaped boobies or something. What was your sex life like before me?"

I asked the question casually, easily, like we could talk about it just as candidly as we did mine. It didn't occur to me until the long silence stretched between us that maybe I was asking a question I didn't actually want the answer to.

"Does it matter?" Theo asked after a moment.

His deflection made my stomach roll, my smile fading.

I shrugged. "I don't know. Humor me. You know all about my past."

"Yes," he agreed. "But I'm eleven years older than you. I've had a lot more time to..."

"Sow your wild oats?"

Theo chuckled. "Something like that."

I traced shapes on his bare chest, fingers brushing the slight hair that dusted his skin as the walls of my throat closed in. "Have you ever had a serious relationship?"

"My lifestyle isn't exactly conducive to long-term or serious engagements," Theo answered. "With anyone — whether friendly or romantic."

"Oh..." I said, and I couldn't ignore the way my heart thumped to life in my chest, hammering in my ears as those words sank in. "So... you've *never* had a girlfriend?"

"I guess it depends what that title means to you." Theo shrugged, and I was thankful I was staring at his chest and not into his eyes when he said, "I've been with many women, some who I could picture a future with, sure. But in the end, they had their own lives and I had mine. The most serious I ever got was seeing them when I was back in their country, or state or city, depending." He paused. "I guess you could say I have international affairs."

Theo laughed with the joke, squeezing my side, but I didn't find anything humorous about what he'd just said.

Because suddenly, after living in a fantasy bubble for weeks, I realized just how completely naïve and stupid I had been to think this would last.

I sat up slowly, tucking my hair behind my ears before I crossed my arms over my chest. "So... I guess I'm Colorado?"

I couldn't look at him when I asked the question, and my entire body chilled once those words hung in the space between us.

Theo shot up from where he'd been reclined, reaching for me. "What? Of course not. Why would you ask that?"

"Because you just said your lifestyle isn't conducive to a long-term relationship."

Theo swallowed. "I did, didn't I?" He sighed, shaking his head and pulling me into him. He held me tight, but I still kept my arms crossed. "I'm sorry, I wasn't talking about you. I was referencing the women I've been with in the past."

"But how is this any different?"

At that, Theo scoffed, pulling back to frame my arms with his hands as his eyes searched mine. "Are you kidding?"

When I didn't answer, Theo motioned for me to crawl into his lap, and he wrapped me up in his arms again, kissing my forehead.

"You, Aspen Dawn, are different in every possible way. You have ignited a spark in me that no one else ever has, or ever could. I desire you for my own more than I desire *anything*."

Theo fell quiet, and though I wanted to melt at his words, my stomach churned with anxiety that he could be lying. Or even if he wasn't lying, even if he *did* feel that way now — how long could it possibly last?

The new and exciting feelings we were experiencing now would fade.

And then where would we be?

"I want to be with you," he whispered, kissing my neck. "Now. Tonight. Tomorrow. Next week. For as long as I can see my life, I see you in it."

Tears pricked my eyes, and I sniffed them back, burying my head in his chest. "How can you be so sure, if you've never been serious with anyone else?"

"That's exactly *why* I'm sure," he said. "Don't you see? Since I laid eyes on you, I have lost all desire for every other woman." Theo chuckled. "You've bewitched me."

Again, I wanted to believe him, but it was like there had been warning bells going off in the distance and I'd had on noise-canceling headphones. Theo's admission of his past relationships — or lack thereof — had ripped those headphones off.

And now, I couldn't ignore the blasting whistles and horns and giant red flags warning of the pain to come.

The longer we were there in that bed, the more the smoke seemed to clear. I saw it all so clearly, so suddenly. I saw the beautiful fantasy I'd lost myself in, the magical possibilities I'd convinced myself were abundant.

In reality, I was just a billionaire's current fascination.

And just like this summer vacation, I wouldn't last.

We wouldn't last.

"Hey," Theo said after a moment, tilting my chin until our eyes met. "I'm sorry I gave you any reason to doubt me. Or us. Or what we have." He frowned. "Just... give me a chance, okay? I'll prove that I mean what I say."

My heart squeezed hard in my chest, but I nodded, anyway, and Theo dragged me down into the sheets with him until we were curled together. He kissed the back of my neck, rubbing my hip and thigh with his fingers to soothe me until his breaths slowly evened out into soft snores.

But once again, I found myself in a sleepless night.

And the reason for my restlessness was a lot less fun this time.

CHAPTER
TWENTY-FOUR

"You sure you don't want me to spike this next cup?" Emma asked the next day, her eyes sympathetic as she made me another steaming cup of tea. It was a gray and foggy day, which was wildly uncharacteristic of the island, and everyone from the crew to the locals were in a tizzy over it.

Theo was working — or so he said. It was the first time since Joel left the boat that he'd spent a full day at his computer. He was locked up in one of the state-rooms, and other than breakfast, I hadn't seen him all day. When I *had* seen him, earlier this morning, he'd seemed distant, like he had something on his mind, and I couldn't help but wonder if he was thinking over what we'd talked about the night before.

If he was realizing just as I was that what we had could never last.

"I'm sure," I said on a sigh, thanking Emma with a smile as I wrapped my hands around the mug. "I tried that once, remember? Didn't work out well for me."

"Yeah, well, you were trying to drown your sorrows in a very poorly made vodka cranberry that would have knocked an experienced drinker on his ass."

I smiled, but it fell quickly, my stomach rolling again just as it had all night. Tea was about all I could think about consumption wise, and even that, I had to sip slowly.

"You going to tell me what's going on?"

"I'm not sure I know what to say."

"Is it Joel?" she asked. "Because it's okay to miss him, even if he was a grimy, cheating thief of a loser."

I chuckled. "Weirdly... no. I haven't thought about Joel in weeks. Maybe because, to me, our relationship had been over for a long while before either of us admitted it." I paused, staring at my hands a while before I met Emma's gaze. "Does that make me an awful human?"

"No. You're much kinder than me, I'll tell you that much. You and Theo both. Because *I* would have had all their sorry asses thrown into Italian jail if it were my call." She reached for another mug, pouring herself some tea, too. "So if not that, then what?"

I chewed the inside of my cheek. "Just realizing that the fantasy world I've been living in all summer is going to leave a nasty mark when I wake up and it's all gone."

"Gone?" Emma frowned. "What do you mean?"

"Come on, Em," I said, leveling my gaze. "Theo Whitman is a hot billionaire who could have anything and any*one* he wants. No woman has ever tied him down. And now I'm supposed to think *I* have a chance?"

Emma let out a slow exhale, studying my face. "Well, anything is possible."

I snorted. "Yeah. I think I heard that in a Disney movie once." I sighed. "I don't know how this hasn't been on my mind from the start, from before either of us even gave in to each other. I mean, Joel aside, what did I think was going to happen? I feel…" I tried to swallow the bitter pill of what I was about to say but came up empty. "I feel like an absolute fool."

"You're not a fool," Emma said. "And hey, who says it has to be forever, you know? Why not just enjoy it now, have some fun, and at the end of the trip… well…"

"I let him go," I whispered, and my eyes blurred with tears instantly. "*God*, why does that feel like an impossible thing to ask of myself?"

Emma smiled sympathetically, pouring some scotch into her tea. "Not everything amazing in life is meant to be kept forever," she said, toasting her cup to mine. "Sometimes, we're just meant to enjoy a little slice of heaven, or learn a lesson, or grow into someone new." Emma shrugged then. "I don't know what's to come between you and Theo any more than you do, but I do know one thing for certain."

"What's that?"

"If you had the chance, right now, to go back and undo it all in the name of saving yourself from heartbreak?" She smiled. "You wouldn't."

My throat tightened again, so fiercely I thought I'd lose the ability to breathe altogether. But then I smiled, because she was right.

Why did she have to be right?

Even after the conversation with Emma, I couldn't let go of my anxiety. It stuck to me like tree sap, following me all around the ship as I tried to busy myself. By the time I gave up and headed back up to the cabin, it felt like my anxiety was permanent, like I had sprouted a new limb that would be a part of me forever.

And when I opened the door and found the suite empty, Anxiety whispered that this was the beginning of the end.

I had asked too many questions.

And now, I'd chased him away.

Theo didn't come to the room that night, not before I laid down around nine and not any time after. I knew, because again, I couldn't sleep, and every little sound had my eyes popping open, hoping to see him crawling into bed next to me. I wanted to apologize, to take back everything I'd said and pretend like none of it mattered. I wanted to go back forty-eight hours and stay in my blissful unawareness until I had no choice but to crash on the cold, hard ground.

Theo's steel eyes haunted the eerie dreams I had that night when I *did* occasionally slip into a state of sleep, like even my unconscious brain was hell bent on reminding me how much I'd screwed things up. And when I woke to the bed still empty and the morning light streaming through the windows, I sat up and hugged my knees to my chest, finally succumbing to my tears.

This really is it.

I was still rocking in a ball like that when Wayland knocked on the door, and I told him to come in, although the last thing I felt like was seeing or talking to *anyone*.

"Good morning, Miss Dawn," he said, like I wasn't a complete mess before him. His eyes were kind and wrinkled at the edges like always, his smile polite, voice calm.

"I told you to stop that," I said.

He shrugged. "My apologies. Habit, now that you and Mr. Whitman are..."

Wayland paused, not finishing that sentence, and my stomach cramped because I wasn't sure there was anything to even finish that sentence *with*.

"Just call me Aspen. Okay?"

Wayland smiled. "As you wish." He held up the carafe in his hand then. "Claude is making breakfast now, but I thought you might like some coffee."

He set down the carafe first, followed by one mug — not two.

"Will Mr. Whitman be joining me?" I asked, hoping I didn't sound as pathetic as I felt.

"Unfortunately, he's already gone to shore. Business. I'm sure you understand," Wayland said.

I nodded, throat squeezing tight again. "Of course," I croaked out.

He watched me for a long time, and I felt the weight of his sympathetic eyes until he sat on the bed next to me. "We have a saying in Jamaica, one my mother said many times to me." Wayland paused, furrowing his brows before the thickest accent I'd heard yet from him made an appearance. *"De more yu luk, de less yu si."*

He poured some coffee into the mug he'd brought for me then, handing me the steaming cup.

"The more you look, the less you see?"

Wayland nodded. "Exactly. It's a reminder that it's impossible for us to know all the details about everything in life. And usually, the more we badger ourselves to try to figure it all out, the narrower our scope of understanding becomes."

I frowned, staring at the black liquid in my cup and watching the steam rise slowly.

"What I'm saying is, I can see that you are troubled — and perhaps what's troubling you most is that you're trying to get a concrete answer for something that may not require it. Perhaps letting your mind rest is the best cure for what ails you."

Wayland arched his thick, dark brow at me then, tapping my knee before he left me. But regardless of how beautiful the sentiment behind what he'd shared, I still slumped back into the bed once he was gone, determined to waste the entire day away there.

It didn't matter that the sun was back, that it was a perfectly beautiful day on one of the most gorgeous islands in all of Greece. There was nothing I could do to block out the black clouds hanging over my heart, and they were all-consuming, the kind of despair that couldn't be erased by anyone other than the person who caused it.

I didn't eat breakfast. I didn't eat lunch. I didn't do anything but lay in bed, wafting in and out of a restless sleep. I was too tired to do anything active, but too anxious to let myself fully rest. It was the most exhausting push and pull, like an unrelenting barrel of waves taking me under over and over, barely letting me catch my breath in-between.

Sometime in the late afternoon, Wayland knocked again, and this time, he entered carrying a piece of clothing on a hanger covered by a black fabric protector.

"I've been instructed to take you to shore at six this evening, Miss—" he caught himself, smiling sheepishly at me as he said, "Aspen." He hung the mysterious clothing item on the back of the closet door. "You are to wear this."

I sniffed, squinting through my hazy sight at the black bag, then at Wayland. "Where am I going? Will Theo be there?"

"I'm afraid I don't have any further information," Wayland said, but there was a small smirk on his lips, and he ducked away before I could pepper him with more questions. "I'll meet you on the main deck at ten til six."

"Wayland!" I tried, but he just waved me off and shut the door behind him with a soft *snick*.

I sighed, staring at the black bag hanging on the door like it was a bomb waiting to go off. I didn't know why my anxiety was prickled even more at the lack of information and demand to be ready to go ashore, but it was.

Is he kicking me off?

Is he going to take me to dinner and then have Wayland pack my bags?

Is this it, is this when I let him go?

I steeled a breath against the onslaught of *what ifs*, wrapping myself up in the bed sheet and tip-toeing over to the closet. I unzipped the bag, and when I did, I gasped.

Hanging inside was a cream, long-sleeve top that weaved together in the front in a stunning criss-cross of thick, ribbed wool. It had a deep but elegant V neck, and around the hanger, there were three delicate gold neck-laces of varying size to illustrate how they should lay on my neck. The shortest was just a chain choker with small balls of gold, the next was slightly longer with a small key, and the longest ended with a gold heart about an inch wide.

Below the sweater, there was a gray knee-length skirt with pockets and a thick cotton belt that tied around the waist. There was a clip to the side that held a tortoise shell thin-strap watch. And finally, at the bot-tom of the bag, were simple nude flats.

I tilted my head to the side, unable to fight off the smile at how much I loved the entire ensemble. It felt strangely... *me*. The colors were neutral, but the style was fun and quirky, as if Theo had jumped inside my head and picked out exactly what I would love to wear if I knew anything at all about fashion.

And yet... I was confused.

This wasn't his usual choice of a long, flowy, sparkling dress to take me out on the town to wine and dine. And besides, we were on an *island*... why in the world would I need long sleeves?

I searched the bag for a note, but found nothing, and one look at the clock had me panicking at the thought of figuring out what to do with my hair and makeup in the hour I had to get ready.

So, for the moment, I put my anxiety on hold and flew downstairs to find Emma, begging her to help me.

She obliged with a squeal of delight, and at six o'clock sharp, I was on the tender with Wayland and headed to shore.

CHAPTER
TWENTY-FIVE

Theo wasn't waiting for me at the dock, like I expected. Nor was he in the sleek black car that picked me up and drove me across the island. I was alone in my thoughts as the sun set over the water, and my knee bounced along to the lovely Greek music playing on the driver's radio.

We pulled to the side of a narrow street about twenty minutes after leaving the dock, and the driver told me I would need to walk the rest of the way, given the nature of Santorini's cobblestone alleyways and stairs. He handed me a slip of paper with clear directions on it, as well as a phone number, in case I got lost. Then, I was on my own.

It was like walking in a dream as I followed the directions through the tiny streets to my next destination. The setting sun cast the white buildings in brilliant shades of orange and pink, the sky slowly faded into dusk, and all over town, lights began to flick on one by one. There was a gentle breeze rolling off the water, and I was thankful for the long sleeves now that I felt how the sun setting could call in a cooler evening.

I checked the directions twice once I arrived at the destination — a bustling white building with a bright blue roof nestled between a hotel and a restaurant. There was a considerable crowd inside the building, from what I could see through the glass front doors, and two couples offered me polite smiles as they pushed past where I hesitated and let themselves in, too.

The sign above the doors read γκαλερί τέχνης.

Which meant I had zero idea of what was inside.

An older gentleman brushed past me, and when he saw the unsure look on my face, he smiled, opening one of the glass doors and gesturing for me to enter. I returned his smile as best I could, trying to soothe my stomach with a warm palm pressed against it as I slid past him and inside the building.

No, not just a building.

A *gallery*.

I blinked like I'd walked in from the blinding light of the sun, adjusting my purse on my shoulder as the gallery came into view. It was a small space, quaint, all-white walls and black ceilings with a mosaic-tiled floor. There were two thick wall-like dividers in the middle that separated the one room into four sort of aisleways, each one lined with artwork. The lighting was low, mostly just the up-lights illuminating the art, and soft jazz played from a speaker in the corner.

There were at least a few dozen people inside, the sound of laughter and chatter and the clinking of drinkware combining with the music to set a pleasant ambience. It was like a party, but I had no idea who the guest of honor was, what we were celebrating, or why *I* was here.

A lean woman dressed in all black approached me with a tray full of champagne, but I declined with a smile, confusion setting in more and more as I waited by the door for Theo.

I searched the crowd, but didn't see him.

I searched the alleyway outside, but didn't see him.

I scanned the crowd and the gallery again, and still, I didn't see him.

But what I *did* see that second time around was so unbelievable I pinched my side to make sure I wasn't dreaming.

I tilted my head, heart picking up from a trot to a gallop as my brain tried to fight me with logic. It screamed at me all the reasons why there was *no way* I could possibly be seeing what I thought I was.

I let my feet carry me blindly across the entryway of the gallery to the first piece of artwork hanging on the wall, muttering *excuse me's* as I weaved through the crowd, and the closer I got, the more my brain quieted, leaving only my racing heart to pulse in my ears.

There was no refuting it.

There was no trying to talk myself out of the possibility of it being real.

The photograph in the frame was *mine*.

I covered my lips with shaking fingertips, eyes bouncing from one end of the photograph to the other. It was one I'd taken on the island of Capri, three children playing kickball in the yard with the white limestone cliffs stretching up to touch the sky behind them, the sun's rays peeking through thick white clouds, specks of dark and light green foliage peppering the hills of houses. I remembered the way the sun coming through the clouds seemed to almost cast a golden hue over the entire island that day, and how I'd felt that piercing light into my very soul when I took this photograph. It was seeing the pure joy on those children's faces, watching the way they ran unabashedly forward, onward, without fear or hesitation. They laughed and played and capturing that moment made me feel like I had plucked the fruits of innocence and peace straight from the tree of life and tucked them away into my heart forever.

The photograph was framed by a warm wood that only brought out more of the glow in the photograph, and there was a soft pool of light cast over it from the lamps shining on each side.

I wasn't sure how long I stood there, blinking, swallowing back emotion, trying to understand. But when I finally turned my head to cast a glance down the rest of that first aisle in the gallery, my heart stopped altogether before kicking back to life with a fierce *thump thump thump*.

Every photograph in that aisle, and the next, and in the entire gallery was mine.

"Oh my *God*," I whispered under my breath, shaking my head as I walked on jelly legs to the next photograph.

It was the one from Nice of the couple on the seawall, and as much as I loved seeing it printed and framed, I loved the expressions of those who were viewing it even more. There was a young couple, much like the one in the photograph, who stared at the picture a while before giving each other a knowing look, their hands clasping, cheeks blushing as if they knew the secret the couple in the photograph did, too. And an older woman behind them looked at the photograph with solemn eyes, her fingers twisting around the bare ring finger of her left hand. I wondered if there once was a gold band there, one signifying a love that was never supposed to die.

I weaved in and out of the guests of the gallery, chest tightening more and more with every step that revealed a new piece of my art. I watched as the patrons pointed and nodded, listened as they whispered how each one made them feel, and all the while, my brain was still trying to convince me none of it was real.

I must be in a dream.

I must have fallen asleep on the boat.

This can't possibly be happening.

But when I rounded the corner into the last aisleway, there was no fog or haze or dreamy state of mind. There was only a giant photo of me looking over my shoulder, the sunset over Positano behind me, my eyes bright and wide and glistening in the setting sun.

It was the photograph Theo took.

Emotion warped my face, but I schooled it, crossing my arms over my chest as I slowly made my way to read the plaque next to it.

Aspen Dawn, photographer of all the pieces included in this special Dawn of the Med exhibit. Taken by Theo Whitman, exhibit sponsor and philanthropist. Sunset in Positano, Italy.

I rolled my lips together, shaking my head as tears flooded my eyes.

The gentleman who had held the door open for me earlier quietly came up to stand beside me, his eyes flicking from me to the photograph Theo had taken. He smiled widely, gesturing to the photograph and saying, "You?"

I nodded, laughing and swiping away the fat teardrops that slipped over my cheeks with the smile.

The man looked back to the photograph, then at me, and his hands reached forward to take mine in his own. He bowed a little, kissing my knuckles, and said something that sounded like *panemorfi*.

I made a mental note to look up what it meant later.

With another sweet smile, he dropped my hands, glancing at the photograph of me one last time before he left me. And I stared at the happiness reflected in my eyes in that photo for a long time before I turned, too, and promptly lost my next breath.

Standing there in the center of the aisle was a devastatingly handsome Theo Whitman.

He wore a cream tailored suit with a simple, thin black tie that somehow made him look like he was part of the exhibit, himself. His hands rested easily in his pockets, his hair gelled into a perfect swoop, and he watched me with bent brows as I slowly made my way toward him. I stopped with a few feet between us, clasping my hands in front of me and searching his gaze.

Theo looked like he hadn't slept any more than I had, and the wrinkle between his brows told me he didn't know what to say, or what to do, but that he was anguished. We watched each other for a long time, the music and background noise of chatter fading out more and more, as if we were the only two people who existed at all.

"You did this?" I asked after a long pause.

He nodded, closing the space between us. His hands reached out tentatively at first, but when I didn't pull away, he slipped his hands to hold me at the small of my back, his piercing eyes watching me over the bridge of his nose.

"I wanted you to know the truth."

"What truth is that?" I whispered.

Theo swallowed, his Adam's apple bobbing hard in his throat. "That I love you."

I choked on a soft sob, covering my mouth with trembling hands as my eyes flooded again.

"That I believe in you this much," he said, looking around at all my photographs hanging in the gallery as he stepped into me even more. When his eyes found mine again, they seemed to peer into the very depths of who I was. "And that I believe in *us* even more."

I closed my eyes, releasing the tears that had been building. Theo thumbed them away, pressing his lips to my forehead and holding me tight.

"I don't care about your past. I don't care about mine. Nothing else matters to me, other than the future you and I can make *together*. And I know what I said about my lifestyle the other night," he said, pulling back to look me in the eyes. "But we will find a way. We will make it work. Because if I've learned one thing this summer, it's that now that I know you exist in this world, I cannot live without you existing in *mine*, too."

I shook my head, leaning into where his palm framed my face. "I can't believe you did all this..."

"I did it to prove to you that I'm not going anywhere, and that what we have is real. You don't have to be scared of it disappearing." He paused, thumbing my jaw. "Do you believe me now?"

I laughed, swiping away the tears that were let loose with the notion. "I believe you are crazy, and impulsive," I said, but then I locked my arms around his neck and brought his lips down to mine. "And the most brilliant, thoughtful, *incredible* man I have ever known."

"Anything else?"

I nodded, swallowing down the knot in my throat before I whispered, "And I think I love you back."

Theo smiled against my kiss before deepening it, his arms wrapping me up tighter, and just as we both groaned at the way it felt to be connected, I pressed my hands into his chest.

"Wait," I breathed, looking around the gallery. "I don't understand... how did you do all this?"

Theo shrugged. "I have my ways."

"Ways you can't tell me, huh?"

"A magician never reveals his secrets," he said. "But let's just say I made a sizable donation to the gallery in exchange for a little help with tonight's event."

I chuckled, looking behind him at all the guests admiring my work. "I can't believe all these people are looking at my photographs."

"Not just looking at them. *Falling in love* with them," Theo said, and he turned so that we were both facing the gallery, tucking me under his arm. "You know, we've already had thirteen offers to buy."

My eyes must have popped out of my head because Theo laughed and kissed my cheek, squeezing my hip gently.

"Don't look so surprised."

"I... I just never considered..." My gut did a full-on somersault, and I swallowed down the sudden rush of nausea that I couldn't pinpoint the source of. "Did you sell them?"

"No," Theo answered quickly. "That wasn't the purpose of tonight. But I *can* sell them. If you'd like me to."

I frowned. "How much did they offer?"

At that, a grin spread on Theo's lips. "The one you took in Nice of the man and woman facing opposite directions on the bench. You know the one?"

I nodded.

Theo leaned in to whisper in my ear. "Four-thousand euros."

I slapped his chest, shoving him away as I shook my head over and over and he just laughed at my expense.

"You can't be serious!"

"But I am," he said. "So, should I sell it?"

I just stared at him with my mouth hanging open, but then something in my heart squeezed tight, and I frowned, glancing down the hallway lined with my art. Every picture hanging in that gallery was a little piece of me, and though I'd always dreamed of sharing those little pieces with the world, I'd never considered that someone might want to purchase that little piece of me and take it home with them.

"How about this," Theo said after a moment, pulling me into his arms again. He waited until my eyes were back on him before he continued. "I'll have the curator collect the information of the potential buyers and let them know we'll be in touch. That way, you don't have to make any decisions tonight. Okay? If you decide to sell, we'll arrange it. Otherwise, we'll have them all shipped back to New York."

I smiled, shaking my head as my fingertips played with the lapel of his suit jacket. "I feel as transparent as wax paper with you around," I said. "You can see what no one else can, what not even I can."

"I feel the same way when you look at me," he said, thumbing my chin. He smoothed the skin along my jaw, over my cheek, his hand slipping back to cup my neck.

When I leaned into the touch with a sigh, he swallowed, his jaw set. "I'd like to take you home now."

"Would you?" I asked, arching a brow playfully.

He nodded, and without another word, he swept me into his arms and out the back door of the gallery, leaving the guests and my photographs behind.

My feet had no sooner touched down on the plush rug in Theo's master suite before his lips covered mine, warm and soft, his breath a long sigh of relief. It was like he'd been waiting for this moment all night, to have me alone and all to himself, and now he was reveling in the way it felt to wrap me in his arms.

I felt the same way.

After the last two days of uncertainty, of anxiety spirals and hopelessness, all I wanted was for Theo to consume me. I wanted him to cover me up in all that he was, until I could no longer tell where he stopped and I began.

I pressed onto my toes to deepen the kiss, sliding my hands up and over his shoulders under his jacket so I could push it down his arms. Theo released his grip on me long enough to help me strip him, and then he was doing the same to me, gently fingering the bobby pins out of my hair first until it fell down over my shoulders in long, curly waves.

I worked his tie next, and his hands tugged at the bow securing my skirt. I unfastened each button of his dress shirt and he broke our kisses long enough to strip my blouse overhead. It was completely silent, save for our breaths and the soft sounds of skin on skin, of fabric hitting the floor, of hearts thumping to life more and more with each touch.

When we were both fully nude, Theo wrapped me up in his arms again, the warmth of him meeting the warmth of me as we both exhaled together. He ran his hands back through my hair, tugging until my neck was arched, chin to the ceiling, and he kissed me hard and long, as if that kiss was his only chance to show me how he truly felt about me.

As if what he'd done for me tonight hadn't already illustrated that perfectly.

Still, I leaned into that kiss like it was the vessel bringing me home until Theo scooped me up in his arms again and gently laid me down in the cool sheets of his giant bed.

I'd had Theo in a multitude of ways, ways that I was certain now no other woman ever had. I'd had him on his knees in the shower, tasting me and driving me to orgasm with one leg hooked over his shoulder. I'd had him pounding me from behind, his hand wrapped tightly around my neck until I had to tap his arm and beg for oxygen. I'd had his cock in my mouth, him groaning out instructions and guiding me until he pulled out and painted my chest with his release.

So many ways. So many nights and mornings and long afternoons. So many times now, I'd seen that man undress, and felt his hardness inside me, and known the ecstasy that came at the mercy of his fingertips, his tongue, his throbbing, thick member.

But I'd never had Theo Whitman like *this*.

I'd never had him quiet and trembling, his eyes locked on mine as he slipped between my legs and pulled the sheets up until they covered us like silky fog. I'd never had his arms tucked under me, his hands wrapped around my shoulders, thighs spreading my own until I opened for him. I'd never had his shaky breaths washing over my skin as he positioned himself at my entrance, never stared into his adoring eyes as he pressed inside me, never felt the difference between being fucked by Theo and having him make sweet love to me.

I gasped when he flexed all the way inside me, and Theo caught my breath with his mouth over mine, kissing me softly, surely, as he withdrew and flexed inside again. This time, I moaned, chills racing over my skin at the sensation of having him so deep. Theo kissed along my neck, my collarbone, over the swells of my breasts before he pressed up onto his elbows so he could look down on me.

On us.

His mouth parted as he looked between us, at where we met, at where his long length pressed inside of me again and again. It was so erotic, watching him watch us, and when he lowered himself back down again, it was with a needy kiss, a sweep of his tongue over mine, a desperate pull of my shoulders, a whisper of *more*.

My orgasm built slowly but fiercely, like a volcano formed over millions of years. It burned inside me, singeing the bones of my rib cage, melting the walls of my heart. I felt every spark, every lick of the flame until it bubbled out of me, and I dug my nails into Theo's back, holding on as he picked up the pace to drive me over the edge.

I cried out, back arching, Theo's name on my lips as I found my release. I realized then that Theo was there, too, grunting and gripping me just as tight as he came undone inside me. It was the first time we'd come together, that we'd been so wrapped up in each other that our bodies caught fire at the same moment.

We trembled in tandem when we were both spent, Theo's slick forehead dropping to my chest as I sheltered him with my arms. I kissed his hair, and he squeezed me tighter where he held me, our breaths slowly evening out.

"I love you," Theo whispered against my chest, and I couldn't stop the tears that pricked the corners of my eyes at such a sweet sound.

"I love you," I whispered in return.

We fell asleep wrapped in each other in a tangle of arms and legs and silky sheets, with our hearts soaring, our souls on high. At the core of who I was, I truly felt like nothing could touch us, like nothing and no one could ever rip us apart.

For the first time all summer — perhaps all my life — I felt secure, and safe, and sound.

And in the blissful, nescient sleep I slipped into with Theo's arms around me, I didn't hear the distant crack of thunder warning me that I was wrong.

CHAPTER
TWENTY-SIX

Two days later, we anchored outside of Athens on a balmy August morning. It was the last place Theo had work to tend to, and he was desperate to wrap up and spend a couple more weeks on a *true* vacation with me before we headed back to the States.

Back to the States — *together*.

It made me giddy any time I thought of it, flying in his private jet back to New York City. I had no idea what would happen after that, what my parents would think when I told them everything that transpired over the summer, or where we would live, or if I'd go back to Colorado and he'd stay in New York. There was so much to discuss, which was another reason Theo was anxious to get his work done so we could have the time to figure it all out.

He was off the boat as soon as we anchored, and I watched the tender take him to shore as I sipped my coffee and breathed in the fresh sea air. I was still all bliss and sunshine, high off love when an idea struck me.

"I want to make Theo dinner," I told Emma, slightly out of breath by the time I found her down in the crew mess. She was trying to have her own breakfast in peace — coffee and a blueberry scone — but she chuckled at the sight of me and gestured for me to have a seat across from her.

"What do you have in mind?"

"Well, back home, I learned how to make a *delicious* pan-fried trout from my mom. It's kind of a rite of passage growing up in Colorado." I cringed. "Any way we could find some trout here?"

Emma chuckled again. "Aspen, you're dating a billionaire. The word *impossible* doesn't apply to you anymore. Not with money like that at your fingertips."

I blushed, tucking my hair behind my ear. "Well, I want to pay for dinner, too. Here," I said, fishing my card out of my pocket and handing it to her. "Charge it to that."

"You know we have a card specifically for getting provisions, right?" Emma asked with an arched brow.

"Yes, I know, but I haven't spent a single dime of my own money in what feels like forever and I..." I rolled my lips together, thinking of all Theo had done for me, and how I desperately wanted to do something special for him, too. "Just let me do this."

Emma shook her head on a smile, but took my card anyway and told me to give her a list before noon so she could get everything I needed.

I spent the better half of the morning planning out the meal, considering what type of salad I wanted to make, what appetizer and dessert would complement the trout, and thinking of the best wine pairing. Even though I didn't drink, I knew Theo appreciated a good bottle of wine, and I wanted the night to be perfect.

Once Emma had my list, she took the second stewardess to shore for provisions and I changed into my swimsuit, climbing my way up to the sun deck with a fresh lemonade in hand, thanks to Claude. I spent the afternoon sunning and reading and waiting for four o'clock when I could video chat my sister without her killing me for calling too early.

"Well, if it isn't my *too-busy-traipsing-around-Europe-to-call-home* sister," Juniper answered with a yawn, her dorm room still completely dark. I knew by now she was back at CU, and when she flicked on the lamp on her bedside table, I smiled at the familiar set up of a dorm similar to the one I had called home for four years.

I smiled even more at the familiar sight of my tired sister with a messy bun piled on top of her head.

"Good morning, Juni," I said cheerily. So much so that she groaned and rolled her eyes before sitting up more in bed.

"Morning. A little too *early* in the morning for my taste." But she smiled with the jest. "It's good to see you. We haven't talked in forever. How the hell *are* you?" She paused, frowning at the screen. "I guess the better question is *where* the hell are you."

I laughed, getting up out of my chair and walking the phone over to the railing. I showed Juniper the coast of Athens in a slow panoramic while she groaned in jealousy.

"I can't believe that's your life right now."

At that, I turned the camera back around to face me with a grimace. "Um... do you have a Keurig or something there in your dorm?"

"Yes," she said, cocking a brow. "Why?"

"Because you're going to need some caffeine for everything I'm about to tell you."

I hadn't talked to Juniper or anyone back home since before Joel left the boat. Everything had just happened so fast, and then I was caught up in Theo, and before I knew it, a month had gone by.

So, I started where we left off last time, telling my sister about my frustrations with Joel, how he wouldn't talk to me about the pool party incident, and how things just got colder and colder between us while everything between Theo and I sparked into a hot flame. I told her about Capri, about Joel breaking up with me and how I was supposed to be kicked off the boat, but then lo and behold it ended up being *him* who was kicked off. I told her about the grand theft and how Theo asked me to stay and filled her in on all that had transpired between me and Theo since.

There was a myriad of emotions coming from her end, from red-faced punches into her pillows at what Joel did to me, to running her hands back through her hair like a crazy person as she tried to understand everything that went down, to leaning her chin on her hands close to the screen, swooning over Theo's little gallery surprise.

By the time I finished, I'd practically worn a hole in the sun deck from pacing back and forth, and Juniper was on her third cup of coffee.

"Say something," I said after a long silence.

She shook her head, sipping her coffee with a dazed look on her face. "I'm speechless. I mean... I'm *appalled* at Joel. I have no idea what got into him."

I sighed. "Me either. Part of me wonders if maybe he was doing more than just drinking..."

"You think drugs?"

"Maybe," I said. "He just wasn't himself. Or if he was, then I didn't know him at all, and the boy I fell in love with never really existed."

"Maybe he has always led two lives, you know? The one here and the one on yachts. I mean, I can't imagine living that lifestyle." She arched a brow then. "Well, okay, I can imagine living it the way *you* are now, but not as crew."

I laughed.

"Seriously — you're dating *Theo fucking Whitman*, Sis." She lowered her voice as if someone would hear her. "He said he *loves you!*"

"I know."

"And you're yachting around the Mediterranean on a million-dollar yacht."

"I know."

"And he rented out a whole freaking *gallery* and filled it with your photographs!"

I chuckled, flushing so hard I pressed my cool fingertips to my cheeks. "I know. I know!" I sighed on a smile. "How is this real?"

"Your guess is as good as mine," Juniper said with a chuckle. "But I'm happy for you. Because *you* look happy. Happier than I've ever seen you. You have this new way about you, like... like you're confident, and sure."

I smiled again. "That's how I feel with him. It's like I've been waiting to be this person all my life, but I was afraid or something. I don't know."

"He brings out the best in you," Juniper said softly.

"Even better — he makes me feel like the worst of me is still worthy of being loved."

Juniper clasped her hands over her heart. "Stop. I need to watch a rom-com stat."

I laughed, and then we launched into conversation about school and her volleyball season. We laughed together thinking of what Mom and Dad would say when they found out about me and Theo, especially if I ended up moving to New York. And before we ended the call, Juniper made me promise that I would bring Theo home to meet her before we settled.

She also made me promise her a trip to the Bahamas since Theo's friend owned an island down there.

I ended the call with my already high spirits floating even higher, and just in time for Emma to bound back onto the ship with dinner supplies in tow. The sun began to set over the water, and I rested my hands on the railing, watching the golds turn to purples and blues with my heart full and light in my chest.

Everything was absolutely perfect.

A couple hours later, I bopped along to a HAIM song in the galley while seasoning the trout. The sun had fully set, and Theo would be back on the boat any time now. He'd sent me a text letting me know he was wrapping up and had to make a few stops on his way back to the boat, but it wouldn't be long.

I was so excited you would have thought I was about to accept a Pulitzer Prize rather than serve my boyfriend dinner.

Boyfriend.

I giggled at the title.

I felt free in a silly sort of way, dancing alone in the kitchen. Once Emma had dropped the provisions off earlier, I gave her and the rest of the crew the evening off, encouraging them to go explore Athens. At first, she'd declined, insisting that Theo would be upset if they went without his permission. But I gave her a look to let her know it wasn't so much a suggestion as a *hey, I want the night alone with Theo, so get lost*. She'd laughed and thrown her hands up in surrender, letting the rest of the crew know, and they'd taken the tender to shore where Wayland would wait for Theo to bring him back onboard.

Captain Chuck was still here, though, up in the pilothouse. I hoped he couldn't hear my horrible singing as I moved my hips to the beat, but honestly, even if he could, I was too wrapped up in my happy feelings to stop myself.

As I prepped the fish and the appetizers, I couldn't help but smile, thinking back over the past few months. There had been so much pain, but also so much new discovery that the hurt was worth it. It was almost impossible for me to try to remember the girl I'd been when I'd first stepped foot on this boat, when my stomach had turned so violently I thought I'd be ill.

The me who existed then had been quiet, and shy, and reserved. She'd been lost, not knowing who she was or where she was going, not confident enough to even look a stranger in the eyes for longer than a quick moment. She hid behind her camera and lived life through the people she captured, never even considering that she could live a full life of her own.

I couldn't remember that version of myself, but I would always remember the way I felt that first time I laid eyes on Theo Whitman.

My stomach did a little flip at the memory, and I shook my head in disbelief that I could call him mine now. He'd be back soon, and I'd be serving him dinner, and then we'd end the night tangled up in each other.

I bit my lip, doing a little dance as I moved the trout over to the hot pan on the stove. It was already bubbling with butter and garlic and herbs, and when I gently lay the filet inside, it all sizzled to life.

"Mmm," I hummed, doing another little hip shake. "Perfect."

Suddenly, there was a thunderously loud thump from somewhere upstairs.

I paused, frowning as I waited to hear if anything else came after. "Chuck?" I called. I didn't even know if he could hear me all the way down here.

After a moment of nothing else, I shrugged, tending to the trout and singing along to the stereo again. But then there was more noise, something like the faint sound of voices and steps on the stairs.

I frowned, pausing the music, but then silence blanketed me.

"Theo?" I called up the stairs, wiping my hands on the dish towel. "Is that you?"

I heard the faint murmur of voices again, and I wondered if Emma and the crew had come back earlier than expected. Or maybe it was Wayland and Theo, or Theo talking to Captain Chuck.

I didn't want to leave the fish unattended, but I took a few steps up the stairs and called out again.

"Hello? Everything okay?"

For a long moment, there was nothing but silence.

Then, someone rounded the corner upstairs, and it was so dark that they were nothing but a shadow at first. I narrowed my eyes, trying to peer through the darkness, and when my vision steadied, my heart leapt into my throat.

No.

It can't be.

But it was.

Joel slowly descended the stairs, one by one, taking his sweet time as his glazed eyes narrowed in on me. His dark hair was greasy and matted, his eyes hollow and underlined with dark circles.

I backed away with every step he took down until my hips hit the counter of the galley island.

"Well, well, well," Joel said when his feet hit the bottom stair. He stood there for a minute, taking in the scene — the trout on the stove, the half-made salad in a large bowl, the mixing bowl full of what would have eventually become a cheesecake. When his eyes met mine again, I noted how red they were, how wide his pupils were dilated, and my stomach shriveled up at the sight. "Look who's still on board. What a lovely surprise."

"Joel," I whispered.

"Oh, baby," he cooed with a wicked grin, taking a few more steps toward me. "I always did love it when you said my name."

My eyes flicked to the gun in his right hand, and I swallowed, heart throbbing in my ears. I'd never seen Joel *hold* a gun, let alone shoot one, not in all the years I'd known him. And that only made me fear the situation even more.

"Look, I don't know what's going on," I said, holding my hands up as I backed away more, slowly, one steady step at a time across the galley. "But Theo doesn't have to know you were here. Okay? Just... just go, and I won't say a word."

Joel tilted his head at that, frowning for a second before he let out a loud laugh. "Oh, Theo will know I was here," he said. "Especially because his precious little safe is being drained upstairs right at this very moment. I wish I could stay to see his face when he finds it empty, but alas," he said, holding his hands out wide as if that sentence could finish itself.

I forced a steady breath, even though my heart was pounding so hard I thought I would pass out. I didn't know how Joel got here or who was with him, but one thing I knew for sure was that he wasn't himself. He was on something, he *had* to be. Only drugs could have his skin that thin and ghastly, his eyes underlined with dark bags, the whites of them stained with red. His pupils were still wide, even in the galley light now, and they were constantly bouncing, like they couldn't focus at all.

With whatever was in his system and that gun in his hand, I needed to tread lightly.

"Joel," I said softly, and this time I took a tentative step toward him instead of away, hoping it would settle his defenses. "This isn't you."

"Oh, this is *very much* me," he sneered back, glaring at me with a menacing gaze.

I shook my head, but Joel slammed his hand on the wall before I could argue further.

"You don't think I have a right to be pissed off?!" he screamed. "I have worked my ass off for *years*, Aspen. Years! And that prick took away *everything*." He narrowed his eyes at me then. "Including *you*, it seems."

I didn't want to argue that it was *Joel* who had thrown his future away when he committed his grand theft, especially not since he apparently hadn't learned his lesson. So I just nodded, holding my hands out like he was a wild animal and I was trying to coax him into a cage.

"I understand," I said.

"No, you don't. You *don't* understand, Aspen. And you know what? *I* don't either."

I frowned.

"I don't understand why you," he said, pointing the gun straight at my chest as he took a few more steps toward me. Fear prickled at the back of my neck, but I held my chin high, not backing down. "Are still on this fucking boat."

The fish started to burn, the smell of charred meat only adding to the nausea rolling through me now. Joel's gaze shifted to the stove, and then he smirked, shaking his head.

"Are you cooking for him, Aspen?" he asked, tilting his head when he looked at me again. "Did he hire you as a new chef?"

I swallowed as Joel started circling me like a shark, and when he was behind me, I looked around desperately for something to defend myself. The knife I'd been using on the fish was on the far side of the island, but if I moved slowly and kept him talking, I thought maybe I could grab it.

"No," Joel answered himself, shaking his head with a click of his tongue as he rounded me again. He was tapping his chin with the barrel of the gun like it wasn't a deadly weapon that could blow his face off with one wrong move. "That wouldn't make sense. You've always been a *terrible* cook."

I slowly stepped away from him, backing around the edge of the island.

"You're not wearing a uniform, so I can assume you're not a new stewardess, either. So, why else would you be here, in his galley, on his boat, a full *month* after

I, your boyfriend and the whole reason you were here in the first place, was kicked off of it?"

Slow steps. Inches at a time.

"Unless of course…" Joel smiled, shaking his head before he lunged at me so quickly I screamed and slammed into the back galley counter where the sink was, crying out at the flash of pain through my hip. "You're fucking him."

"Joel, please," I said, holding my hands up to ward him off. "You're scaring me."

"Am I?" he asked, his eyes manic, the smile that slid over his lips like that of a man on the edge of reality. He let out a long, unhinged laugh, his head tilting back with the gesture. Then, he steadied, his gaze falling back on me. "Oh, baby, I'm sorry. Come here."

He held open his arms, the gun still wrapped in his right hand, and his eyebrows pinched together as he watched me.

"Come, let me hold you," he said again, gesturing for me to come to him.

I stood rooted in place, heart thundering in my chest. My eyes flicked to the knife on the island, and that hesitancy made Joel snap.

He growled, his arms swinging wildly until he found grip on the crystal wine glasses I'd picked out for the evening. He smashed one and then the other, little specks of crystal flying all around us before he threw the bottle of wine at the door, too. It splintered into a mess of glass and red liquid as he heaved in a beastly breath, his nose flaring, jaw muscles ticking incessantly.

"I SAID COME HERE!"

I jumped at the command, tears pricking my eyes as I walked toward him, all the while looking at the knife on the counter longingly.

Suddenly, the trout caught fire on the stove, sending up a large flame, and it caught Joel's attention long enough for me to dive for the knife.

But I didn't reach it.

I was scrambling for the handle of it over the countertop when Joel cursed, and just as my fingertips touched the wooden grip of the weapon, I was struck in the back of the head.

I didn't register it at first. It felt like it was happening to someone else, like it was a movie and I was just a member in the audience. I felt the blow hard and quick, heard the *clunk* of what I assumed was the butt of his gun hitting my skull, but it didn't hurt. The force of it sent me hurling against the island, though, and I tried to catch my fall, but my head was already swimming.

My arms didn't lock to catch myself, and so my head flew forward from where the blow struck me from behind, bouncing off a corner of the counter. I felt that sickening *crack*, and it seemed to signal to my body that it was okay to feel the first one, too.

I tumbled to the ground as my hand stretched out and missed the knife, knocking it to the floor with me, but too far out of reach.

When I landed, it was with a thud that rendered me immobile.

The pain hit me all at once, the throbbing at the back of my head, the sharp, shooting pain from the cut on my crown, and the panic that no matter how I tried, I couldn't move.

Blood leaked into the corner of my eye, and when I looked up, Joel was towering over me with a twisted smile. In the commotion, the pan I'd been searing the trout in had toppled, too, and now there was a small, but building, fire behind Joel, casting his silhouette in a burning haze.

"I didn't want to believe it when Ivy told me." He shook his head, nose flaring, eyes growing wilder and wilder. "She said she saw you two together. She said Theo was fucking you, but I told her it wasn't possible." He laughed at that. "I said, *not Aspen. Not my sweet girlfriend who barely fucks* me, *let alone anyone else.* Guess the joke's on me, huh?"

I didn't have strength to respond, not even to remind him that he was cheating on *me*, too. He wasn't innocent. He wasn't a victim. I wished with everything I had in me that I could reach the knife, that I could drive it into his foot and run away, that I could escape this monster once and for all.

But I couldn't do anything but lie there.

Joel shook his head the longer I went without responding, and then, he reared back and kicked me hard in the stomach. "I should have never brought you on this boat, you ungrateful bitch," he seethed.

I think I groaned. I think I doubled over in pain, but my head was so fuzzy, my vision darkening, that I couldn't be sure of anything anymore.

"Better yet, I should have kicked your boring, prude ass to the curb years ago. God knows I could have had any girl I wanted at CU." He paused. "But there's just *something* about you, Aspen Dawn," he added with a smirk, tilting his head as he watched me writhe on the floor. "Seems Theo has fallen under your spell, too."

Then, he leaned down close enough for me to see the veins popping out in his forehead.

"But here's my promise, baby," he whispered, not giving a single care to the fire spreading more and more, the black smoke thickening around us.

I wanted to cough.

I *needed* to cough, but nothing came.

"If I can't have you? No one can."

Joel tilted his head one way and then the other, watching me, waiting for a reaction. When he didn't get one, he stood straight again, and like a slow-motion nightmare, he pointed the gun directly at my head.

And I knew now what it was.

That feeling I'd had that first day on the boat, when the sun was high and warm on my neck in Barcelona — the way my stomach had somersaulted like we were in a deep sea storm even though we were still tied up at the dock.

It was a warning.

I didn't see it then, didn't recognize it as anything more than nerves and maybe a little sorrow swimming in my gut.

But now, with the blood pooling around my head, soaking into the teak and my hair all the same, I understood.

It was a warning.

The universe knew long before I did the way this all would end, and it cautioned me the only way it knew how.

But I ignored it.

Now, as the blackness invaded my vision, the splitting ache at the crown of my head going numb, I caught one last glimpse of the man responsible for it all and I wondered how I never saw it coming.

How did I never see what he was capable of, when pushed, when threatened?

How did I ever let him hold me, kiss me, have me in every way there is to be had?

How did I fall for the lie those eyes told, for the heart within that chest, for a man so evil?

They say love is blind, and in most cases, I imagine that means you look past the faults of those you love — how they leave the cap off the toothpaste or throw their dirty clothes on the floor — or perhaps past your own inhibition telling you that maybe you could do better, that maybe you deserve more.

In this case, it meant death.

Through the fiery haze, the smoke and the flames, the broken crystal and the last fragments of my heart — I saw the smirk of victory on his face.

I tried to ask him why, but it came out as a cough instead, the blood around my mouth bubbling with the effort.

And then, everything went dark.

CHAPTER
TWENTY-SEVEN

Everything came in flashes and sounds.

Crackling.

A flash of Joel flying backward.

Gunshot.

A flash of arms and legs on the ground, of smoke swirling, of fire.

A voice.

Theo's worried eyes flicking between mine, his hands on my face, his words indiscernible.

Stay with me.

Was that what he said?

Sirens.

The night sky. Stars. Flashing lights. Smoke.

It all went black then, but for what felt like only a blink before I heard the faint sound of beeping.

It was soft at first, then louder, and louder, until it felt so loud I thought my head might split. I willed my eyes to open, but they wouldn't for the longest time. My lids were too heavy. My response time was too slow.

When I finally cracked one eye open, a young woman stood above me, calling out something to someone. The words sounded like distorted music, a blurring of sounds and syllables.

"Theo," I tried to say, but my throat was dry, raw, unable to make a sound.

The woman shined a flashlight into each of my eyes, and then she offered me a smile.

Rest, she said in a thick accent.

And I did.

With permission from that stranger, I slipped into a deep, almost coma-like sleep for what felt like years. I was haunted by fever dreams, but they came in the same flashes as before, disappearing just as soon as they came to fruition.

I came to with that same low beeping, only it was more tolerable this time. My eyes opened a little easier, too, and I blinked several times, taking in my surroundings.

I was in a hospital.

That much was easy to discern from the bed I was in, the tubes hooked up to various parts of my body, the thin gown I wore, the machines beeping and humming. There was a television hung directly across from me playing an old movie with Greek subtitles flashing in yellow along the bottom of the screen.

I blinked again, eyes trailing over the blanket that covered me, the IV in my arm, all across the room until I found Theo.

He was sleeping in one of the chairs by the window, his long legs stretched out in front of him, arms crossed over his chest, head back, mouth slightly parted. His eyebrows were furrowed like whatever he was dreaming about made him unbearably angry. And there was a thick bandage tied around the top of his left arm.

My heart surged in my chest, the need to touch him, to hold him and have him hold *me* so urgent that I couldn't move fast enough. In fact, I could barely move *at all*, and when I tried, I groaned as my body protested with an aching stiffness and numbed sizzle of pain.

Theo's eyes shot open, and when he saw me, he scurried to his feet and ran to the side of the bed.

"Aspen," he said, his voice nearly a desperate cry as he reached me. I said his name in return, but it came out just a whisper.

He swept my hair away from my face and I leaned into the touch, tears flooding my eyes once we were connected. I didn't miss the way his own eyes glossed over, which gave me permission to let the first tear free.

Theo thumbed it away, taking both my hands in his and kissing my knuckles as he let out a long exhale. His hair was dark and oily, mussed like he'd had his hands dragged through it for days. He wore the same thing he'd been wearing the morning he left the boat when we docked in Athens, but there was dried blood on the fabric of his polo and dress pants now.

"Are you okay? How are you feeling?"

"Tired," I croaked, trying to sit up.

Theo rushed to help me, holding me steady while he propped pillows up behind me. Once I was more upright, he dragged the chair he'd been sitting in over beside the bed, wrapping my hand in his once again.

"Do you need anything? Water?" He frowned. "Maybe I should call the nurse."

"No," I said quickly. "Not yet. I just want you."

Theo nodded, his brows bending together as another long exhale left his chest. "God, Aspen, you scared me. I thought…"

He swallowed down his next words, and I squeezed his hand in mine. "I'm okay," I assured him, and then my weak hand reached out to brush the bandage on his arm.

"It's fine. Just a little bullet graze."

My eyes shot open wide. "Bullet graze?! Theo!" The words felt like sandpaper against my sore throat.

"I'm okay," he said again. "I promise. It's you I was worried about." He swallowed, brushing my hair back again as his eyes washed over me, over all the tubes and wires sticking this way and that. "You lost a lot of blood."

My chest tightened at the look of pain on his face, and with that same breath my heart surged, because I'd never felt more loved — not ever before.

"What happened?" I asked after a moment. "Where are we?"

"It's a long story. We can talk about it when you're rested, okay?" He frowned again, looking at the door. "I think I really should call the nurse."

"Theo," I pleaded, squeezing his hand. "Please. Tell me."

He sighed, but nodded, handing me a small cup of ice chips from the table next to him before he began. I didn't realize how thirsty I was until the first chip touched my tongue, and I eagerly tipped the cup back for more.

"It's hard to explain," he started. "I'm still trying to understand it all myself. But long story short, Joel, Ace, and Ivy snuck onto the boat after the sun went down. They were there for the safe."

"Celeste?"

Theo shook his head. "She wasn't with them. Judging by the way she was acting the day we fired them, I don't think she wanted any part of what they were doing. Not anymore."

I nodded, sucking on another chip as he continued.

"Wayland told me on our way back to the boat that you'd given the crew the night off. What neither of us realized was that while we'd discovered four of the rats involved in that grand theft, we'd left one onboard."

I frowned.

"Eric," he clarified. "Our bosun."

"No!"

Theo nodded. "Apparently, he was the head of the whole thing. He befriended Joel early on in our trip, told him about his successful thefts from yachts in the past, and before the end of the night, he had him and Ace in on the deed. Ivy and Celeste weren't a hard sell, especially not once they started formulating a plan."

I chewed my cheek, trying to understand through the fog in my head. I wondered what kind of pain relievers they had pumped into my system. "So... Eric was with them?"

"No, actually. He went to shore with everyone else, so as not to look suspicious. But apparently, he'd been feeding Joel, Ace, and Ivy information ever since we left. He'd even hooked them up with some of his guys to get them to Greece once we left Italy. Those same guys were the ones who provided the guns they had." He swallowed at that. "They were just waiting for the right time to strike. And when you sent the crew to shore for a night off..."

"I gave them the perfect opportunity," I finished for him with a groan.

"Hey, it wasn't your fault, all right?" Theo assured me, bringing my knuckles to his lips. He kissed all four of them before resting our hands on the bed again. "But yes. I was off the boat, Wayland was waiting to bring me back, the crew was gone." He shrugged. "No one but Captain Chuck."

"And me."

"And you," Theo agreed. "Which, from what I can gather, Eric left that part of the equation out. When questioned about the whole night, he told the Athens authorities that he hoped you would just stay out of the way and the three thieves could get on, get what they wanted from the safe, and get off without you being any the wiser."

"What was in that safe that they wanted so badly?"

"Cash. I had a pretty good amount of it in there, just in case. Wayland thinks they might have been trying to steal my identity, too, or at least utilize it long enough to open up a few cards. I had all my travel documents in the safe — passport, business visa, even my Social Security card. I also had a few credit cards in there, so they could have been trying to rack those up before they were found out. Or open new ones. It's hard to really say."

I shook my head. "How did they think they'd get away with any of this?"

"Well, if there wouldn't have been a fire, and if Joel wouldn't have gotten caught up in... in..." Theo couldn't even say the words. "If things would have just been a little different, they might have gotten away with a large amount of cash and enough cards to do some damage to my credit line."

My heart lurched into my throat with another thought. "Oh, God. Captain Chuck? Is he okay?"

"Ace knocked him out with a blow to the head. He lost quite a bit of blood, too, but yes, he's okay."

"I heard him," I said. "I heard this loud thump, and then voices, and then…" Tears flooded my eyes again as I recalled the memory. "And then Joel was there, and it all happened so quickly. He… I think he was on something. He looked… *evil*."

"Cocaine," Theo explained with a heavy sigh. "Among other things, we think, but they found a baggie of cocaine in his pocket. If he was mixing it with anything else, or taking a lot of it, well… it doesn't surprise me he didn't seem himself."

I swallowed, remembering how cold and lifeless his eyes were. "He… he hit me," I whispered, touching the back of my head. My eyes widened when I felt thick stitches, and I winced at the feeling of my fingertips against the raw skin there. "I was trying to get to the knife, but I couldn't reach it. I fell and hit my head again," I remembered, touching the crown of my head next. Another batch of stitches was there. My eyes caught Theo's. "He had the gun pointed at me," I whispered. "He was going to kill me."

Theo's nose flared, and he shook his head, pulling me into his arms. It was awkward, the way I was hooked up to the various machines and bags of fluid, but Theo held me, anyway, pressing a kiss to my hair, my forehead, and finally, my lips.

He kissed me long and slow, both of us inhaling and exhaling together like we hadn't taken a real full breath until that very moment.

"I'm so sorry I wasn't there," Theo whispered against my lips. "I'm so sorry he hurt you, that I didn't stop him in time."

I shook my head, emotion strangling my throat. "I thought... I thought I saw you."

"I must have gotten there moments after you passed out," he explained. "Wayland and I knew something was off as soon as we pulled up. There was smoke billowing out from the lower deck, from the galley, where you two were. But we ran into Captain Chuck first, and he was badly injured. Wayland helped him into the tender and then we went looking for you." He paused. "We found Ace first."

"Oh, God. What happened?"

Theo shook his head. "Hard to really say. It was all so fast. He fired a few shots, but Wayland wrangled the gun free." Theo covered his bandaged arm. "I got a little graze, but nothing serious. Wayland knocked Ace over the head with one of the vases on deck, and when Ivy saw us, she fled — along with a duffle bag full of cash. We think she took the jet ski, but we couldn't be sure because we knew we had to find you and get you off the boat."

"So she's gone? She never got caught?"

"She did, by the Greek police. Wayland called them as soon as we saw the smoke coming from the boat. By the time we were down getting you, they had already pulled up, along with the firefighters."

I shook my head, trying to take it all in. "And Joel?"

Theo's jaw ticked. "I walked in on him standing over you with the gun pointed at your head, and I swear, Aspen, I just... I blacked out. All I could think about was getting you to safety." He swallowed. "I'm ashamed to say I beat him to a bloody pulp first, though."

Theo really did look ashamed of himself, and I squeezed his hand to encourage him to continue.

"I lunged so fast he didn't see me coming, he was too focused on you. The gun went flying out of his hand and I had him pinned and I just... lost it. Wayland had to tear me off him, and then he threw Joel on his shoulder like a bag of potatoes while I carried you up the stairs." He scoffed then. "Part of me wanted to tell Wayland to just leave Joel to burn."

I shook my head. "You did the right thing."

Theo shrugged. "I don't know. Regardless, by that time, the police were already on board. They took Ace and Joel to shore while another boat searched for Ivy, and Wayland and I took you and Chuck in the tender." He smiled a little then. "There was an ambulance waiting for us at the dock. And then..." He gestured to our surroundings. "I'm sure you can infer the rest."

I leaned back into the pillows. "Jesus... what a nightmare."

Theo nodded, sighing again as he leaned in to kiss me. "The worst one of my life."

We pressed our foreheads together, resting for a while before my eyes shot open again. "Emma? The rest of the crew?"

"They're fine. No one was harmed."

"And what happened to Joel and Ace and Ivy?"

At that, Theo shrugged. "Not sure. They're in custody now, I'm sure we'll have an update sooner or later. But for now, just know they're somewhere where they can't hurt you. Or anyone else."

My heart heaved a relieved sigh at that. "I just can't believe this all happened." Suddenly, my stomach bottomed out again. "Oh God, Theo. Your boat! *Philautia!*"

"It's okay," Theo said on a chuckle. "The fire spread pretty quickly, and with all the commotion on board, it was first priority to vacate it before anything else." He shrugged. "She suffered too much damage to salvage."

"No!"

He laughed again. "It's *okay*, Aspen. It's just a boat."

I scoffed. "I don't think anyone else on this planet would agree with you that it was *just a boat*."

"What I mean is, it's not important. It's material, something that can be replaced. You, on the other hand," he said, his brows bending together as he pulled my knuckles to his lips again. He kissed them softly. "Are not."

I tried to smile, but my stomach was still so tied up in knots I barely managed it.

Theo swallowed. "I thought I lost you."

My face twisted with emotion, and I pulled him into me, awkward as it was over the bars of the hospital bed, until his lips met mine. I held that kiss for as long as he'd let me, and then Theo pulled back, taking my hand in his again and watching me with tears in his eyes.

We stayed like that for a long while, Theo holding my hand in his and kissing my skin with soft, feather-light touches as his eyes flicked between mine. The more we were silent, the more at ease I felt. I savored every warm touch of Theo's hand, thankfulness filling me like helium in a balloon.

We were alive.

We were okay.

Nothing else mattered. Not right now.

I let my eyes close, let the relief flood me like the warm water of a bath after a long day. Theo kept his hold on my hand, and then I felt his fingertips brush against my face, and I leaned into his palm with a smile.

"Aspen?"

"Hmm?"

"Marry me."

I nearly choked on my own spit as I sat up, eyes flying open again. I stared at Theo like he'd just confessed an addiction to watching foot fetish porn, and it only made him grin.

"What did you just say?"

"I said, *marry me*," he repeated, and he laughed when my eyes got even wider. "I don't care if it's crazy. I don't care if no one else understands it. I love you," he said, and he emphasized each word of that last sentence with his eyes searching mine. "I love you, and I don't want to — no, I *can't* lose you."

I bit my lip against the emotion crawling up my throat, watching Theo with tears blurring my vision.

"Say you'll be mine forever," he pleaded. "Say it, and I'll be yours forever, too."

I choked on a mixture of a sob and a laugh, nodding as more tears flooded my eyes until they started pouring over my hot cheeks.

"Yes?" Theo asked, his eyes widening.

"Yes," I whispered. "I'm yours."

His next exhale was on the wings of the biggest smile I'd ever seen spanning his face, and he pulled me into his arms so quickly and so completely that it set off more than one of the machines I was hooked to. Alarms rang and still he held me, and kissed me, and I laughed and kissed him back until two nurses ran in yelling at us in Greek first and then in English to let go of each other.

Theo finally released me but held my hand tight even as the nurses fixed the wires and tubes. They started checking my vitals then, asking me questions about pain level and asking me to perform various tasks.

All the while, Theo was there at my side, holding my hand and smiling at me like an absolute loon.

He *was* crazy. We both were.

But I wouldn't have it any other way.

CHAPTER
TWENTY-EIGHT

One Month Later

"**D**ear Ms. Dawn," Theo read from the letter in his hand — the one I repeatedly tried to jump up and snag for myself, but he kept out of my reach. "It is with great pleasure that I write to you with an exciting offer that I hope you will receive with as much enthusiasm as I have sending it."

"Theo, give it to me!" I tried to jump again, but he spun away from me, waltzing over to the oversized window with a reading nook that overlooked Central Park. The leaves were just beginning to turn, their greens fading to faint shades of orange and yellow and red.

We'd been "home" at Theo's penthouse in New York City for two weeks now, flying back to the States on his jet as soon as we were both cleared from the hospital and took care of the affairs with the yacht in Athens. We were set to fly to Colorado for him to meet my family in just two days.

That was, if he was still alive by then, because I was about two seconds from strangling him if he didn't give me the mysterious letter that came addressed to me that morning.

"My name is Dorothy Hammerstein, and I was blessed enough to be in Santorini on the night of your stunning exhibit at the Blue Top Gallery. I was also surprised to find such exquisite work from a photographer unbeknownst to me, and even more surprised to find that my generous offer to purchase my favorite photograph of the lot was declined."

I waited until Theo was by the couch, then I jumped on top of it, launching myself onto his back and clinging on like a monkey. He laughed as he caught me, but still kept the letter out of my reach as he continued.

"Admittedly, I broke the rules of the gallery and snuck a few photos of your work to show to my boss. I'm hoping you will forgive me once I tell you this next part, which is that we would like to offer you a large sum of money — to be discussed in person — for the photographs that were on display at the gallery that evening, as well as a permanent spot on the *TIME Magazine* photography team."

"Oh my *God!*" I squealed. "*TIME Magazine*?!"

Theo ignored me, continuing. "Your photographs haunt me still to this day, Ms. Dawn, and I look forward to the day when the rest of the world gets to have their hearts split open and their minds warped the way I did that evening in Greece. Please give me a call at the number below at your earliest convenience to discuss the details further. Until then, may your focus stay sharp.

Respectfully, Dorothy Hammerstein, Director of Photography, *TIME Magazine*!"

Theo said the last part in almost a giddy squeal of his own before he dropped the letter to the ground and reached for where I was saddled on his back. He spun me around to face him, wrapping me up in his arms and kissing me hard.

At least, until I pinched his nipple and made him drop me.

"Ouch! What the—"

But he was already laughing as I dove to the ground for the letter, reading it over again myself.

I shook my head in disbelief, and then I shot Theo an accusatory glare. "Did you do this?" I asked, slapping the letter against my palm. "Did you invite this woman or pay someone off? Because I swear, Theo, if you—"

"I didn't, I didn't!" he said, laughing as he dropped down to the floor with me. He pulled me into his arms with a wide grin. "This is all you, Aspen. All. You."

I stared at him for a long time, brows furrowed, shaking my head over and over. I read the letter again, then a third time, and even then I didn't believe it.

"I think I'm in shock."

Theo chuckled, and then he fished something out of his pocket, and for the first time — at least that *I'd* ever seen — a faint blush touched his cheeks. "Well, hopefully this won't add to that."

"What?"

Theo swallowed, holding his fist out in front of me. When his fingers uncurled, there in the center of his palm was a teal Montana sapphire ring so big and beautiful I lost my breath at the sight of it.

"Theo..."

"I know it's different," he said, picking up the ring. It looked small between his large thumb and forefinger. "And we can return it and get what you want, if this isn't it. But... I wanted something blue, like the water was the day I first met you, and the sky." He paused. "And your eyes. God, this sounds so corny now that I'm saying it out loud."

"I love corn," I said on a laugh that made tears spring to my eyes. "Kettle corn. Creamed corn. Corn on the cob."

Theo chuckled, too, holding the ring up and waiting for me to offer him my hand. When I did, he held it in his own, thumbing my skin as his eyes searched mine. "I know I asked you this already in the most romantic way, while you were hooked up to an IV in a hospital bed."

I laughed.

"But I want you to know that I'm just as serious now as I was then, and that if you put this ring on your finger, I will do everything in my power to give you the happiest life."

"And if I don't?"

"Then I'll jump off the roof."

"Theo!"

"Kidding," he said with a smile. "Sort of."

I shook my head, wiggling my fingers where he held them. "Put it on me, already, you big ball of cheese."

Theo grinned, sliding the white-gold band over my knuckles. When the ring was in place, I pulled it closer, inspecting the elegant pear shape of the sapphire, the twinkling shades of teal and turquoise and almost a green-blue that made up the stone, and the tiny diamonds that framed it on either side.

Then, I looked into the eyes of the man I would call my husband, the man I never saw coming, the man who changed my life in just one unforgettable summer, and I wondered if God was having a laugh, if He was looking down with a big bucket of popcorn at the wild love He'd made out of the messiest of situations.

"This is a conditional yes."

"Conditional?" Theo asked, arching a brow.

I nodded, and then I climbed into his lap, pressing a long kiss to his lips before leaning in to whisper in his ear. "You've got to pass the baby sister test to be official."

Theo barked out a laugh at that, tickling my sides before he pulled me to stand and swept me up into his arms. "I'll buy her a Maserati," he said. "That oughta win her over."

I smacked his chest with a laugh, but it faded quickly when he kissed me hard and deep, carrying me through the penthouse to the master suite. He laid me gently in the sheets, and I rubbed my fingers over the fresh pink scar left from Ace's misfired bullet.

"I'm going to make you the happiest woman in the whole damn world," Theo said, kissing my neck, down my chest, over my navel once he peeled my shirt up. "Mark my words."

I pulled on his arms until he crawled back up, granting my plea for another kiss. This time, I deepened it, wrapping my arms around his neck and holding him to me as my heart surged in my chest. I caught a glimpse of the ring shimmering on my finger, and with that, there was no use in trying to fight back the tears that stung my eyes when I pressed my forehead to his and told him the most irrefutable truth.

"You already have."

The End

EPILOGUE

Eight Months Later

"**Y**ou've already shown me this video," I pointed out to Theo as we rode across the bustling city of Miami. "Like, a dozen times. Before we left New York, on the jet, in the hotel, and now—"

"Just wait, there's more to it. They added on an extra minute at the end."

I laughed. "I really don't think an extra minute is going to show me anything I haven't already seen."

"Just watch."

I rolled my eyes but let Theo tuck me into his side as he showed me the video playing out on his tablet. It was the one the naval architect team put together to show Theo his new yacht, the one he'd had built in supersonic speed. It usually took at least three years, but with money like Theo's... well, let's just say he made his own timelines.

It was a gorgeous, albeit humid day in Miami, and we were on our way to see the yacht for the first time in person. We likely wouldn't be able to take it out just yet, but Theo was so anxious to see all his design dreams in real life that he couldn't wait any longer. We'd flown in last night, and as of now, didn't have a date picked for when we'd return to New York.

I leaned into Theo's chest as the video played on the screen, showing the four-deck mega yacht. As incredible as it was with its beach club extended off the stern, its oragami-like sleek engineering, its sauna and gym and pools and hot tubs and staterooms that made *Philautia* look amateur, I really *had* seen it a dozen times, and so I let my mind wander as my eyes watched the screen.

It was easy on a day like today where the sun was high in the sky and there was a warm breeze coming in off the water for me to think back to that first day I saw Theo almost a year ago now. And as if that first summer we had together wasn't enough of a crazy whirlwind to last a lifetime, the last eight months had shown me that life with Theo would be anything but boring.

We'd made a home in his New York City penthouse, and while I wished every day could be a vacation, it wasn't long after we returned from the trip to Colorado where Theo met my parents that Theo had to get back to work. And while he spent his days in the Manhattan Envizion office, or flying around the country for different conferences, events, speeches, and more, I started my own career.

With *TIME Magazine*.

It had stunned me, walking into that office for the first time. I'd been shocked at how kind Mrs. Hammerstein had been when she greeted me and introduced me to her team. And I'd *literally* fallen out of my chair when she offered me a quarter-of-a-million dollars for one of my photographs I'd taken in Positano.

And that was just the beginning.

Not only had she published that photo on the cover of the February issue, but she had also offered me a job. And ever since, I'd flown to a dozen different countries capturing photographs for what I considered the most influential magazine in the world.

The dream I had always thought would be just that — a dream — had become a reality.

And Theo was by my side the entire way.

It was hard sometimes with both of us traveling and working. At one point, we went three weeks without seeing each other even once. Of course, that made for a memorable night in the sheets once we were together again. And no matter where our jobs took us, we always knew we'd come back home to the other.

That made it all worth it.

It'd also been a dizzying rush getting used to the lifestyle Theo led. He was one of the world's most eligible bachelors, and when news broke that a college graduate somehow stole his heart enough for him to propose, there was no hiding from the paparazzi and onslaught of reporters begging for an exclusive interview. For the first few months of us being back in the U.S., we couldn't leave our house without a dozen cameras and microphones shoved in our faces.

But things had quieted since then, especially since we'd kept our lips sealed about wedding plans. The truth was that we really hadn't made many plans *at all*, thanks to life being so hectic.

But they didn't need to know that.

"Okay, here's the new part," Theo said, and I chuckled at how giddy he was.

On the screen, the camera panned the master suite for the first time. It had many of the same art deco features that Theo loved in *Philautia,* like the geometric lines and cold metals combining with the warm wood and pops of color. There was an oversized bookshelf and luxurious sitting area with a blush rug and a navy statement chair that looked so comfortable I knew I'd lose days there reading.

But as much as it had Theo, the room also had bits of *me.*

On the white couches, there were faux fur throws, and the coffee table looked almost like a sliver of wood from a giant tree that had been varnished and stained and fitted with two industrial-looking metal legs. The comforter on the massive bed was a beautiful southwestern pattern that reminded me of the one my parents had, and there was a glass-covered gas fireplace lining the far wall, nestled beneath three gorgeous photos of the Rocky Mountains.

It was like the interior designer had taken 1920's New York City and married it with 1980's Colorado — all with a modern flair, of course.

I touched the screen with my fingertips, shaking my head in awe. "It's so... *us.*"

"I thought so. And," Theo said, unwrapping his arm from where it held me long enough to dig into his briefcase on the floor. "I saved a special spot on the bookshelf for this."

He pulled out an elegantly framed photograph, but not just *any* photograph.

Mine.

The first one published on the cover of *TIME Magazine.*

My eyes watered as I looked from the frame to Theo and back again.

"I told you, didn't I? That day you found me sitting by the sun deck pool. I told you you'd be published in *TIME*, and that I'd have it framed when you did. And what was it that you'd said back to me?"

"That even if I ever did, you wouldn't remember who I was."

"And how did that theory turn out?"

I shoved him playfully just as his eyes snapped to the screen. "Oh! Okay, watch. This is the best part."

The same drone video that I'd seen time and time again showed us the wide shot of the yacht then, and the way the navy blue water glistened around the fresh teak was just as magical as the first time I'd seen it. But then, the camera cut to a view from the starboard side, and I saw what Theo was so excited about.

Written in elegant white script with gold embellishments was the name of the boat.

Dawn's Light.

I smiled, glancing up at where Theo was watching me rather than the screen. "Dawn's Light?"

He nodded. "Do you remember that night in San Marco, when I told you how you have this light about you?"

It clicked together then, and I hid my blushing face in his chest. "Theo..."

He lifted my chin until my eyes met his. "I told you people either want to bathe in it or dim it so it doesn't outshine their own." He smiled. "But what I didn't say was that it was your light that saved me, that woke me up from merely existing day in and day out. I am living now. *Truly* living. And it's all because of you."

I shook my head, peppering him with kisses before I held his gaze, my eyes flicking back and forth between his. In that moment, all that we'd been through, all that we'd accomplished together, and all that we'd shared flooded me like a warm ray of sunshine. The feeling was sweeping, so much so that I felt compelled to pull Theo into me even more and say two words.

"Marry me."

Theo laughed, kissing my nose. "Hey, don't steal my line."

"I mean it. Marry me. Today."

"Today?"

"Today. On our new boat," I said, glancing at the screen. "I know we'll have a big ceremony — I mean, my family would kill me otherwise, and I know your parents would, too. But... let's get married today, just me and you. No one needs to know. It can be our little secret."

Theo smirked. "I like the sound of that, but there is *one* little problem..."

"And that is?"

"Well, we won't exactly be alone."

I frowned, not understanding. Sure, I knew the architect team would be there, and maybe the interior designer, but wouldn't it be relatively easy to ask them to leave for a while?

Before I could press further, we pulled up to the marina, and Theo took my hand in his, helping me out of the car and guiding me down the dock.

We passed sailboat after sailboat, yacht after yacht, each one of them grandiose in their own unique ways. But nothing compared to the sight at the end of the dock where Dawn's Light rested in all her three-hundred-forty-eight-feet glory, shining in the mid-afternoon sun.

And when we made it onboard, I understood what Theo meant when he said we wouldn't be alone.

I saw Emma first, standing on the main deck with the same warm smile she'd offered me when I met her last year. My jaw dropped at the sight of her, and then I tore off in a sprint and crashed into her with a fierce hug I didn't want to release.

"Nice to see you, too," she said with a laugh.

"Emma! What in the world?" I pulled back, holding her in my hands as I looked her up and down. "What are you doing here?!"

"Getting Dawn's Light ready to cruise, of course," she said with a wink. "And I have some pretty good help, too."

Her eyes flicked behind me then, and Wayland was there, shaking Theo's hand before offering him a cold glass of champagne.

I gasped, flying across the deck and into his arms — which opened just in time to catch me. He laughed and gave us a little spin before he set me back down on the dock.

"Ah, I see he did manage to keep the surprise, eh?"

"The *best* surprise!" I said, squeezing him again before I looked at Theo. "I don't understand, I thought we weren't going to be able to take the boat out yet?"

Theo shrugged. "So I told a few little white lies... Captain Chuck is here, too. He'll join us later."

"What else do you have hiding up your sleeve?"

He tucked his hands into his pockets, looking around with an innocent whistle, but then his eyes locked somewhere behind me.

When I turned, I nearly burst into tears.

Both of our families were sitting in the main salon — his parents talking to mine, and of course, Juniper lounging back behind them on one of the sun decks.

"Go put your swimsuit on, loser!" she yelled, sipping the fruity drink in her glass before she added. "You're missing all the great sunshine!"

I laughed as tears filled my eyes, and then Mom was up out of her chair and hugging me while Dad shook Theo's hand. Theo hugged his father next and kissed his mother's cheek while my dad wiped a tear from the corner of my eye before it could fall.

"I think you've got a pretty special one here, Aspen," he said, glancing at Theo.

As if I didn't already know.

And as Wayland turned up the music and Emma refilled drinks, the rest of the crew who I'd yet to meet yet worked together to get Dawn's Light out onto the water for her maiden voyage. Juniper danced in her swimsuit, my parents swapped stories with Theo's, and all the while, I stared at him from across the salon with a heart fit to burst.

I found myself remarking how beautiful and unexpected life could be, at how sometimes, in the most precious moments, not even a photograph taken by the most talented photographer in the world could truly capture all the magic.

And as Theo crossed the room and put his arm around me, kissing my hair before he looked down lovingly into my eyes, I knew one thing was for certain.

Whether tonight, next week, a year from now, or ten years down the road, I was going to marry that devastatingly handsome man.

And when I did, I'd vow to fall in love with him a little more every day, knowing it would be the easiest promise to keep.

Want more Aspen and Theo? Check out this bonus scene (http://www.kandisteiner.com/bonus-content) where Theo meets Aspen's family for the first time!

A NOTE FROM THE AUTHOR

Thank you for reading *Close Quarters*. I hope you enjoyed reading this angsty goodness as much as I enjoyed creating it.

If you liked this book, check out my new box set – *The Pain in Loving You* – where you can read THREE of my angsty all-time bestsellers. You'll get *Weightless, A Love Letter to Whiskey,* and *Make Me Hate You* all in one epic collection.

You might also enjoy my Becker Brothers series, following four rowdy brothers in a small town in Tennessee as they solve the mystery of their father's death – and find love along the way. Keep reading for a sneak peek inside!

Three of my very close friends also released new books this month, and I cannot recommend them enough. Check out *Hold the Forevers* by K.A. Linde if you want more angst, *Bet the Farm* by Staci Hart if you're ready for a rom com after all this tension, or *Eastern Lights* if you want to feel the kind of love and emotion only a Brittainy C. Cherry book can bring.

I also love to hang out with my readers online. My favorite place to hang out is Instagram, but I'm also on TikTok if that's your jam. And, my group on Facebook gets exclusive giveaways, sneak peeks, and more – so come hang out.

You can also sign up for my newsletter (http://www.kandisteiner.com/newsletter) if you don't want to do all the social media, but also don't want to miss any new releases from me.

And again, thank you for picking my book out of the millions you could have selected to read. I truly appreciate it.

MORE FROM
KANDI STEINER

The Red Zone Rivals Series
Fair Catch
Blind Side
Quarterback Sneak
Hail Mary

The Becker Brothers Series
On the Rocks
Neat (book 2)
Manhattan (book 3)
Old Fashioned (book 4)
Four brothers finding love in a small Tennessee town that revolves around a whiskey distillery with a dark past — including the mysterious death of their father.

The Best Kept Secrets Series
(AN AMAZON TOP 10 BESTSELLER)
What He Doesn't Know (book 1)
What He Always Knew (book 2)
What He Never Knew (book 3)
Charlie's marriage is dying. She's perfectly content to go down in the flames, until her first love shows back up and reminds her the other way love can burn.

Close Quarters

A summer yachting the Mediterranean sounded like heaven to Jasmine after finishing her undergrad degree. But her boyfriend's billionaire boss always gets what he wants. And this time, he wants her.

Make Me Hate You

Jasmine has been avoiding her best friend's brother for years, but when they're both in the same house for a wedding, she can't resist him — no matter how she tries.

The Wrong Game
(AN AMAZON TOP 10 BESTSELLER)

Gemma's plan is simple: invite a new guy to each home game using her season tickets for the Chicago Bears. It's the perfect way to avoid getting emotionally attached and also get some action. But after Zach gets his chance to be her practice round, he decides one game just isn't enough. A sexy, fun sports romance.

The Right Player

She's avoiding love at all costs. He wants nothing more than to lock her down. Sexy, hilarious and swoon-worthy, The Right Player is the perfect read for sports romance lovers.

On the Way to You

It was only supposed to be a road trip, but when Cooper discovers the journal of the boy driving the getaway car, everything changes. An emotional, angsty road trip romance.

A Love Letter to Whiskey
(AN AMAZON TOP 10 BESTSELLER)
An angsty, emotional romance between two lovers fighting the curse of bad timing.
Read Love, Whiskey – Jamie's side of the story and an extended epilogue – in the new Fifth Anniversary Edition!

Weightless
Young Natalie finds self-love and romance with her personal trainer, along with a slew of secrets that tie them together in ways she never thought possible.
Revelry
Recently divorced, Wren searches for clarity in a summer cabin outside of Seattle, where she makes an unforgettable connection with the broody, small town recluse next door.

Say Yes
Harley is studying art abroad in Florence, Italy. Trying to break free of her perfectionism, she steps outside one night determined to Say Yes to anything that comes her way. Of course, she didn't expect to run into Liam Benson...

Washed Up
Gregory Weston, the boy I once knew as my son's best friend, now a man I don't know at all. No, not just a man. A doctor. And he wants me...

The Christmas Blanket
Stuck in a cabin with my ex-husband waiting out a blizzard? Not exactly what I had pictured when I planned a surprise visit home for the holidays...

Black Number Four
A college, Greek-life romance of a hot young poker star and the boy sent to take her down.

The Palm South University Series
Rush (book 1) FREE if you sign up for my newsletter!
Anchor, PSU #2
Pledge, PSU #3
Legacy, PSU #4
Ritual, PSU #5
Hazed, PSU #6
Greek, PSU #7
#1 NYT Bestselling Author Rachel Van Dyken says, "If Gossip Girl and Riverdale had a love child, it would be PSU." This angsty college series will be your next guilty addiction.

Tag Chaser
She made a bet that she could stop chasing military men, which seemed easy — until her knight in shining armor and latest client at work showed up in Army ACUs.

Song Chaser
Tanner and Kellee are perfect for each other. They frequent the same bars, love the same music, and have the same desire to rip each other's clothes off. Only problem? Tanner is still in love with his best friend.

ACKNOWLEDGEMENTS

First and foremost, I want to thank my mother – La-Von Allen. If it weren't for you, I never would have had the confidence or strength to chase my dream of being a writer. Thank you for always encouraging me and making sure I knew that I could do and be anything I wanted to. I love you.

Close Quarters was unlike anything I'd ever written before, and when it came to yacht life, I had a lot to learn. So, I want to give a special shout out to Jack and Becky Hamm, who provided invaluable knowledge and resources to help me get this right. Thank you for sharing your stories and listening to me yack about all the ideas I had. I appreciate your patience and love more than you know!

It takes a team to make a book come to life and really shine. Thank you to my amazing alpha, beta, and Charlie readers. I literally could not do this without you. Kellee Fabre, Trish QUEEN MINTNESS, Sarah Green, Zainab M., Carly Wilson, Dee Lagasse, Becky Hamm, Maggie Ehrgott, and Sasha Erramouspe – without your valuable feedback, this book would be trash. So, thanks for making it smell better.

Tina Stokes, thank you for being the world's best PA and the most loving, caring, amazing friend. I'm so lucky to have you in my corner.

A giant thank you to Elaine York of Allusion Graphics for editing and polishing up this bad boy. I love that you always work with my crazy timelines, embrace my hair-brained ideas, and even leave me sweet little love notes in the middle of all your critique. You're such a light. Love you.

Valentine PR, your team constantly amazes me with their attention to detail and out-of-the-box thinking. Thank you for being amazing.

If you bought this book because of the cover, then you'll have to join me in thanking the incredibly talented Lauren Perry of Perrywinkle Photography. I'm so fortunate to work with her to bring my characters to life, and this shoot was one of my all time favorites she's ever done for me. Thank you, Lauren, for working your magic!

There are so many people who likely would have never even HEARD of me or this book without the love and support of our blogger community. Thank you to each and every single one of you who shared the cover reveal, teasers, read an ARC and blasted on release day. You are the heartbeat of this community and I appreciate you more than you know.

A special shout out goes to my group on Facebook, Kandiland (http://www.facebook.com/groups/kandilandks), where I feel like I can truly be my weird self. Thank you for always encouraging me and being just as excited as I am about new projects. Oh, and for not judging me when I told y'all I was obsessed with Theo Whitman... a character I created... so therefore, myself? That's real love.

Finally, thank YOU, reader who even read through the acknowledgements. You're awesome. You had a million choices when it came time to pick a book to read, and you picked mine. It is because of you that I am able to live a life I've always wanted, sharing words with others across the world. I hope we can do it for many years to come.

ABOUT THE AUTHOR

KANDI STEINER is a bestselling author and whiskey connoisseur living in Tampa, FL. Best known for writing "emotional rollercoaster" stories, she loves bringing flawSed characters to life and writing about real, raw romance — in all its forms. No two Kandi Steiner books are the same, and if you're a lover of angsty, emotional, and inspirational reads, she's your gal.

An alumna of the University of Central Florida, Kandi graduated with a double major in Creative Writing and Advertising/PR with a minor in Women's Studies. She started writing back in the 4th grade after reading the first Harry Potter installment. In 6th grade, she wrote and edited her own newspaper and distributed to her classmates. Eventually, the principal caught on and the newspaper was quickly halted, though Kandi tried fighting for her "freedom of press." She took particular interest in writing romance after college, as she has always been a die hard hopeless romantic, and likes to highlight all the challenges of love as well as the triumphs.

When Kandi isn't writing, you can find her reading books of all kinds, talking with her extremely vocal cat, and spending time with her friends and family. She enjoys live music, traveling, anything heavy in carbs, beach days, movie marathons, craft beer and sweet wine — not necessarily in that order.

CONNECT WITH KANDI:

→ NEWSLETTER: bit.ly/NewsletterKS
→ FACEBOOK: facebook.com/kandisteiner
→ FACEBOOK READER GROUP (Kandiland):
facebook.com/groups/kandischasers
→ INSTAGRAM: Instagram.com/kandisteiner
→ TWITTER: twitter.com/kandisteiner
→ PINTEREST: pinterest.com/kandicoffman
→ WEBSITE: www.kandisteiner.com

Kandi Steiner may be coming to a city near you! Check out her "events" tab to see all the signings she's attending in the near future:

→ www.kandisteiner.com/events

9 781960 649003